GW00726649

#SHARKGIRL

By Christian Darkin

978-1-9998930-4-0
First printing 2021
Rational Stories
www.RationalStories.com

About The Author

Christian Darkin is the author of more than fifteen books for adults, young adults and children. As a journalist in the UK, he has written on science and technology issues for newspapers such as The Times and The Guardian as well as dozens of newsstand magazines. He is also the journalist behind three science documentaries and the scriptwriter of a Doctor Who spinoff film. You can talk to Christian on Twitter at @animateddad.

Also By Christian Darkin

Land of Monsters – The kids who discovered America
Lab Grown Meat Bites Back –a young adult sci-fi thriller
Deadly Placebo – an adventure in pseudoscience
The Skull – a middle-grade adventure
Act Normal – a series of chapter books for children

Thanks so much to Rebecca Byrne and Teresa Taylor for helping me out with the complexities of Robert's character Thanks also to the Crystal Palace Writers of the Triangle for suffering my first drafts, and making suggestions which made the whole book stronger. And as ever, thanks to my wonderful girlfriend, editor and PR champion, Rachel for everything.

Prologue
THE AMAZON JUNGLE. COLUMBIA.

Utterly alien. Deafening. Louder than a storm. Louder than anything he had ever heard. It grew from a growling rumble to a throbbing roar that seemed to beat from his own heart. A sound like the pounding of a waterfall over a cliff-face, raining down onto hard rock. It filled him with a confused fear.

Then the thing came in low. A strange, angular bulk glowering just above the treetops. Darkening the sky. Bringing the whole jungle to thrashing, desperate life with the wind from its spinning wings. It was a hulking, impossible shape, sweeping, swinging back and forth above them as though hanging heavily from a vine lowered out of the clouds themselves. The blast of wind rushed downwards, forcing Eena and the rest of the hunting party to throw themselves to the hot, damp ground, hugging it, terrified. It felt to him as though the world had turned to churning chaos. He dug his fingernails hard into the leaf-mulch, hooking them between the fine roots. At any second, he thought, the wind could shift and he would be sucked upwards into that monster, and the slicing beams that span above it. He held fast until it passed over them, and the dislodged leaves settled over their naked bodies like a green blanket.

Eena opened one eye, and focused it on his hand, clutching the ground in front of him. A tarantula, disturbed by the churning leaves, crawled across it. He felt its weight, heavy on the back of his fist. The scratch of its pin legs. But still he didn't dare to move. He waited until it had passed on its way, the sound from above slowly moving off.

Eena slowly stood, still shaking, leaves tumbling from him, and looked around. Today was his sixteenth birthday, though in a world where dates were not marked, and the plants flowered all year, the concept would have been meaningless to him.

The rest of the group emerged from their hiding places. The red and black stripes of body paint hiding their shapes until they moved, they appeared to resolve themselves from the trees. They looked from one to the other, confused. Terrified. Juro, Eena's brother, this hunt's leader, was listening in frozen wide-eyed intensity to the throbbing roar - his breath held in his chest until the sound fell below that of the singing insects.

Eena swung the blowpipe from his back. Something in him needed the security of it in his hands, but there was nothing to aim at now. The thing was gone. He gripped the pipe, drumming his fingers against the bamboo as he looked around.

The Huaro had no word for helicopter. Unseen by outsiders for generations in the green-roofed world of the Amazon rainforest, they had never needed such a word. They were going to need one now. In the coming months, they were going to learn a lot of new words, and a lot of new things to fear.

Juro caught Eena's eye, and slowly straightened. He nodded at his brother, and gestured towards the tallest tree. Eena knew his brother's thoughts instantly. Juro wanted him to go up and see where the thing was going. What it was. He turned, assessing the tree. It presented no great challenge. Eena had the long arms, and long fingers of an expert climber. The best in the group. Best in the tribe maybe. He grabbed a nodule of vine, and started to pull himself up.

Eena could move almost as fast upwards as he could on the ground through the thick forest, but his heart was still thumping as fast as the throb of the thing's beating wings. The thought of what he might see when his head cleared the canopy filled him with dread.

*   *   *

2,500 miles away, in a city Eena could not have imagined, an office block rose forty floors into the sky. Metal-framed, gold-tinted windows presented a shining flat surface. Eena could probably have climbed that vertical face all the way to the top floor, where Lincoln Drier, the man whose commands had ultimately launched the helicopter, sat studying the slow decline of his company's stock. Nobody outside the board knew it, but things were a lot worse than they seemed. The company was on the edge. The Amazon project had to work. It just had to. Everything was at stake.

If Eena had been there, naked, his black and red striped skin standing out against the empty blue sky, his poisoned blowpipe at his back, hanging outside the window, Lincoln Drier would not even have noticed. The flickering green and red figures on his screen completely absorbed him.

*   *   *

Eena climbed, almost running up the twisted ladder of vines that led to the canopy. Below him, Juro's and the others' eyes were on him, but they were tiny now, and dark against the forest floor as his eyes adjusted to the sunlight filtering through the high leaves. He heard Juro's whistle of encouragement, and a couple of seconds later, broke through into the empty air at the top of the tree.

Around him, the treetops formed a single green cascade from Eena's tree to the violet distance in all directions. The landscape undulated with mountains and valleys. Cloud hid the highest peaks, mist rose in patches here and there, but the treetops covered everything except the wide, yellow, muddy swirl of the river down in the valley.

Everything Eena had known or imagined was before him. It was a world without oceans, roads, cities, deserts. The forest was all there was and all there ever could be.

Then he saw it. On the other side of the valley. It could have been a fly, or a bird, but somehow it wasn't. Its path was too firm. Its turning circle, strange. Spinning around its centre, its tail held straight out, rigid. Its body was angled slightly down as it swept back and forth, swinging around. As he watched, it banked around, close to the mountain at the other side of the valley, and then levelled out heading straight back towards Eena.

From a speck at the other side of the valley, it grew with frightening speed. Nose down. Tail up. Its voice roaring louder and louder. Eena looked down through the trees and whistled a warning. Below him, the others started to run, scattering into the undergrowth.

He looked back up. It was close now, its black body shining with hard angles. It slowed to a halt. That sound, impossibly loud now, vibrating through his whole body. The tree swinging as he clung to it. The thing hung in the air so close he felt as though he could touch it. It hovered in front of him for a moment, as though it were alive, watching him. Did it see him? He couldn't tell.

Suddenly it twisted. A huge door slid open on the side of its body and he could see a man now inside it, encased in black cloth. Eyes covered with shining glass like the eyes of a giant insect. He leaned out, holding something. A stick. Red brown. About the length of his forearm.

He threw it down into the trees. Eena watched it drop, spinning through the canopy to the forest floor below. It seemed to be flickering. Glowing at one end.

The door slammed shut and the machine reared backwards, rising up until it was about twice tree-height above him. Eena watched it go. It was impossible not to. The largest, heaviest, most terrifying object he had ever seen in motion, and it was flying like a bird. No, not like a bird. A bird couldn't hover motionless in the air. More like an insect. A giant, metal fly that could swallow him whole. What was it doing?

A white light lit the jungle from below like lightning, and there was a sound like every sound Eena had ever heard compressed into a single moment. It tore his attention from the sky to the ground. The tree shook. Three others nearby folded in splintering destruction, down into the forest, and were instantly replaced by one single towering tree of fire, its trunk burning his face, and its branches spreading high above him in orange flame.

In a second, the tree of fire was gone, plummeting upwards, turning to black smoke. He clung onto his bending, swooping tree. Felt its trunk straining, starting to splinter. His eyes were seared with bright darkness. He screwed them up tight, and held on for his life.The dirt, and leaf mulch, and creatures of the forest floor rained down around him, dead, blackened and torn apart by the force of the explosion.

The tree steadied. He opened his eyes, and they adjusted. Blurry, smoky but slowly clearing. He rubbed a hand across them. There was a great hole in the jungle. A dark brown pit of exposed earth, and shattered branches, and slowly setting debris.

The birds, even the insects were silent in the emptiness after the blast, but on the other side, a huge tree, tied by vines to one of the falling ones, was being dragged towards him. As he watched in terror, its trunk fractured, and it tipped, falling towards his own tree.

Above him, the metal thing was swooping down again. Closer this time. He swung down under the canopy, racing hand over hand down the huge trunk, half falling, half climbing, grabbing at vines and branches to slow his fall. Mid way down, he felt the whole thing shake under him as the falling tree struck it. He lost his footing, swung by one hand around the trunk, just hanging on, still a more-than-deadly fall above the forest floor. Nothing was beneath him to break his fall if he dropped now. Just a dizzying drop into the carved-out raw earth surrounded by broken trees.

He scrambled for a hand hold, and looked up. The falling tree was still coming. Broken at the top, and slowed by its tangle of vines, the tree's canopy was sweeping down towards him, snapping and scraping his tree clean of every branch and clinging plant as it came.

No point trying to flee it. He clung on until it swept onto him and felt the thick thatch of leaves and branches tear him from the trunk, and grasped for something - anything to hold onto as he fell.

His fists closed on loose leaves. Flailing vines caught under his arms. He fell with the tree. Tumbled in its now-horizontal canopy. Slowed slightly by the friction of leaves against the trunk. Slowed enough to survive? He couldn't tell. For a moment he glimpsed fur. A troupe of monkeys had been in the other tree. They were falling now, with him, screaming as they went. Sure-footed in the trees, but unable to comprehend their destruction, they fell as chaotically as he did.

In what seemed like a second he crashed into the forest floor. It was a pit of broken trees and churned mud. He scrambled to his feet. Breath hard. Fingers raw and shaking. Scratches from the tearing branches stinging every part of his body. Around him the monkeys were scattered dead or dying. A mother cradled her baby against her chest. It was still living, protected somehow by its mother's body. The tribe hunted monkeys for food, but never the mothers. Never the babies. It was a rule. Killing the babies was wrong. Unfair. It looked up at him. Huge eyes, round. Screamed. Eena bent towards it. Scooped it up. Just then, he saw, out of the corner of his eye, the glowing stick spinning down beside him and vanishing beneath the leaves.

Eena turned and ran, desperately flinging himself over logs and through waist-deep fragments of shredded green canopy. He grabbed handfuls of roots and vines and leaves and hauled himself forward, legs whirling, pounding into the loose ground, arms flailing past and through the destruction.

Behind him came the explosion.

It hit his back - a wall of sound and heat, throwing him high into the air. It seemed he was flying, and then his shoulder hit a tree, sending him spinning to the ground. He got up, scrambling, still holding the baby monkey, and fled blindly into the forest, not stopping until he reached the river where he threw himself face down in the mud, shaking and gasping, his back and face still burning with the heat, the smell of the smoke still in his nose, the baby monkey clung hard to his back.

SIX MONTHS LATER.
THE ENGLISH CHANNEL.

A dinghy bumped out across a cold, grey, empty sea. They had rounded the Isle of Wight, and were now heading straight out into the English Channel. It was a small craft with a single, tiny outboard motor, struggling under the weight of its three occupants and their hastily grabbed luggage. Celeste Nardani pushed the boat urgently through waves it was never designed for. Time was short. If they made it to the ship before it set off across the Atlantic, they would get passage. If not - well, it was best not to think about that.

Celeste was sixteen. She dressed practically, not for show: army issue camouflage trousers and jacket. Short hair. Not a crew cut, but definitely a boy's style. It wasn't easy to rebel against parents like hers, but Celeste had nailed it. This time, she had absolutely nailed it.

They sat in front of her, sullen and wet. Dad, nervous, ragged, eyes darting. Mum, tired, limp.

Celeste's brain was stuck on repeat. Three days now and still she buffeted between emotional states the way the boat buffered between waves. One second airborne. The next, plummeting down to crash hard into the floor of water between the waves, sending a sheet of shattered liquid over the whole family. Regret to anger. Guilt to a strange sort of grim pride. She hadn't slept. Had barely eaten. The bruises were hurting more now than they had in the underpass.

She gripped the tiller, and stared between her parents out to their destination in the distance. They were running again, and it was her fault. Of course it was her fault every time. The Nardanis had always been what most people called "alternative". To successive sets of polite neighbours, Mum

11

and Dad were "the hippies" or "the weirdos" who'd just moved in. Lazy stereotypes followed them wherever they went and Mum and Dad didn't seem to care.

Celeste, however, felt every insult. Every snide remark reminded her that she did not belong with the rest of the world. But while Mum and Dad could cope with being 'weirdos' because they had each other, Celeste knew she did not belong with them either. She had no-one.

In each new town, gossip, mistrust, and unfocused anger hung like a cloud of poison in the air. Just visible at first, but then growing and concentrating until finally something would happen and Celeste would snap. Mum and Dad would never defend themselves and they would never be there to defend her either. But sooner or later, Celeste would always be forced to fight for them.

It was a pattern Celeste knew well enough. Someone would say something about them, or pick on her for being one of them, and Celeste would hit back. Hard.

Only then would the family close in. Not of course to confront the real problem, but to avoid it. Avoidance of conflict was like a choreographed dance for the Nardanis, and all of them knew their roles. Dad would say something crazy about the government. Mum would announce a sudden passion for some other town. They'd pack up and move on. Nobody ever needed to allocate blame, or have any uncomfortable conversations. Nobody pressed charges. And Celeste never had to decide whether the blame lay with her family, the town or herself. That was how it had always worked.

But this time it was different. This time they could not exchange tight smiles and decide that it was "about time" to move on. Dad's latest conspiracy could not be blamed. Mum brightly talking of an exciting adventure was not fooling any of them. Celeste's parents were going through the motions because it was all they knew how to do, but nothing could disguise this one. It was on her. And this time, they were running for real.

Mum flashed a concerned smile across the boat at her. She had the tired look of a skull, grinning from behind a sheet of long, dry hair which hung limply down to her waist. Her gypsy skirt was soaked. Its tassels slapping wetly against her ankles.

"We're not running away," she had protested, as they had stuffed a few possessions into a couple of floral carpet bags in the middle of the night, and bundled them into the car. Those same bags, now wet through, lay on the floor of the boat. Mum looked over at the ship growing on the horizon. It was more than a silhouette now. A green hull, white boxy shapes on top. Faster, apparently, than it looked.

"I'm actually looking forward to this!" said Mum. "It'll be exciting." Celeste did not answer. Eventually, Mum said, "It's just a little holiday. Until things calm down. You know that, don't you?" Typical Mum. She was wrong, and Dad, despite his paranoia, was right. Things would not calm down. Not this time.

If Mum had sent Celeste to school like a normal kid, none of this would have happened. Probably. She'd have GCSEs. Friends. A life. Probably. But being home-schooled - especially when your mum had no sense of boundaries, humour, or time - was an excruciating, frustrating and suffocating business. It left Celeste out of place between her parents, and out of place anywhere else. What felt like a dark, angry hole had opened up inside her where the normal life of a teenager ought to be.

Dad tilted his head up so that the now ragged neckline of his beard showed as he scanned the skies.

"Can you hear that?" he said. Celeste shook her head. She couldn't hear anything except the outboard motor, and the boat slapping the waves. "Drone" he said. He pointed to three white specks in the sky. "They've been following us since we left shore." Drones were Dad's absolute favourite conspiracy. He saw them everywhere. Every unknown noise. Every dot in the sky. He was convinced the government was using them for surveillance. Dad had a deep suspicion that everyone, from the government to the media to NASA was part of the Illuminati - a global conspiracy possibly involving aliens. Doctors were suppressing herbal cures. Google was reprogramming people's minds using psychological suggestion. Oil giants were hiding the truth about impending environmental catastrophe.

But Celeste's eyes were sharper than his. "They're seagulls," she said. Was Dad getting worse? She hoped not, or that would be another thing to blame herself for. Her parents were irritating idiots a lot of the time, but they didn't deserve this.

On the other side of the boat, Dad raised his eyebrows in his trademark 'That's what they want you to think' expression. He was a paranoid fantasist, and Celeste's actions had handed him the perfect opportunity to run with that paranoia, but she knew that when he had said it was time to run, he had been right. This time, being shunned by the community and told off by the police was not going to be the end of it.

Up ahead, the shape of the *Green Crusader* had grown on the horizon. Was it moving already? Leaving them? With the movement of the dinghy crashing through the water, she couldn't tell. She checked the fuel gauge. Almost empty. If she went too slowly and conserved fuel, they could make it easily, but the ship would be gone. If she went too fast, they'd run out before they reached it. She made the call, and opened the throttle fully. The boat surged forwards.

2.

Eena stood on the edge of the clearing. Juro was by his side. His brother had survived those first blasts. Eena's warning whistle had given the hunters just enough time to scatter, but even six months on, the burns on Juro's back and all down his left arm had still not healed. They were still too sensitive to apply the red and black camouflage, so his skin in places was pink and raw. On Eena's shoulder, the monkey shifted its position. With nowhere else to go, it had stayed with him since the blast. Now it tilted its head to peer through the trees to the ironwork beyond.

Juro held his spear. It was as tall as he was. Not a weapon to hunt, but one to show strength. Eena shot him a questioning glance. The brothers were going against their family. Against the whole tribe. Was he certain?

Juro narrowed his eyes, but he didn't answer. Instead, he crouched. By his foot was a pool of water. It should have been clean and clear. Instead, it was dark. Its surface swam with a sheen of dim rainbows. Juro dipped his hand into the pool, just for a second, and when he drew it out and held it up right in front of Eena's face. It was jet black and shining and covered from wrist to the tips of his fingers. A viscous coating flowed, thickly down his arm. Juro said nothing, but his meaning was clear enough.

It had something to do with the outsiders. Somehow they had made the earth angry and now dark water was soaking up through it. After the thing in the sky, and the explosions splintering the trees in the clearing, they had returned, lowered down on ropes. They had felled more trees close to the river and created a wide, bald patch of land large enough for the flying things to land.

16

Day after day the men came, bringing more strange cargo. Crates, hauled out of the flying monsters, were broken open to reveal things that rolled around the clearing on tracks like the bellies of snakes so huge and strong that they could push down whole trees. Clanging huts swung from the flying things on ropes as they were lowered in to be guided by strange-clothed, shouting men into position. In the centre, a tower rose red and black, but taller and wider than any tree trunk. It was brought in one piece at a time as the brothers and the other tribesmen watched secretly from the edges of the jungle. At the top of the tower, the outsiders lit a fire that burned day and night, in a plume of flame taller than ten men standing on each other's shoulders.

And soon after they came, the dark water started to weep, stinking from the angry ground. Now the whole clearing smelled of it. The men dug rough pits, and poured it into them through pipes, channeling it down towards the river.

Gradually all the water started to smell, and darken. The rainbow sheen covered the river. The water the tribe bathed in. The water they fished in. The water they drank. Fish floated to the surface, silver on their sides and curled over in dead shoals. They drifted into the banks. Parrots appeared, flapping on the ground, the bright reds and greens and blues of their feathers matted and scuffed with black smudges. Only the rainwater was clean. Soon after that people from Eena's tribe had started to get ill. Sick, dizzy, vomiting. Some had grown pale and quiet. Others were feeling pain in their stomachs, their throats, their heads.

Time and again, Eena had watched his brother arguing that they must try to make contact with the outsiders, make them understand, but the rest of the tribe had said no, their stupid legends holding them back. Legends of the last time outsiders had visited, killed, enslaved, and forced the Huaro tribe to fracture, to flee deep into the jungles and hide. But that was so long ago, before Eena and Juro's grandparents' grandparents. Surely the outsiders must have changed by now?

Eena and Juro could not have known that it was a hundred years since the British Empire's need for rubber killed so many of their ancestors. They could not have known that the new outsiders sought something else from under the jungle. And they could not have known that this small clearing was just a test-bed for something much, much larger.

Eena watched his brother. There was a solid-set determination on his face. They would do this together, or Juro would do it alone. Juro turned, and despite his misgivings, despite his fear, Eena followed him. The two brothers stepped forward out of the clearing and into plain sight.

3.

The boat bounced and crashed towards the ship. Celeste fought to keep it upright and on course. The little dinghy was built for cruising the shoreline, not the infamously choppy waters of the English Channel, but it was all they could get hold of at such short notice. They had obtained it from some confused holidaymakers in exchange for their beaten up old estate car. Dad, conducting the negotiation, must have looked every inch the fleeing criminal. The waves were getting rougher now, and the engine was straining. Celeste had real doubts that the craft would make it.

She hated herself. Not for the fight. Not even for what had followed. Those girls had asked for that. But she hated herself for being such a sad-act in the first place.

It wasn't as though she'd ever even been to that stupid school. They'd only moved to Milton Highbury, a couple of months earlier, so what on earth had possessed her to start hanging around outside the gates, pressing her face up against the green metal bars like an animal staring jealously into a zoo? Her eyes had filled inexplicably with tears she could not define. Anger, bitterness, loss - she had no clue.

She remembered the moment it had started. She had been on her way to the computer shop, hoping to pick up a motherboard for a new computer she was building, when a gaggle of girls erupted from a bus in their blue-checked uniforms talking loudly and excitedly. They were her age, on their way to school, and for a minute or so, she had shared the pavement with them, walking side by side, ignored amongst them as they buzzed about their imminent GCSEs.

The feeling that hit Celeste as the girls turned in through the school gates, and left her, had been completely unexpected. It had only been a moment. Just a glimpse of a world she would never be a part of. But it had torn into her. Every girl of her age was preparing for exams. Everyone but her, and suddenly, she felt totally alone.

She started to stalk the girls. Following them to school. Watching through the gates as they filed from lesson to lesson. Exam to exam. How did she imagine it was going to end?

She should have realised - should have known from experience - that while she watched, they were watching her back. They talked about her. That weird girl from that weird family, on her own at the gates, and they had decided to teach her a lesson.

It had happened so quickly she hadn't have time to react. She had been walking through the subway on the way back to the bus stop. Suddenly, one of the girls was behind her, grabbing her hair. She kicked out and tried to turn, but she was pulled off-balance, and fell hard onto her side. Then they were all around her, kicking her over and over. She couldn't tell how many. Six, maybe. They were laughing. Jeering. She fought to fend off the blows with her hands, but there were too many. She felt them in her stomach, her shins, her face.

If she'd been thinking straight, she would have stayed down and waited for them to leave. She should have limped home, chalked it up to experience and moved on. That was what she should have done. It would have been better for everyone. But she didn't stay down. She felt a sharp impact to her cheek, forcing her head back hard against the subway wall. She smelled her own blood, and something inside her flared like an igniting match. Here we go again, she thought.

She kicked out. One went down. She was on her feet in a second, and striking out with everything she had. Head down, seeing nothing. Just feeling her way through the fight. A ball of blind fists. She remembered shadows, bodies, her blows landing. Theirs must have landed too, but she did not care.

Other people always fought too carefully. Trying to avoid pain. Looking for opportunities. Trying to inflict the precise amount of damage they thought it appropriate to inflict. Socially polite fighting. Celeste did not understand why. She fought like a cat. No restraint. No hesitation. As though every fight was for her life. If she left scars, she left them. If she broke bones, she broke them. If she had had a stick she would have used it. Or a knife or a gun. To win a fight, you did not have to be stronger, or faster. You just had to not care. While your opponents were making threats and testing weaknesses, you had to go nuclear early.

In seconds, it was over. There was blood on her fists. A throbbing in her head. But no pain. The girls who were still standing were staggering away. She must have been kicked a dozen times, but she could feel nothing. Nothing except her breath and the throbbing of her own pulse and anger still blindingly strong.

Could she have stopped then? Possibly. Should she have? Of course. But these were just a few girls. It was the school that needed to be punished. The whole stinking place.

Because while Mum was not much of a teacher, Celeste herself knew how to learn. And in the years when the other girls had been studying French and Physics Celeste had found herself another teacher. With no limits on her Internet access, and no bedtime since she was five, Celeste spent her nights scouring the online world. By the age of ten, she knew how to strip down and rebuild a computer. By fifteen, she had followed every black-hat hacker on the planet.

Now, her fury still growing, she turned, walked out of the subway and into the library. The librarian may have looked up, and noticed the strange bloodied girl marching into the computer room, but Celeste was not challenged as she sat down at a terminal, hit the dark web, and sent a trojan straight through the school's firewall. The school's security was weak, an old school with aging teachers and creaking IT. They didn't understand their vulnerabilities. They would understand them soon enough.

She opened up a window displaying a direct link to the school's protected drives, and she deleted everything. School records. Test results. Pupil data. Exam papers. Lesson plans. Everything from the hockey fixtures to staff wages. She wiped the lot. When they got into school the following morning, ready for the final GCSE exams, the teachers would find everything had gone, and it would serve them right. If she had burned the school to the ground in the night, it would have done less damage.

Celeste was half-way home before her head finally cleared, the full consequences started to dawn on her, and she realised she would have to confess to Mum and Dad.

Dad, of course, had assumed the black helicopters of the Illuminati would be landing on the lawn. Mum had initially thought it would all blow over. But Celeste knew what she had done. A cyber-attack on that scale meant prison. No question. And they would find out who did it. She had been clever enough to hack the school, but she had made little attempt to disguise herself. They had until the morning to make their escape.

It was 2 am when Mum had finally accepted the seriousness of the situation. Celeste could tell she had got it because she had suddenly remembered Rose and Annette, a couple of semi-retired roaming eco activists the family had met at a festival the previous summer. Rose and Annette had enthused about the joys of volunteering on environmental protest ships in an unending stream of earnest words from the moment they pitched up camp next to the Nardanis until the moment the festival ended. By comparison to this wall of sound, the music had been but a minor irritation. Now, Mum suddenly recalled their conversation and fished out a decorated notebook in which she had scrawled their phone number.

Mum had made the call and it was answered immediately despite the time. The ship was due to leave for South America, and Mum signed them up on the spot. If they could make it before the ship left and volunteered to help on the ship's mission, they would be welcomed on board. The family had stuffed their bags and ran - off to join the hippy equivalent of the French Foreign Legion: *The Green Crusader*.

A wave hit them hard, and jolted Celeste and knocking the tiller to the left. She struggled to correct it. They were close now. She could see the hull, curving up and out of the water a few hundred metres in front of them.

But something was wrong. The ship was starting to move. Behind the vessel, water was churning as the propellers started to spin. The ship began to pick up speed. It was leaving without them. On deck, she could see just one person. A man in a yellow jacket, scanning the horizon with binoculars. As she watched, the figure lowered the binoculars and turned his back. He hadn't spotted the little boat in the water.

Celeste acted instantly. She steered away from the ship - no point trying to catch the vessel - and instead headed for a point just in front of it. There was just one chance. If they could intersect the ship on its course before it picked up too much speed, they might just get close enough to be heard shouting.

She felt the boat bank to its new course, and, as they sped over the water, the two crafts slowly began to converge. In a few moments, their boat was just in front, the Green Crusader bearing down on them faster and faster as they bounced over the water on a direct collision course.

It was high above them now, the prow like a cliff-face, curved out over them. The Green Crusader was not, Celeste just had time to realise, very green anymore. The paintwork on the hull was filthy, speckled with rust and scratches. She had seen photos of the ship, new and shining, cutting through the water. But right now, as its shadow fell across them, Celeste reckoned she could get through the bodywork with a kick. The ship had seen better days - but not recently.

A second later, the outboard sputtered and died. Celeste looked down in horror. Out of fuel. The dinghy drifted to a halt directly in the path of the huge vessel. It was right on them, now. They began to shout, all three of them, yelling at the tops of their voices. The ship kept coming.

Suddenly, a figure appeared, pointing over the edge of the railings. Celeste recognised Rose. Annette's head bobbed into view next to her. She pointed, shouted something. Then there were more figures, peering over. The ship veered to the left, slicing past them just a metre away, slowing, its wake almost overturning the little dingy.

The rocking subsided, and the ship came to a halt, towering above them.

Celeste breathed a sigh of relief. Mum smiled.

"Ready?" she said as though they'd just secured the last spot in a carpark.

Now there were figures starting to appear all along the side of the ship. Celeste scanned them. If the people of Milton Highbury thought her parents were weird, they'd have a field day here.

4.

"You'd better come see this." Samuel's wide, sloping shoulders appeared in the doorway of the stifling metal office Zoila Chavez was forced to call home. What was it now? It wasn't enough that she had to put up with this place. What made her life impossible were these constant interruptions. The local workers seemed to have no idea what they were doing, and no respect for the chain of command. She had worked damn hard to get control of this project but still the workers fought her every step of the way. They couldn't get used to being ordered around by a woman. Well, that would have to change. If she were to keep the project on track, she would need to make an example, and soon.

She stood, and slammed her pen down on the desk. It made a hollow metal sound. The desk was a piece of tin with sharp, unfinished edges, but the pen was thick and heavy and gold. It was a present, as it happened, from the president. Zoila was used to roughing it, but she knew what luxury was like too, and if this job came through the way it ought to, she would never have to sit in a tin box in the jungle ever again.

Everything here was filthy, everything seemed to be alive, and everything wanted to either drink her blood or waste her time. Civilised accommodation couldn't come quickly enough to this disgusting place. The man in the doorway had proved himself useful in the past, but Samuel hadn't been hired for his brains.

"Come now," Samuel said in a deep, stupid voice. He turned and lumbered off. Zoila reluctantly followed him, stomping outside away from the fan that was her only respite from the heat. She swore under her breath.

In the compound outside, everything had stopped. The workers had abandoned their machines and were clustered at the edge of the clearing. Zoila pushed her way to the front of the crowd. She didn't have to take this idleness, and it was time they learnt that.

What she saw, stopped her in her tracks.

Two men - boys really - naked and painted in red and black stripes - were standing at the edge of the trees. The older boy was holding a long spear, waving it around, and shouting in some strange language. Zoila noticed he had deep burns down one side of his body and arm.. The younger one was silently standing by, watching. On his shoulder sat a little monkey, screeching.

They looked like something from prehistory. Zoila knew that there were tribes living in the jungle which civilisation had never made contact with, but there were so few of them, and the jungle so huge, that she never expected to meet one.

In any case, the initial explosive charges dropped into the jungle by helicopter should have scared off any natives lurking in the valley. These people must either be deaf or stupid, but their presence in the valley was a problem. A big problem.

Spear Boy stepped forward, focusing on Zoila. He shouted in his strange language, waited for an answer, then shouted again. Zoila shrugged. He looked at Monkey Boy - perhaps he could communicate.

"What do you want?" said Zoila, loud and slow. Monkey boy didn't react. Spear boy carried on shouting and waving aggressively. The workers crowded around, Zoila straightened. This was all she needed.

Even now, the cutters were powering through the jungle, flattening and tarmacing to create the roadway that would link this site with the main road 200 kilometres away. Once that happened, they would no longer be limited to what they could bring in by helicopter. The trucks could come in. The tankers could go out. Things would start moving a lot faster then. But Zoila had a lot to get done before that could happen. A lot. And the crew were unsettled. Disrespectful. Discipline was breaking down.

Zoila understood. The ecology here was amongst the richest and most valuable on earth, and the native peoples were some of the last un-contacted tribes on the planet - living as humans had lived hundreds of thousands of years ago.

She was well briefed on all that. She had read the reports. In fact, the early part of her job had been showing the various government agencies and charities and the world's press just how conscious the company was of its responsibilities not to upset the delicate balance here. She had been good at it too. If it hadn't been for her assurances that the work would be done sensitively, they would never have got the go-ahead. PR was everything, after all. But now, everyone on site, workers and natives alike, needed to know how seriously Zoila took those responsibilities.

Spear Boy was still shouting and waving. He looked angry. Monkey Boy was still standing back, quiet. Probably just along for the ride.

Zoila remembered what the boss, Lincoln Dryer had told her when he'd given her the job: "Nobody gives you respect," he had said. "You gotta take it."

They needed a clear signal, and it was Zoila's job to set the tone.

She waited until Spear Boy paused for breath, holding his spear up high above his head. She looked straight at him, pulled her pistol from the holster in her jacket pocket and levelled it. The boy looked at it, head on one side. He'd probably never seen a gun before. It hardly mattered. The idea wasn't to scare him. Zoila shrugged, and shot him square in the chest.

The boy's knees buckled. He was dead before the surprise hit his face. Monkey Boy stared, wide-eyed for a second, trying to take in what had happened. Zoila turned the gun towards him. The boy turned and fled, wailing into the forest. The monkey bounded after him, screeching as it ran.

The crew stared at her. Two dozen tough-guys, sweating and dirty. Eyes wide, mouths hanging open in shock. They looked in silence at her, then at each other. She holstered her gun.

"Clear that away," she said, gesturing to the body, "and then get back to work." The workers reacted, obeying instantly. In a single second, she had changed everything. Nobody would be questioning her authority ever again.

Back in her tin office, Zoila flipped open her laptop. The natives looked pretty harmless. Once Monkey Boy got back to whatever camp or tree house those savages lived in, the rest - if there were any - would probably vanish. Best for everyone if they did. There was plenty of forest for them. The workers had all been brought up with superstitions about the rainforest people. Rumours of cannibalism. Rumours of magic powers. All nonsense, of course but it was just the kind of thing that might spook the hired help, and more delays weren't part of the plan.

The security in this place was hopelessly low-tech. And this little incident might be just the excuse Zoila needed to bring in a bit more firepower. It would make her look better. Build her role up. After all, the harder this job seemed to Lincoln Dryer and the rest of the board, the better Zoila herself would look when she pulled it off. PR was everything.

5.

A rusty crane swung out from the deck of the Green Crusader, and lowered down a set of ropes. Mum and Dad strapped them to the dinghy to allow it to be hoisted on board.

Suddenly, the crane pulled tight and caught Celeste off balance. The little boat jerked and tipped as it was yanked out of the water. Somehow, Celeste's phone dropped out of her pocket and into the wet bottom of the boat as she gripped the rubber float tight to avoid being thrown overboard. On the floor, the luggage shifted and one of the bags slammed hard into her foot, its buckle scraping her shin. Her phone skidded across the floor towards a puddle of water. Whoever was operating the crane was not doing it very well. She leant down and grabbed the phone just before it was submerged.

They started to ascend in sickening, swinging jerks pitching one way and then the other. The bags slid back and forth, slamming into Celeste's leg again and again, forcing her against the side of the boat closest to the ship's hull. She fumbled with her phone, cold hands struggling to hold onto it.

As they rose higher, the swinging got worse. Celeste stuck out her foot to stop the pile of bags crashing into it. The bottom one stopped, but the top two simply slid on top of her, hitting her in the ribs, and pitching her half out of the boat. Her arm was hanging down below her, outstretched towards the water, phone held just in her fingertips now. She stared down, five metres into the grey sea, churning and frothing against the barnacled side of the ship and cursed whoever was driving the crane. She scrambled back into the boat just as the dinghy swung in towards the ship again, trapping her hand painfully between their little boat and the hull. Her knuckles scraped and she felt something crack under her fingers. Her heart sank.

She pulled her hand back, and looked down. The phone's screen was broken. A spider's web of white cracks spread from the corner out across the screen. Great. The crane driver was in big trouble now.

The crane lurched again, and the boat cleared the top of the deck. It swung inwards, scraping them over the railings and dumping them on a flat portion of deck in a little alcove. On one side, she spotted a control console. A pillar blocked her view of its operator.

Celeste scrambled out, clambering angrily over the boat's rubber sides. She gripped her phone in her hand. There was blood seeping from her knuckles, and it smeared across the screen. She marched up to the console and held out the phone in front of her.

"Look!" she said, waving the cracked screen. "Were you trying to kill us?"

The crane's operator looked up. Celeste did a double take. She was expecting a smock-wearing hippy. Either that or some pretentiously manicured hipster. This was neither. It was just a boy. He couldn't have been much older than she was. He was tall. Messy blond hair, topping a face that looked as though it had done stuff. Hands too big for him still gripping the crane's twin joysticks. He was folded in deeply layered thick clothing. Loose jeans, a heavy jumper. A yellow waterproof. She realised it had been him on the deck with the binoculars, failing to notice them.

The boy turned. Grinned. A smile that turned into a laugh. A smile that made her want to either smile back or kick him in the groin. She resisted both urges and just stared him out until he saw she was serious, and the smile died on his face.

"Keep your hands inside the boat," he said, "didn't anybody tell you?" His accent was strange - a mish-mash that didn't seem to come from anywhere. There was American in it, a little South African or Australian, and something else she couldn't place.

"No!" she said, shifting from one foot to the other. "Nobody told us anything." The boy shrugged. His eyes were brown. Almost black. A gust of wind threw a burst of spray across one side of his face. He wiped it away without blinking or looking away from her. She was suddenly aware of what she must look like to him. Bleeding. Soaked. Waving her broken phone at him like a spoilt child. Well, she had a right to be angry - how was she supposed to know what to do? And anyway, all he had to do was get the boat onto the deck without throwing them all in the water, or beating them to death against the side. How hard could that be?

She opened her mouth to ask him, but at that moment, the crew descended.

If you could call them a crew.

A spinning gabbling crowd of Bohemian patchwork knitwear and henna tattoos. Men in checked shirts with impossibly manicured beards. Others, braided and pierced so that they resembled Hollywood pirates - if Hollywood pirates were unarmed and wore no animal products. Women in dreads and layered hemp, and T-shirts with angry motifs. Nobody, Celeste noticed, under forty. Mum and Dad would fit right in.

They waved and greeted and hugged and bundled Celeste and her family away. The boy vanished behind a swirl of ethically-sourced ponchos and somehow Celeste found

33

herself in the heart of the ship, where a welcome meal was being doled out in the form of thick, hearty soup and flatbread, brown food which she devoured at a rate that surprised even her.

6.

All in all, there were about twenty crew including her parents. Everyone except Rose and Annette were strangers, but they were all horribly determined to make Celeste and her family welcome. While she ate, Celeste's crimes were quickly outlined by Mum and Dad.

Her parent's account was a work of art. Improvising around each other, they quickly made her act of petty revenge-fuelled vandalism seem like a blow against the institutions of the state. Celeste said nothing. If that was what they wanted from a daughter, then fine. She wondered if they really believed it.

One thing was very clear. Mum and Dad's wild enthusiasm for the ship's mission was not faked. The voyage may have been forced on them, but they embraced it wholeheartedly. The more they learnt from the rest of the crew, the more excited they got, and the more cynical Celeste became.

Because, apparently, this bunch of misfits were on their way to confront the world's biggest oil company. Their arrogance was breathtaking. This crew of well-meaning volunteers was about to save the Amazon rainforest. How? With a rock concert. Dad must have caught Celeste's skeptical expression because he grabbed her by both shoulders and assured her that this protest would send shockwaves across the world. After all, the Pale Riders were playing - the ancient band had re-formed especially after forty years to do this one gig. If that didn't stop the bulldozers, Dad was certain, nothing would. Way to stick it to the global conspiracy, thought Celeste. The Illuminati would be quaking in their boots.

In reality, of course, the whole thing was a pure, stupid waste of time, but Celeste said nothing. Because, for the first time in three days, both her parents seemed genuinely happy. She felt a tiny wave of relief as she watched them. Her responsibility for looking after Mum and Dad, protecting them from the world and themselves, was temporarily lifted. This may be a floating asylum, but for the first time in years, they were in a place where she wouldn't need to get into any fights to protect them.

She just hoped that when they arrived, she would be able to stand at the back where her camouflage would allow her to blend into the rainforest.

She looked up. The crew were gathering in a circle, her parents, joining it, Mum trying to attract her attention. On the other side of the room, somebody was unzipping a guitar case.

Celeste had been to enough gatherings with her parents to know where this was going. Some cringing singalong was about to spontaneously erupt, and if she didn't act now, Celeste knew from experience she'd be forced to express her creativity in some horrific way just to prove she was part of the group. She did not want to sing folk songs. Not now. Not ever. As the circle closed, Celeste quietly opened the door and slipped out of the room.

Safely outside on deck, Celeste hauled out her phone. She hit the button. It lit up. Not broken, at least. The screen was visible too, mostly. A small tangle of cracks in the corner shattered the icons slightly there, but the touchscreen worked, and the display was readable.

Now for the important part. She had done her research online while the family had driven to the beach from which they were setting off. That meant they were locked in for the four week journey across the Atlantic, through the

Panama Canal, and down to Columbia. That meant weeks of empty ocean with nothing but seasickness, mind numbing boredom and her parents' earnest eco-tourist friends for company. And for Celeste that meant one overridingly vital question needed to be answered:

Did they have Wifi?

She tapped the phone.

TGC Network:

Signal Strength: Fair

She punched the air. Now all she needed was the password. Looking up, she could see, at the highest point of the ship towards the back, a white, bulbous dome. A forest of antennae reached up behind it, and a metal tree sprouted satellite dishes in white and grey, all pointing out and up in random directions. That was the communications hub, but the router could be anywhere. She had to find it because, if it were like every other router she'd ever seen, it would have the password printed on the bottom of it. People cared about security, but they hardly ever cared enough to change the default password.

She walked to the very back of the ship where the wide, flat expanse of the helipad was bordered by railings. The hub was above her now. She could see its looming shapes. She opened her phone again.

Signal Strength: Poor

That meant two things - three actually. First: the router was closer to the front of the boat than the rear. Second, it wasn't strong enough to cover the whole ship. And third, whoever had fitted it was too dumb to realise that a cheap booster would have given them good access throughout the whole ship.

This was good news. If the Wifi didn't cover the whole ship, then she could track it down. She made her way along the narrow walkway that led down the side of the ship almost to the prow. On one side, metal doors lead into the vessel. On the other, torn chicken wire stretched between overpainted rusty struts was all that separated her from the drop into the grey ocean churning past below. Cold spray sprinkled her face and left little drops on her screen, but as she walked, she could see the signal strength growing. She was getting closer.

By the time it was registering as **Excellent,** she had reached the end of the walkway and struggled up a set of metal stairs.

In front of her was a curved door, with a small window. She peered through. It was filthy and scratched, and its two layers of glass had somehow lost their seal, so that the inside was misted by a grimy blurring haze. But from inside, she could see the spark of blinking LEDs and the reassuring blue glow of computer screens. It must be here. She turned the handle and stepped through.

7.

She was standing on the bridge. A curved console in pale cyan, sloping, filled the room. Above it, a view out on a huge three-sided window to the front of the ship and the sea beyond. A row of phones in black and red. A radar scope. Lights, gauges, and readouts. Hundreds of buttons and controls. Four computer screens were moulded into the console. In the centre, on its own section, the ship's wheel stuck out from the main panel.

Once, it had probably looked state-of-the-art. Now, it was a mess. The whole console was dirty and scratched. The underside was rusting. One of the built-in screens was dark and broken, and a replacement had been clumsily wired in, and stuck to the top of it using gaffer-tape. An ancient printer was balanced on one end of the console.

And Celeste was beginning to suspect she knew why the ship was in such a state, because, right in the centre of the control room, hand resting casually on the wheel, that familiar dumb grin on his face, was the boy. If he steered the ship like he operated the crane it was a wonder they were still afloat.

Suddenly aware that she had stared at him for too long without saying anything, she said the first thing that came into her head. "What's the Wifi code?"

The boy shrugged. "I don't know," he said.

Celeste blinked at him. How could he not know something as basic as that. "How long have you been here?" she said.

"All my life," he said simply.

"And you don't know the Wifi code?" she stared at him incredulously.

"Never use the World Wide Web," he said. World Wide Web? What decade was he from?

At that moment, her eyes flicked to a little white box stuffed under the control console - green light flashing. The router. Grimy. Cracked. Sitting in a puddle of water. It looked as though it had been wedged there and forgotten about. What kind of operation was this?

The boy let go of the ship's wheel and held out his hand.

"You're Celeste, right?" he said.

"How do you know?" said Celeste.

"You volunteered because you did a hack or something?" he said. "I'm Peter - the captain's son." Did a hack or something? He was so dumb it was sort of cute.

"I didn't volunteer. I was volunteered," she muttered. "Where is the Captain? We haven't even seen him yet."

"He's in his cabin," said Peter.

"I thought he'd want to meet us."

"He doesn't," he said. "He doesn't like talking to the volunteers."

"I get it," she said.

"No, you don't," said Peter, "He only cares about the ship. The volunteers and the money they pay to be on board are the only thing keeping it from sinking. He needs you, but he doesn't like you. He thinks you're all a bunch of hypocritical eco-tourist tree-huggers and he'd dump you all in the sea if he could."

"I like him," she said. "What stops him?"

Peter shrugged. "Me most of the time," he said. He must have caught her expression, because he added, "He's not so bad. He just has bad days." He smiled. "If you're lucky he won't come out of his cabin until we hit the Panama Canal."

"OK," said Celeste.

40

"Sorry about your phone." Peter said after a long pause.

"It's OK," she said. "Still works."

"You're home-schooled?" said Peter.

Celeste nodded.

"You can always tell. Me too." Celeste's eyes widened.

"Your Mum? Is she on board?" Peter shook his head. "Your Dad?" There must have been a bit too much disbelief in her voice. The captain didn't sound like much of a teacher. Peter shrugged.

"You know how it is."

"Yea," said Celeste. She knew how it was all right. Peter was beginning to seem a bit more interesting.

"Lots of people come on board," he said. "You'd be surprised what you pick up here."

"Like operating a crane?"

Peter looked embarrassed. Celeste smiled. "And a ship," he said. "Want a go?" Peter stepped away from the controls, gesturing to the wheel.

"Really?" she said. He shrugged.

She gingerly reached out and touched the wheel. It moved so easily, it took her by surprise. It was almost loose.

"There's a - an autopilot, right?" She tried to sound casual.

"Yea," Peter let go, and then moved to the main console, flicking at a couple of switches.

"What are you doing?" she said.

He paused.

"I just turned it off," he said. Celeste jumped. Her hands flew away from the wheel as if there were electricity passing through it. You weren't supposed to leave the bridge of a ship under the control of a sixteen-year-old girl, were you?

41

Surely, there must be some kind of law about that. Peter laughed, and it occurred to Celeste that this was a ship at sea. No laws. Nobody's jurisdiction but the Captain's. And the Captain was sulking in his cabin.

She looked over at Peter. And she'd always thought *she* had no boundaries.

Ok, thought Celeste, if he wants to play games... She laid her hands back on the wheel. How hard could it be?

She slowly turned the wheel. The change was gentle, but it quickly started to build. Nine hundred tonnes of metal turning underneath her, cutting through an unimaginable weight of water. She felt the ship dip slightly to one side, forcing her to shift her weight to one foot. The vibration of the engine through her body changed a little. Then she felt it in her spine. Her stomach. Not just the change in the ship, but the slow-building realisation that she was in control of it. This huge vessel was turning just through the movement of her hand. She laughed involuntarily. The boat tipped more severely. A strange thrill spread through her body. It was a feeling she couldn't see, or describe, like the movement of the ship, but it left her heart pounding and her hands shaking. She pulled the wheel harder, forcing it to one side. Felt the whole ship bank, leaning into the turn. Engines wined and struggled, gauges flicked. Screens lit up with red warnings.

"Gently," Peter said. "They're eating soup back there." He had moved behind her. He placed his hand over hers, guided it back, turning the ship back to its original course.

"You like to push it, don't you?" he said.

She shrugged. "I can do it," she said, moving his hand away.

She brought the wheel back to its original position, still feeling adrenaline through her body. The engines calmed. The red gauges settled back. She looked at him as calmly as she could. He looked serious suddenly.

"Can I ask you a question, Celeste?" he said, his eyes not leaving hers. "Why are you here - on this boat? You could have gone anywhere."

Celeste shrugged. Not a question she was expecting. She felt herself blushing for no reason she could explain. What did he want her to say? "I want to do something to help - I... " she stuttered. "My parents - " Peter sighed suddenly and looked away. The intensity gone from his eyes.

"Wrong answer," he said. He flicked a switch on the dashboard. The autopilot light blinked on. Without looking back at her, he walked out and slammed the door behind him.

For a moment, Celeste stood in silent shock in the empty bridge. The lights of the control panels glowed and flickered. The floor vibrated with the slow throb of the engines. Celeste stood, staring after him. What was that about? What had she done?

She followed him out onto the deck. He was fiddling with the railings at the side of the boat. They were rusted right through, the safety rail hanging on by a corroded shard of metal.

"What are you doing?" she said.

"I'm going to need to fix this up." He wobbled the rail. It rattled loosely. "One good push and someone could go right over the edge," It sounded like a threat.

"Mum and Dad said there were other young people on board," she said. "Are they like you?"

Peter looked at her. Suddenly his face looked harder. "They're busy." He went back to his work. Celeste stared at

43

him. What was his problem? Arrogant idiot. Didn't he know what she'd been through in the last three days?

"Ok!" she said at last." You asked me why I was here. Well, I don't know! OK? I didn't ask to come on your stupid boat! I hate the place and every stupid hippy on board. Your boat is a wreck. Your Dad is a waster. And I'm sick of all your stupid, fake worthiness! You all act like you're going to save the world, but who do you think is going to take notice of some dumb concert and a few placards? Nobody, that's who! This whole damn trip is a waste of time!"

Peter looked up, slowly. His face changed. A tight smile twitched at his lips.

"Better," he said. "Much better."

"What?"

"Engine room. Zero six hundred hours tomorrow." he said, and he turned and vanished down the metal steps into the bowels of the ship.

8.

Celeste made a quick trip back to the cockpit to flip the router over. Underneath the faded code was stuck to its bottom. She laughed despite herself. The password was "PASSWORD".

She tapped it into her phone and felt it buzz repeatedly with a day's worth of push notifications. All spam.

For a second, she let her hand rest on the wheel again. Felt a strange impulse to turn it. To punch into the autopilot, set them on a different course. Any course. She remembered a YouTube clip of a cruise ship hitting a pier. Thousands of tons of metal grinding into cars, buildings, tearing itself and everything in front of it to pieces. It looked like fun. She tapped her fingers on the wheel, then drew them back. She closed the door of the cockpit, and made her way back along the gangway to the mess.

Inside, the evening was in full swing. She could hear the music spilling out through the metal door and onto the gangway. It was getting dark now, and yellow lights had appeared along the grey horizon, clustered - France maybe. But the ship was running parallel to the coast. Celeste knew they weren't due to land, or park, or whatever it was ships did, for weeks yet. Assuming the rusty crate made it that far, those little yellow dots were going to be her last sight of civilisation before they headed out across the Atlantic.

It was the hippy party or nothing. She gritted her teeth and stepped through the door.

Somebody had brought a guitar. Predictable. A gawky, bearded man she was later introduced to as 'Ace'. His wife/partner, Dianne was a proud, but ultimately talentless Flautist. Beside them a multiply-pierced and deliberately shaggy-dreadlocked white guy had used up his meagre luggage

45

allocation on a double bass.   Maurice, she later learned. Celeste pictured him wrestling it onto a dingy and rowing it out to meet the ship.

Celeste watched from the edge of the room as they played. Artistic differences between the musicians had already started to surface. The guitarist husband clearly wanted to rock out. Ace hammered at the body of his instrument, tapping out a beat as he strummed, but the double-bass player was having none of it. Maurice owned the rhythm with his deep, resonant sound and he was taking it slow. The washing certainty of Pachellbel's Canon in D. Eight notes repeated without variation over and over. The other players could do what they willed with the melody, but the rhythm was going nowhere.

A girl got up from the audience. About Celeste's age. Blonde. Shining. Spinning in a thin dress spattered in primary reds, yellows and greens.   It looked vaguely Indian in a touristy sort of way, the kind of thing you'd only ever wear to let people know you'd been to India. The girl wore it like it was part of her dance and she danced like everyone was watching. They were. Celeste hated her instantly.

"Darling!" Annette had spotted her. Welcoming arms opened at the other side of the room, and she swooped forward. A loose knitted shawl forming blood-red net wings. Celeste was dragged into her group. Mum, Dad, Annette, and Rose, all talking at once. Light, friendly scalding.

"Where were you?" "We have to introduce you to..." " Have you heard about.." Half sentences running into each other, over Celeste, trailing off, changing tack, or lost in the music. Names, connections, little anecdotes that ran into each other.   Someone called Jane was at the same protest as...

Somebody used to run a falafel van at the festival where…
Someone else had been the artist who… Shared moments all
designed to welcome her, initiate her into the group that was
being forged for the long journey ahead.

Celeste realised instantly that this was a vital moment,
this initiation. In her parents' flighty lifestyle, group bonding
happened fast and irrevocably. It was an essential part of
being rootless. Ruthlessly efficient networking sessions turned
strangers into lifelong friends, and forged close-knit
communities in minutes. And she had missed it. The messy
re-cap being hurled at her from all directions was
indecipherable. In the minutes she had been away, they had
developed a language she was not party to. Her parent's
friends were trying to include her, but it was too late. The
group had been formed, and again, she had missed it.

But that hardly mattered now. She was on the outside,
looking in. Again.

Well, fine. Celeste didn't want to join this merry crew
anyway. The old hippies could do what they liked. There was
something else going on on this ship, and even if she didn't
know what it was, she was determined to be a part of it. She
let the conversation wash over her until Maurice's slow
repeated melody and Ace's constant attempts to jump-start
folk rock blended with the gabbling voices and the sway of the
ship and the unselfconscious dance of the whirling blonde girl.
Celeste drifted away, wondering what Peter had meant. What
was going to happen at 6am in the engine room? It would be a
bit early in the morning for a clumsy pass. She hoped that
wasn't it. That would be disappointing and she'd hate to have
to snap his wrist.

She wasn't sure how long it was before she became
aware of a sudden silence. She refocussed her eyes from her

own internal space to the faces around her, all turned now to the improvised stage. A figure was stumbling in front of the musicians. Hands up in front of him in a gesture which could have been meant to silence the room, or just to steady himself, he lurched to a halt.

Great. The captain was a drunk mess. Even amongst the disheveled volunteers of the Green Crusader's crew, he stood out like a tramp at a wedding reception. A thick wide-check shirt covered his chest, open two buttons down and showing an indistinct black-only tattoo beneath. The sleeves were either never present, or had been roughly cut off to turn the garment into a tank-top with frayed, unfinished edges. The check had probably not always been the grey, green colour it was now, but salt and oil and careless use had taken their toll. Below the shirt, blue jeans. Loose and held up with a wide belt and a country-and-western buckle bearing a dull metallic pirate insignia. Above it, a face that looked like it had been dragged down into a fierce snarl by a thick black moustache, the shape of a downturned horseshoe, around his mouth.

His hair was pulled back into furrowed lines which started as neat groves at his forehead, but ended in an untidy tangle at the back. It shone with grease. His eyes were pinheads hidden under a creased and heavy eyebrow, and ringed by drooping bags maybe three times the size of the eyes they hung from. His skin was creased and marked, scraped and potholed, as though it had been the subject of meteor collisions over millions of years. The captain had the kind of face that would have trouble looking any way other than angry. He could have managed 'disgruntled' maybe at a push.

"Early start!" he said. The accent was Latin. Mexican maybe. Nothing like his son's. Peter must have gained his skin from his mother, and his twisted accent from a hundred volunteers. Celeste wondered what he'd inherited from this man. Very little, she hoped. "New ones, with me." The captain turned and shambled towards the door, not even making eye contact. Mum and Dad exchanged glances and shrugged.

"Come on then!" said Mum, switching suddenly into adventure mode. She stood up brightly and headed after the captain. Dad and Celeste followed.

9.

"In here." The Captain led them down into the interior of the ship, and along a thin metal corridor. Either side, doors, painted pale blue green over bubbling rust, lined the wall. He stopped outside one door, and pushed it open.

"Cosy!" said Mum. Celeste put her head around the door. The room was impossibly cramped. Two narrow bunks, one both side, and above another with steps going up to it, crushed against the ceiling. Between the two beds there was enough space for one person to edge their way from the door to the tiny porthole, but only if you turned your feet sideways and crab-stepped your way.

"No chance!" said Celeste. The captain raised his eyebrows. It looked like it took him considerable effort. "I'm not sleeping in the same room as them!"

Mum smiled. "Come on, it'll be fun!" Celeste shot her a look, then turned to face the captain. He grunted.

"We can't all sleep in there!" said Celeste.

"There's nowhere else," mumbled the captain and turned to shuffle away. His path was blocked by Annette and Rose.

"Whatever are you putting them in there for?" said Rose. "That's the tiny room!"

"There's nowhere else," repeated the captain.

"Don't be silly," said Annette. "The ship's only half-crewed. You said it yourself." The captain mumbled something unintelligible. Annette turned to Celeste. "You have one of the empty berths, dear," she insisted.

"They're not made up," said the captain. "No linen. Anyway they're full of stuff." Annette pushed past him.

"Nonsense!" she said. "We've got sheets you can have!" Rose grabbed Celeste's hand and bustled her off down the corridor towards another door. The captain shrugged.

"Please yourself," he said and shuffled off. As he pushed past her, Celeste could smell the thick mix of alcohol breath and unwashed clothes.

"Here you go, dear. Nobody in here," said Annette. Celeste tried the door. It didn't budge.

"Put your shoulder against it." said Rose. Celeste did. It scraped open with a sound like tearing metal. Inside was a similar room to her parents' except perhaps a little wider. It smelled of damp and mold and something else that could have been oil, but could just as easily have been whatever the captain was drinking. Two of the beds had mattresses, but the third had only flat boards and a few cardboard boxes. Celeste chose the least filthy mattress and sat down.

"It'll be all right," said Rose, from the doorway.

"Some incense will sort out the smell," said Annette.

The two vanished and returned with armfuls of coloured blankets and something that smoked and smelled both fresh and stale at the same time. Together, they laid a patchwork of fabrics over the mattress and hung the rest so that they draped covering the other bunk and hung down to floor level.

By the time they left, the mould had been covered, and the smell masked. The place didn't look or feel like anything Celeste could describe as home, but it looked like somebody had made an attempt and that, she decided, was the most she could hope for.

She retrieved her rucksack from her parents' room and unpacked it for the first time since she had stuffed it three days earlier. A few clothes, crumpled. Combat trousers, Korean army issue. A couple of hoodies. black. A jacket leather. Three tee shirts. Underwear. A single dress. Simple, black, knee length. A party dress, she supposed, if you were the kind of girl who went to parties. For Celeste, the dress had a more practical value. It was the right shape, and the right thickness. She unwrapped the dress, put her hand up inside it and pulled out the item of value its soft wadding had protected throughout the journey.

Her laptop.

Celeste formed the stack of cardboard boxes on the bunk next to the porthole into a makeshift desk, and hung up her clothes to shield it from anyone watching from the door. A little work area. If she sat on the end of her own bed, with her face just next to the porthole, she could hover her fingers over the trackpad and keyboard on the bed opposite.

She stuck her hand down behind the bed and felt along the dirty wall. She felt a little jolt of joy as her fingers touched what she was looking for. A plug socket. She put the laptop on charge, and powered it up.

Wifi. She must have been somewhere below the router in the bridge, and the signal wasn't great. It flickered between two and three bars. Enough. She tapped in "PASSWORD" and she was online.

Her fingers wavered above the keys. She hadn't dared to look since they'd started running. But now they were on the ship, anonymously, untraceably cut off and heading for international waters, it felt safe to glance at the local news for Milton Highbury.

She was glad she'd waited. She was all over it. Twice. Her family's disappearance was a little paragraph in the local paper. The Nardanis had less of an impact on local life than she'd imagined. Nobody would have missed them at all if it wasn't for the fact that some local boy - doubtless a boyfriend or a brother of one of the girls who'd attacked her - had been caught throwing stones through the windows. When the police had come to take statements, they'd found signs of the family's quick exit, and were still trying to contact somebody to get the windows boarded up. The police had assumed the Nardanis had gone on holiday and were appealing for anyone who could contact the family. Nobody, of course, had come forward.

The cyber-attack on the school was a whole different matter. It had taken a full twenty-four hours of their slow-witted tech team staring at blue screens and empty hard drives before they'd even realised it was a deliberate attack. Once the penny had dropped, the school closed indefinitely, exams were moved, and the story exploded across the media. She'd even made the ITV news. She was pictured in a shadowy reconstruction as a dark figure - a man of course - filmed from the back against the green light of a computer screen filled with vertically scrolling hexadecimal numbers. Absolutely nothing like a real hack, and no mention of the brightly-lit public library in which she'd actually done the deed.

Celeste smiled to herself. It wouldn't last, of course. Even the police would eventually connect the missing family with the cyber-attack, but there was definitely a part of her that enjoyed the sinister super-villain figure she was being painted as.

She wondered what had happened to the girls. Had they been called into the headteacher's office, to explain their bruises? They must know by now that Celeste and her family had vanished. Were they now waking up to the horrific realisation that what had happened to the school was actually the result of their actions? Celeste hoped so.

She closed the lid of the laptop, set her phone to wake her at 5:45am and lay down, letting the sway of the ship rock her to sleep under her borrowed patchwork duvet.

10.

Celeste made her way along the corridor of locked, silent berths and up to the empty mess hall. She had slept in her clothes, and had got used to the early morning ache of her shoulders and legs by the time she got out onto the wide deck behind the cargo doors.

Dawn was a gradient of horizontal stripes. Orange at the horizon, blending to green and then fading slowly to dark blue above her. Below the horizon, deeper, greyer blue. Smooth, running into horizontal ripples close to the ship. The sun, bright and tiny, the only speck of detail outside of the ship itself, almost directly behind them. She was properly alone now. The rest of the planet might as well not exist. That, at least, was comforting.

Still she had a meeting to attend. The engine room, Peter had said. She checked her watch. 6:05am. The sound of the engines were a constant grind that vibrated the whole ship, but she guessed they must be located somewhere towards the back and on the lowest level. Her instincts were right. A set of steps led down, and then down again, and ended in a door marked with a 'Danger of death' sign. Behind it, the engine sound was much louder. She pushed the door. It was locked from the inside.

She knocked. After a second, the door opened. Peter's head appeared. He checked behind her to make sure she was alone, pulled her inside, and bolted the door behind her.

"You're late," he said above the noise of the engines. "Next time, three knocks. A pause, then one more knock. Got it?"

Celeste just blinked at him. "What's going on?" she said.

Peter said nothing, but turned and lead the way towards the other side of the engine room.

The room was long and comfortless, built for machines, not humans. The machines in question were the engines. Yellow painted. Shining once, but now caked in oily grime. They sat in safety barrier cages peppered with hazard signs, and between them, textured aluminium tread-plates formed a path. Celeste kept her hands in her pockets and her head down as she followed Peter through. A warm electrical burning smell rose from the gloom and combined with the sharp smell of metal and oil that felt somehow unsafe.

Air conditioning boxes in dull aluminium snaked across the roof so that Celeste had to weave between them. Each raw metal corner was striped with yellow and black warning tape - evidence that previous crew members had failed to duck.

At one of the engines, Peter stopped, took out an oily cloth, wiped the film of dirt from a gauge, looked at it and shook his head. He wrapped the cloth around his hand, reached deep into the engine and grasped a pipe in his fist. Celeste saw the muscles in his forearm tense as he pushed the pipe. It gave way a little. He withdrew his hand and looked at the gauge again. It flickered, and settled. Peter seemed satisfied.

"The whole place needs cleaning," he said.

"Or scrapping," muttered Celeste.

Peter spun back, waving the oily cloth at her. "Hey! I can say it. You can't," he said. He could have been joking, but there was that edge to his voice. This was his home after all.

"Sorry!" said Celeste.

"You know who keeps this running?" he said. "Me. Just me." He turned and stepped away, vanishing behind a wall, quilted in filthy fabric.

"OK!" said Celeste. "I get it!" She said. She rounded the corner. Behind the fabric covered wall, the engine sound was deadened. In front of her Peter was standing. Beside him, four teenagers, about her age, or slightly older, sat around a foldaway table.

One was the dancing girl from last night. New dress, equally colourful. Up close she was far too pretty.

"Hiya! I'm Rain." She held out a hand, its skeletal fingers drooping.

Rain. Of course she was. She smiled in a free, open way that screwed up her eyes, and showed all her teeth, and suggested nothing bad had ever happened to her. "Dianne and Ace's daughter."

"The band?" said Celeste.

Rain nodded and smiled again. "I don't play," she said, "but I dance."

"I saw," said Celeste.

"Sebastian!" said the boy sitting next to Rain in a voice that boomed with confidence from the back of his throat. "Call me Seb." Celeste immediately noticed the camera hanging around his neck. A big, heavy expensive one. Slightly old-school. The kind of camera a wedding photographer might use. Seb clocked her noticing it. "I make photographs," he said, making a gesture with his spread fingers that implied some kind of magic. "I'm a lens-based artist if you like." Seb had an intense, but constantly moving stare, as though he were sizing everything he saw up for a snapshot.

"Which ones are your parents?" said Celeste. She couldn't

recall seeing anyone on board who looked like they could have sired Seb.

"One doesn't bring them everywhere," he ran a hand through his mop of brown hair as though it wasn't messy enough already. "I'm here to make my gap year mean something." Celeste had seen enough protest marches to recognise his type. Over-confident, over-privileged, over-entitled public schoolboys who thought a social conscience might make them more interesting when they applied for their first job in the city. Seb was right out of that mould.

Celeste's eyes settled on the other two boys at the table. One of them was smiling up at her. Grinning even. He had crew-cut hair and the kind of muscle on his arms and neck that would have marked him out as a night-club bouncer or a rugby player if it weren't for that smile. It took a second for her to clock that the boy was the son of Maurice, the double-bass player, and another second to realise something else. Celeste and her family had spent one Christmas in a commune in Wales. Three out of the eight children she'd met there had Down's Syndrome, and Celeste had learned to recognise something in the look - the body language. She wasn't surprised. The hippy mums she'd met tended to leave having kids to the last minute. Maybe it was because they wanted to behave like teenagers themselves well into their forties. Whatever. It was a thing.

"I'm Robert!" The boy held out a hand still beaming, and Celeste shook it. Robert's handshake was like iron. She let go and rubbed her hand, smiling tightly.

The other boy's face was shaded in a black hoodie. Hunched over the table. He hadn't moved a muscle - not even his eyes. As she watched him, he slowly blinked, looked up at her with an expression that didn't change, and said the single word "Josh," before turning his gaze back down to the table. His voice was deeper than she had expected from his lean face.

"Guys, this is Celeste," said Peter. "Celeste is on the run."

"I hear you take out your school with cyber-attack," said Josh, slowly. . His accent was Eastern European or Russian maybe. "Huh!" It was a sound like a laugh, but without much humour.

"That's a lie!" said Celeste. "It wasn't my school."

"Nice," said Josh.

Celeste allowed herself a little smile. "Ok," she said. "Why all the secrecy?"

"There are two missions on this boat," said Peter. "There's the little hippie concert, and then there's us. We're the other one."

"We're going to do something real," said Rain.

"You are?" said Celeste.

"Yeh," said Peter. Beside him, Josh nodded.

"You five?" The group in front of her nodded.

"Ok, I'll bite," she said. "What is it?"

Peter reached behind a set of pipes and pulled out a manilla folder. He dropped it on the table and flipped it open. The newspaper cutting on the top showed a middle aged-woman in a smart business suit shaking hands with a suited man in front of a Coloumbian flag. Both were grinning broadly. Above the picture, a headline read "Clean oil from the Jungle - agreement signed".

"She originally trained as a nurse, but don't let that fool you," said Peter. "She's a nasty piece of work. Her name is Zoila Chavez - owner of a little prospecting firm with big ideas. She's bullied and lied her way to the top. Her last project involved having a bunch of farmers thrown off their land, then selling it on to a major corporation for open cast mining which left the land around uninhabitable."

"Nice," said Celeste. "So?"

"So about a year ago, she struck oil about fifty miles inland in the Amazon rainforest. If she pulled the same trick there, the results would be devastating," he said.

"She's target number one," added Robert.

"Target number one?" said Celeste. "What are you people talking about?"

"Ordinarily, mining there is heavily restricted and her little company just doesn't have the cash to bribe their way in," continued Peter. "But about six months ago, she signed a deal with this guy." He pulled a shiny press photo of a man in a suit out from the folder. "Lincoln Drier," he said. "Head of PetroMoto, a major player with oil drilling interests all over the world and a reputation for wrecking everything it gets ists hands on. Drier has the cash to buy off officials, and the infrastructure to turn Zoila's little organisation into a global problem. There's a lot of oil in that jungle - enough to fuel global warming for years - and once he gets a foothold who knows what damage Drier could do there."

"Let me guess," said Celeste, "target number two?" She looked over to Robert.

He nodded, refusing to look away. Either he didn't get her sarcasm, or he was choosing to ignore it.

Peter shook his head, "Drier is clever. Whatever crimes his companies commit, he always makes sure there's no link to him. Whatever Zoila does in the rainforest, he'll come out of it smelling of roses. We'll never get to implicate Drier."

"Ok, I get it," said Celeste. "Bad people doing bad things. What are you going to do? Wave some placards?"

"We're going to go into the jungle," said Seb. "We're going to find the drilling rig, take photos and release them to the world. Whatever is going on, we're going to expose it." He waved his camera as though he was the only person who had ever owned one.

Celeste glanced over to Rain, hoping in vain for a shot of realism, but she was staring at one of the pictures in silence. It was a shot of the rainforest being cleared. A tear ran down her face. Celeste fought the urge to roll her eyes. One of those, she thought.

"You're all mad," said Celeste.

"Up to you. You don't have to come." said Josh, his expression unreadable under his hoodie. "Maybe you go to the concert with Mummy and Daddy."

"Have any of you ever been in a jungle?" she said.

"No." said Peter. "Have you?"

"What if you get lost?" said Celeste.

"It's on the river. We take an inflatable. We stick to the river and we won't get lost."

"What if you get caught?"

Peter shrugged. "Taking photos isn't illegal," he said. "What can they do?"

Celeste raised her eyebrows. She could think of a few things.

"What do you say?" said Peter.

Celeste looked from one to the other. The too-pretty hippie dancer girl, Rain. The posh-boy photographer, Sebastian. Sulky Josh - whatever the hell his problem was. Robert. Was he even aware of what he was getting into? And finally, Peter - who looked as though he might just know what he was doing, but with this hopeless bunch as a team, he wouldn't last five minutes in a shopping mall, let alone the Amazon jungle.

Celeste opened her mouth to tell them so, but somehow she couldn't. Maybe it was the way they were all looking at her. Hopeful. Inviting. She couldn't remember the last time a group of people her age had actually wanted her to join them. She hesitated.

"Come on!" said Rain, beaming. Her arms opened wide, demanding a hug. Little bells jingled somewhere around her wrists, or in the layers of her clothing. "It'll be fun!" she said. Celeste felt herself stepping backwards.

"No way," she said. "Not a chance," and she turned and walked out.

11

Up on deck, the ship had become suddenly busy. The captain obviously liked early mornings more than he liked late nights, and he was determined to make sure nobody else on board felt the same way. He had divided the crew into groups and given them tasks while he himself marched between them, pointing and shaking his head dismissively.

One gang, containing Rain's musical parents and about four others, was working its way along the gangway with wire brushes, scrubbing off the rust. In front of them, a huge job. Brown patches spread across every surface. Behind them, scraped and scratched silver metalwork, revealing just how much of the Green Crusader's integral structure had been eaten away by seawater. Celeste had rarely been on a boat, but she could recognise a death-trap when she saw one. The railings that were the only thing stopping careless sailors from pitching into the sea were worn right through in places. In other places there were holes gouged in the deck itself and patched over with riveted plates, now rusting too. Where the various structures of cranes and stairs had been bolted to the deck, the rust had crept into gaps and crevices and through bolts and broken welding, and was eating its way through the ship like a parasite. The scrubbing team's work had only served to highlight the terrible state of the vessel in shining brushed silver.

A few meters back behind the scrubbing gang, Rose, Annette and Mum were crouched, repainting the de-rusted areas. Mum looked up as Celeste approached.

"Hello, darling!" she beamed. "This is terrific fun!" She held a paintbrush. Her fingers were already thick with dull grey paint and there was a stripe across her forehead where she had wiped it with the back of her hand. "Grab a brush!"

Celeste looked down at the area the group had painted; a tiny patch around a pillar. Then she looked out along the gangway stretching in front of and behind them, leading out to the expanse of the rear deck - just one of the ship's levels. All metal. All rusting. The sun was rising, but there was still a cold wind, and even in this flat sea, spray was splashing onto the gangway like little needles on her skin. This was Day One. There was a month of this to go before they crossed the Atlantic and hit the Panama Canal, and easily enough scrubbing and painting to occupy the crew between now and then. Celeste wondered if Mum would be so cheery by the end. She probably would.

"Where's Dad?" she said.

"He's below decks," said Mum, clearly revelling in her use of nautical language. She gestured to a stairway leading down into the depths. Celeste climbed down. Perhaps Dad had a better job. If she wasn't going to hang about with the kids, she'd have to occupy herself with the adults for the voyage. A choice between two types of madness.

Dad's gang's work was only a little more exciting than Mum's. She found him deep in the heart of the ship, where rows of wide pipes emerged from the floor and ceiling, ran along horizontally and then vanished either up or down to feed the rest of the ship. Rings of metal, studded with bolts, circled the pipes, and here and there, hatches and boxes were welded into the piping.

Dad, under the instruction of three other crew members, was unscrewing a hand-sized cap from the top of one of the pipes, and feeding a long metal tape with a weight attached to the end down into the pipe.

"Just sounding the bilge tank," Dad looked up at her. Nautical terminology again. Damn, they were both at it. He turned to Maurice next to him. "Like this?" he said. Maurice nodded, and handed him a tube of what looked like yellow paint.

"There," said Maurice. Dad squirted some paste onto his fingers and rubbed it down a metre long stretch of the shiny tape turning it yellow. Then he fed the tape down into the pipe, letting the weight at the end pull it down until the tangled strip of metal had almost vanished into the pipework of the ship. The end must have been tens of metres below them.

Celeste watched as Dad pulled the tape back up, hand over hand, until he found his yellow mark again. Only now, the bottom half of the mark had turned a deep purple-red. Dad rubbed it with his thumb. Purple, and yellow paint stained his hand, and mixed with the dark black smudges of oil already covering it. Was there any job on this ship that didn't involve getting covered in gunk?

"So that marks where the water comes up to?" Celeste said.

Maurice nodded, but he seemed uncertain. "Is it the right level?"

Maurice looked surprised - as though he wasn't expecting such a question. He shrugged, and screwed the cap back onto the pipe. "I think there's another one down here," he said.

The little group shambled off down the corridor with Dad at the back following the pipes intently with his eyes. While Dad feared electronics, suspecting the dark hand of authority in them, he was a real diesel-head. Cogs and pistons. Engines and machines. They were amongst his more healthy obsessions, and Celeste knew from experience that while he was engaged with practical engineering tasks, it helped to keep his more paranoid thoughts at bay.

"Do you want to show me how to do the next one?" Celeste said. Dad looked at her for a moment, then glanced back up to the ceiling where a network of wires and pipes criss-crossed.

"If someone wanted to bug this place, it'd be easy," said Dad. "There are a million places you could hide cameras and nobody would ever know."

Diversions helped, thought Celeste, but with Dad, nothing was certain. She smiled, and left him to his machines, climbing back up to the open deck and making her way across to the stern of the ship where she could peer over the railings and down into the water as the ship ploughed a widening furrow through it.

Behind them, the horizon was flat and empty. England felt as though it could be another world, Milton Highbury and what she had done there, a myth. Certainly everyone on the ship was busily constructing their own story of it, weaving her actions into a narrative that suited them.

The media had their sinister silhouetted hacker. Mum and Dad had their righteous rebel. The local paper reporting the family's disappearance had used only one word to describe her: troubled. And then there was Peter, and his little gang. Who knew what they thought she was.

In front of her, she watched her past recede. Behind her, a future she could not see or imagine was growing.

12

She felt someone appear beside her, and turned. It was Peter. He leant against the railings, looking at her, but said nothing.

"Shouldn't you be steering the ship or something?" said Celeste.

"It runs itself pretty much in open ocean," said Peter without breaking eye contact. Celeste nodded to the little groups scrubbing and painting.

"So is this what we do for the next month," she said. "Paint rust?" Peter smiled.

"Yep," he said. "Pretty much. Unless being part of our little mission below decks is starting to look more appealing."

"No, thank you," she said. Then she added, "How long have the current crew been on the ship? Only they all seem a bit - amateur. Maurice doesn't seem to know what he's doing."

"We just picked him and Robert up in England."

"And the rest?"

Peter looked out to sea. "Them too. None of them know each other," he said. "That was our third meeting."

"But there must be some experienced sailors on board, right?"

Peter shrugged. "There's me and Dad," he said. "Rose and Annette have been here before, a couple of years ago. The rest are new volunteers. All except Josh."

Her eyes widened. "Let me get this straight," she said. "You can take a ship across the Atlantic with only two people who have ever sailed before?"

"I guess we'll find out," he said.

"Ok," said Celeste, slowly. "So what's the deal with Josh? Are his parents on the ship?" Peter shook his head.

"We - er - rescued him," said Peter. "We got into a disagreement with a whaling ship. He ended up in the water. He was going into cold shock response. His crewmates had to decide between picking him up and going after the whale. They chose the whale. I chose him. He owes me one. If we hadn't taken him on board, he'd have been dead inside five minutes."

"He owes you one - Is that how he sees it?" said Celeste. Peter shrugged.

"It's hard to tell," admitted Peter. "I hope so."

"And Robert..." She paused, not knowing how to finish the sentence. "He's..."

"He's what?" said Peter.

"I mean does he even understand what you're getting him into?"

"Yes!" snapped Peter. "He understands. We all understand."

Celeste wasn't so sure any of them did.

"Hang on," she said suddenly. "You took on a whole new volunteer crew in England?"

Peter nodded.

"So that means your last crew all left at the same time?"

Peter shifted uncomfortably.

"When you got to England."

"The last action didn't go so well," he said. "There were tensions."

"Your Dad?" said Celeste.

Peter shrugged again. "He's not an easy man. And this life isn't for everyone."

"There's something else, isn't there?" said Celeste.

Peter paused for a long time, searching the churning foam with his eyes. Eventually, he said, "Once you dock, if five crew members put in an allegation of unseaworthiness you can be investigated. The ship can't leave port if it's unseaworthy."

"And?" said Celeste looking around. The Green Crusader was in quite a state. "I'm guessing your old crew made a complaint."

Peter stuck his hands into his pockets. "They would have done," said Peter. "But Dad chose not to dock. That's why you had to meet us in the Channel."

"And so you just took whoever you could get?" she said, "No experience? No skills? We're the reject crew?"

"We'll be all right," said Peter. "You can't sit around waiting for the perfect moment, and the perfect team. You have to work with what you've got."

"Is that what you're doing downstairs?" she said.

He shrugged again. "I'm doing what I can." The collar of his coat was sticking up, covering his mouth, so that she couldn't read his expression. He could have been annoyed with her, disappointed or just grimly determined.

"With that lot?" she said. "Are you kidding? They wouldn't stand a chance."

He spun to face her. "I know," he said. "Not without you!"

She looked down. Below them, the water was churning. Ribbons of white foam spreading out from the ship's propeller and flowing over the water's black surface.

"I don't know what you think I am," said Celeste.

Peter shrugged. "I think you're like me," he said. "I think there are people who talk about stuff. And then there are people like us who actually do it." He turned around to face the huge bulb of the radio transmitter on the highest point of the ship. "Maybe I'm wrong."

Celeste didn't answer, but she didn't look away.

"Anyway, I have stuff to do," said Peter, eventually. "That safety rail still needs fixing. Don't want to lose anyone overboard before we get to the jungle." He walked away.

13.

Breakfast was hearty and late enough to feel like lunch. Sausages (with a vegetarian option). Hash browns (with a carb-free option). Thick slices of homemade bread (with a gluten-free option). The food just kept coming out of the little galley until everyone had had enough. The new crew may not be sailors, but they were fair cooks, and well enough used to making do. Summers camping at the Glastonbury Festival hadn't been entirely wasted.

On one side of the mess, Mum's team and Dad's sat together, swapping stories over hot instant coffee. Other groups joined them as they came in, waiving paint and oil stained fingers as they detailed their little victories over the rust and decay. On the other side, Peter, Rain, Robert and Seb sat, talking intently. Josh sat with them, silently, hands wrapped around his coffee, staring into it.

Celeste took her food and chose an empty table. Was this how it was going to be from now on - her eating alone while the others bonded over their dumb plots and pointless battles?

Eventually, she took her plate down to her cabin and set it on one of the boxes on the bed next to her laptop. She flipped the computer open, and opened up Google maps.

Taking a bite of sausage, she switched from the map view to satellite imagery. Where she was searching, a map would be no good. She started with their destination.

She had learned a little more about their official mission by listening to her parents and the others talking in the mess. The concert was actually planned to take place on board the ship - with the cargo deck acting as a stage. The ship itself would sit in the opening of the river along which the symbolic first barrels of oil would be exported. A little bunkering boat crammed with freshly drilled oil would make its way out of the jungle and the barrels would be loaded onto an oil tanker moored at the quayside. It would be a ceremony staged by Drier and PetroMoto for the benefit of the press to show that the rainforest was open for business. But when Lincoln Drier held his press conference on the quay, the Green Crusader would be there to obstruct, disrupt and drown out the company message. Not dumb, thought Celeste, but ultimately pointless. It wouldn't change a thing.

In another tab, she did a quick search for the history of oil drilling in the Amazon. It wasn't pretty. In 1964 a huge oil company set up a drilling operation on the border between Colombia and Ecuador. The result was the poisoning of 4,400 square kilometres of forest, accusations of cancer and birth defects amongst the children of local tribes and one of the worst environmental disasters in history. The company tried to cover up its crimes, threatening and bribing judges but in the end it was issued with a fine of $9.5 billion to repair the damage, which still hadn't been paid fifty-five years later. These people played hardball.

Celeste flicked the tab closed, pinched her fingers on the screen, and zoomed down from orbit. The blue coast of Central America resolved itself from pixelated blocks into a wide, muddy delta swirled with brown and green. On the banks, a small port town. From the satellite imagery, not pretty. A messy grid of low-rise buildings spattered along mud coloured roads. Roofs either pure white, or what appeared to be rusting metal. Google street view had yet to penetrate here, so she had to make do with the view from above. A peppering of small boats were visible scattered in the shallows, little arrowheads in white and pale blue pointing randomly to each other.

She pinched again, scaling out above the clouds to get a wider view. Outside town, green fields ran like uneven scales down the snake of the river, eventually breaking up into the solid dark mat of the rainforest. She followed the thick river delta inland. Within a few kilometres, it writhed off into half a dozen hairline thin brown lines that ran off deep into the jungle before each split again and again into smaller tributaries. Get lost in there and you'd be finished.

She zoomed down until the blobs of individual trees were visible, and panned along the first river, swiping the screen, following it until, after a few hundred kilometres, it shrank to invisible veins beneath the canopy.

Nothing. She scrolled back to the delta and tried again with the next tributary.

It was an hour before she found what she was looking for. A little square of grey-brown beside the green-brown river. She zoomed in. A road revealed itself, an erratic crease that ran through the jungle and towards the square the way a wire connects to a circuit board. The road was unfinished. Black tarmac sputtered out into yellow mud and then vanished amongst the trees a couple of kilometres before it reached the rig.

She knew Google Maps was a patchwork of images stitched together from different sources. The wide views were images from a network of satellites. In populated areas, those were augmented by shots taken from aircraft flying at between 800 and 1500 feet and providing much higher quality shots. In the rainforest, that was less likely. If she was lucky, there might be a little more detail. She zoomed again, this time to the maximum resolution.

The square grew into a blurred blob, and then cleared as the high resolution image downloaded, its regular rectangular edges cut into the forest. The shot wasn't bad. She could see detail of all the huts in the compound. The rough courtyard around them. The structure of the drill itself in the centre.

What really stood out, though, was the pure black mark, like a spreading ink stain all along one side of the compound. One of its edges was straight as though it was supposed to be contained, but on the other three sides, it had overspilled, growing into the green and brown clearing. Beside the black mark were several tiny curved black lines like the scratches of some giant creature. Probably, Celeste realised, they were tyre tracks. Something large had driven in and out of the spillage multiple times, leaving black marks on the ground. Next to the black area on the other side, there was what had to be a dump of some kind. She couldn't tell if it was wood, rubble, industrial waste, or a mixture of all three, but the way it was strewn about on the ground made it obvious that this was a tip. In stark contrast, on the other side of the compound, dark objects were stacked in a mosaic of straight rows. Storage for something maybe? It looked like a small site. If all Peter wanted to do was get some photos...

She sent a copy of the satellite map to her phone so she'd be able to check it later without downloading it again, and then zoomed out. And out. And out. The tiny compound was soon lost in the ocean of green. Thick, lush forest. Unexplored. By the time she had zoomed out enough to see the coastline, the scale was enormous. The distance between where the ship would be moored, and Peter's target was huge, and hostile. And the only things linking the two points were a hair-thin half-finished road, and a winding network of riverways. Take a wrong turning, or run out of petrol, or just break down, and nobody would ever find their bodies.

Peter might talk a good fight, but the boy was utterly utterly mad.

14.

The next week went by slowly. The section of railing painted by Mum's gang inched its way slowly down the gangway. Peeling, rusted paintwork was replaced by freshly patched paintwork under which bubbles of rust and ominous looking gaps could clearly be seen. The gangway now had started to look as though it was being slowly eaten by some unseen creature while the rest of the ship still looked more like the monster's waste.

Mum's enthusiasm was undented, her relationship with Rose and Annette strengthening. When they weren't there, Mum talked about them constantly. When they were there, she couldn't get a word in, of course. To Celeste, it seemed as though Mum had discovered not just kindred spirits in the two older women, but two new mothers of her own. She was regressing into a child, following them about, striving to impress them, talking like them. Dressing like them. It gave Celeste the creeps, and left her with the distinct feeling that Mum found having a daughter of her own increasingly inconvenient.

As for Dad, he was beginning to calm. As Celeste had predicted, his fascination for engines was slowly starting to supplant his fascination with conspiracies. Every day, he talked less about bugs and government plots, and more about pumps and prop shafts. He'd almost stopped coming out on deck to squint into the sky, or scan the sea for signs of periscopes.

By the end of the week that he was spending time down in the engine room with Peter, learning what made the boat run, and of course, Peter welcomed the help.

The two of them and in fact the whole crew - adults and youth alike - settled remarkably quickly into a series of routines and rhythms. The ship enforced them in some ways, but it was more than that. People met at the same places at the same times every day. They exchanged the same pleasantries.

"How's the oil?"

"Fine, fine…"

"Breakfast was particularly good today."

"The weather's picking up."

"Better get on…"

There was a weird predictability to it all. Trapped together, in their little bubble of air bobbing in the ocean, the crew were repeating their own routines. Like fish in an aquarium swimming round and round.

For her own part, Celeste felt herself withdrawing. It was a feeling that had an aching inevitability to it. She had been here before. Her parents effortlessly joining groups. Other people making friends. Forming bonds. All while Celeste herself became an unknown quantity, then an inconvenient outsider, then an enemy, or worse, an irrelevance. A piece of the furniture to be simply worked around as though she did not exist.

Peter's little gang had their own patterns too. Seb roamed the ship, camera always at the ready. He seemed always to be leaning over something, or re-arranging something to get the best shot. Never happy, he would spend what seemed like hours setting up a single photo of a rusty bolt, waiting for the sun to be right, arranging flash lights, changing angles. Snapping, then staring at his camera screen, shaking his head and starting again.

Rain scanned the horizon in search of whales nobody else ever saw, or danced on the deck to music that existed only in her head, her long gypsy skirts flowing out behind and around her. Her dancing was unselfconscious, as though she were lost in her own world, but Celeste noticed that it became more spirited when Seb's camera was around as she threw herself around the deck, leaping and spinning in a style that blended ballet and belly seamlessly. For his part, Seb was more interested in the rust.

Robert, never without a wire brush, or a wrench in his hand would have made a better target for her attention. He was always eager to help anyone who would let him, and never more than a few metres from Rain, watching her with soppy eyes.

Josh was seldom seen and then, usually motionless, sitting at a table with a cup of hot coffee. He seemed to exist in a bubble of his own, the curt nod his favoured form of expression.

Peter strode about the ship with purpose and focus. Whether he was directing Dad and the adult crew, or huddling in the mess for long, serious talks with his little group of misfits, he seemed to ignore everything except whatever he was doing at that moment. You were either part of his plan, or you were not. And if you were not, then you didn't matter.

All the same, Celeste had the distinct feeling that he had not given up on her entirely. There were moments. One day, when his gang was together, hunched over and intently whispering, she saw his eyes lift and scan the room for her. When he saw her, there was a slight tilt of the head. A raising of the eyebrows. It was a question. An invitation. A door still open. It lasted just a second, before he tightened his lips, and ducked back down into the group. Celeste thought about it later, and decided his glance was probably just desperation. His plan was a fantasy, Celeste reminded herself. His little group stood no chance of achieving their aim. They'd probably bottle it in the end. They wouldn't even leave the ship. It was hopeless.

He'd admitted as much himself that day on the deck. Without her, he said, they'd never make it.

She wasn't even sure what he'd meant by that. It wasn't as if Celeste had any skills in jungle survival. She hadn't even been able to hack it in Milton Highbury.

A few days later, Celeste was making her way up to the bridge to reset the router - the line had been dropped somehow. It had probably, she thought, simply fallen into a deeper puddle and needed to be fished out - when she heard the voices of Peter and his father arguing inside.

"We'll make the time up," the captain was saying.

"But I don't see why we need to - if you'd stayed on the course we planned we'd have plenty of time to get there!"

"We'll just run her faster after."

"I don't understand. After what? Where are we going?"

"Same place!" said the captain. "Just different route!"

"But why?"

"Because I'm captain and I say so."

"And I'm Chief Engineer!" shouted Peter. "And I say If I run the engines any faster they'll burn out before we get to Panama!"

"Enough!" shouted the captain.

"But I don't understand. Why risk the whole ship just to take a slower route?" There was a pause. "Oh no!" he said, "You're not going to - You can't!"

"I can and I will!"

"I can't let you risk the whole ship!" Through the fuzzy window, Celeste saw a shape that must have been Peter lunge towards the figure of his father at the wheel, trying to push him out of the way. She saw the captain turn, strike out. Peter reeled backwards against the door.

Celeste stepped back as Peter wrenched the door open and stepped out, clutching his eye. For a second, Peter stared at her.

"Where are we going?" she said.

"You think our team couldn't survive a real action?" said Peter. "You may be about to find out." He pushed past her, and stumbled downstairs.

15.

It was four full days before Celeste started to understand what the conversation had been about and by then, the bruise around Peters eye had blossomed, blue, turned yellow, and finally receded to a red crescent. Peter himself never made any reference to it, and neither did anyone else on board. Everyone had little injuries of their own. Pencil-line cuts on their fingers from torn metal edges. Swellings from hitting their heads on low ceilings. Burns from the pipes. Scrapes and grazes from filing and sanding back rust. Bruises from leaning, reaching and kneeling to reach their work as the ship rocked. A black eye was not remarkable here, and Peter wore it as though it were nothing. Nobody but Celeste saw it as anything sinister.

Celeste began to join him when he stood by the railings, preoccupied, a little more thoughtful than usual searching the horizon, she would stand close by, but not intrude on his thoughts, saying nothing.

On the fourth day, they were both standing silently, staring out, when she noticed that a speck had appeared on the horizon.

"What's that?" she said.

Peter shaded his eyes. His expression seemed to grow darker. A moment later, she felt the ship starting to turn gently so that the speck was directly ahead, and the vibration of the engine grew under her feet as they picked up speed. Peter spun around and looked directly up to the bridge. He shook his head.

"This is madness," he whispered, almost to himself. He stalked off, heading down into the bottom of the ship.

Celeste watched for the next couple of hours as the shape grew on the horizon. None of the adults on board seemed to have noticed their change in speed and direction. Peter's gang were noticeably absent. He had obviously called them below decks for some kind of conference.

Meanwhile, the shape got close, she could see now that it was a boat. Its outline, taller and more solid than the 'Green Crusader'. Built for stability not for speed as their own ship had been.

In the water beside them, she started to see orange buoys - a line of them leading away towards the ship still many kilometres away. A fishing net.

They closed on the ship. Its hull was dark blue, and its sides dropped down vertically into the water. Above it, a high, wide bridge in white spanning the ship from one side to the other with a mess of communications ariels rising above it. A huge, solid winch hung out from the back of the vessel, and from it, strands leading down into the water. The whole vessel looked solid, squat. Industrial. Like a factory on the water. All morning it grew closer until there was no room for doubt. They were chasing it down.

One by one, the work-groups on the Green Crusader abandoned their tasks and crowded to the front of the vessel, watching the lonely fishing vessel get nearer and nearer.

Once they were close enough to see the men on the decks, encased in yellow waterproofs, Celeste felt the engines cut and the ship slowed to a halt. Celeste looked up to the bridge where the captain must have been, but the sun was reflecting in the dark glass. She could see nothing.

There was a long, uneasy silence. The group at the front of the Green Crusader stared at the other boat. The fishermen stared back.

Then, a shout in a language Celeste did not recognise, and the great winch on the stern of the fishing vessel started to turn, winding the kilometres long net slowly in. Water poured from it. She could make out the shapes of human-sized fish being hauled from the water. The men turned away from the sides of the ship, back to work.

Suddenly, from behind her, Peter, Rain, Josh, Robert and Seb burst out from below decks and sprinted along the gangway and over to the crane where Celeste's dinghy had first been raised aboard. Another little boat was there now, slightly sturdier than the one Celeste had arrived in, and sporting a large outboard engine. The boat was already attached to the crane. Celeste ran over to them just as Rain, Robert and Seb piled into the little dinghy. Josh was hanging back, uncertain.

"I not go in the water!" he said. His voice was wavering with real fear.

"Why not?" said Peter.

"I know what it's like to drown," he said. "You need someone to operate crane."

Peter nodded. "Ok." He caught sight of Celeste, and paused, half in, half out of the boat.

"What's going on?" said Celeste.

"Illegal gill net fishing," said Peter. "Captain got a tip-off and decided to chase them down. I didn't agree, but now that we're here, we have to do something before he does." Peter nodded in the direction of the bridge.

"What do you mean?"

"He's obsessed," said Peter. "Now you have to decide. Are you with us, or are you with them?" he pointed to the front of the ship where the rest of the crew were milling, confused. Rose and Annette were marching up the stairs towards the bridge. Another small group including Dad were taking a vote.

Celeste looked to the crew, then to the little group in the dinghy, all looking expectantly up at her. What they were planning to do, she had no idea, but given that they were a bunch of untrained teenagers and they were about to hit the open sea to take on a ship almost twice the size of the Green Crusader and full of angry fishermen, it was probably going to be stupid and dangerous. She hesitated.

"Ok," said Peter, his voice level. "Your call." He gave the signal to Josh, and the winch started to lift the little boat.

"Wait!" said Celeste. Without knowing why, she threw herself over the dinghy's floats and onto the wooden floor of the boat just before it swung out over the side of the ship. As the crane swung them out, rocking above the open water, she grabbed one of the handles on the inflatable's floats and hauled herself up so she was sitting on the hard bench next to Rain. She beamed at Celeste.

"I knew you'd be with us," she said.

"I'm not with you - I'm just not with them!" snapped Celeste.

"I knew," said Rain again. Celeste scowled at her.

"Put these on," said Peter, pulling life-jackets out from under the dinghy's bench and shoving them into everyone's hands before fitting his own. She pulled hers on and clipped its fastening. This all felt suddenly real.

"Hold onto something," said Peter, his hand on the outboard. Rain gripped the seat below her with one hand and grabbed onto Robert's arm with the other. Seb, sitting opposite cradled his camera in both hands.

"I hope you're ready for this," Peter said. Instantly, Celeste's stomach was in her throat as they dropped towards the water. Her body seemed to leave the boat for a second. Beside her, Rain grabbed her sleeve. The boat hit the water like it was a concrete floor, and she felt herself slam back into the bench.

"I said, hold on," said Peter. He might have been smiling.

"I'm ok," said Celeste wrenching her arm away from Rain. In a second, the others had unhooked the ropes securing the boat and Peter yanked the engine into life. They shot forward away from the Green Crusader, and towards the other ship, the dinghy bumping over waves.

"Ready?" said Peter. Seb gripped his camera.

"Ready," he said.

"You two?" Peter nodded to Rain.

She reached under her seat and pulled out a diver's knife. Thirty centimetres long. Black rubber handle. Serrated edge down one side, smooth curved blade down the other, ending in a pointed, curved tip. It was a serious weapon. It did not suit Rain, with her sparkly eye make-up and her flowing hair, but she gripped it in her thin, fragile fingers and nodded back. Beside Seb, Robert pulled out a similar blade.

"What the hell?" said Celeste. "What is going on?"

"Dad got a tip-off a few days ago. He still has his sources. It's an illegal fishing vessel catching exclusively for the Chinese market in shark fin soup." said Peter. "This is not going to be pretty."

"Sharks?" said Celeste. "There are sharks here?" She looked around the boat - somehow expecting to see fins cutting the water all around them. There was nothing.

"Don't worry, we're here to help them." said Rain, smiling, her knife still held out in front of her as though she were a priestess and it was some sacred sacrificial blade.

Peter took the boat around in a wide arc to approach the fishing ship, then he throttled the engine down and they slowed almost to a stop. There was a sudden silence.

"We have to go around the ship," he explained. "We can't risk getting caught in the nets, or hitting anything." He brought the boat slowly closer. It was Rain who first noticed the change in the water.

Everyone else was focusing on the ship. The blue hull rising like a high wall, straight out of the water before them. The net, stretched out at the back forming a diagonal wall from the water behind them to the winch at the ship's stern high above them, winding slowly in. They all looked up, saying nothing at the sight of the writhing bodies of sharks being dragged out of the water, dangling by their gills, pectoral fins held stiffly out to the side as though being both hung and crucified.

But as they rounded the rear of the ship, Rain was looking down into the water, her expression one of exaggerated horror.

"What is it?" said Celeste, noticing her face.

Rain reached a hand down and scooped up a handful of seawater. It was not clear. It was red with blood. Rain let it trickle through her fingers, and Celeste followed it down into the sea where the droplets mixed into a deep red oily slick. Her eyes followed the trail of blood back towards the ship.

The others were watching too now. Seb raised his camera, clicked, angled and clicked again. Peter simply turned the boat without a word, and guided it down the blood-river. The dark stream lead down along the side of the massive hull and out into open sea behind them until it dissipated.

As they made their way along, in touching distance from the great hull, Seb continued taking photographs. Of the ship, of the ocean. He pointed his wide lens directly at Celeste's face. She realised she must be showing her confused apprehension.

"What are you doing?" she said.

"Documenting," said Seb without taking his eyes from his viewfinder. "It's what I do."

"Well, document something else," said Celeste. The shutter clicked. She glared at him.

Next to Seb, Robert was tugging on Seb's sleeve. His eyes wide, he pointed out to sea just ahead of them. Seb turned, camera still at his eye, then lowered it slowly, his own face frozen. Rain and Celeste turned to follow his gaze.

There in the water a body writhed. White on one side, dark grey on the other. A shark as long as their boat. Alive, but only just, its tail contorted, whipping around it, back and forth, but Celeste couldn't tell if it was attempting to swim or just writhing in agony. Its head breached the water briefly, and its mouth swung open. Rows of tiny teeth bared as it gulped at the air. Black eyes rimmed in white, perfectly round swiveled in their sockets.

Celeste followed the shape of its body down to where its dorsal fin should have been. Instead, a wide red wound gaped. The fin had been hacked off. On the flanks of the animal, two more gashes where its pectoral fins should have been. The tapering tube of the shark's body twisted again, turning over in the water, unable to right itself, and it began to sink.

Fighting to swim, the white shape of the belly-up shark fell, still twisting down into the depths. Until it vanished from view.

In silence, they turned back to the ship. Peter kept the engine low, and guided them in until they reached the source of the blood-river. A waterfall of blood and seawater was pouring down the side of the vessel, sluicing from the deck above. Chunks and scraps of meat came with it, hitting the water and sinking, or floating away, unrecognisable pieces roughly hacked. Celeste looked up towards the edge of the deck. Whatever was going on up there, it was brutal beyond imagining.

Suddenly, from a gap in the railings at the side of the hull, a shape slid, or was hurled out above them. The shark's torn body turned in midair, head down, jaws open, it plummeted towards them. Celeste threw herself backwards out of its path, and the fish slammed onto the wooden floor of the dinghy.

In a moment, everything was thrashing chaos. The finless, bloody shape looped in on itself in the little boat, and then sprang back, its long whip of a tail blurred back and forth powered by the solid muscle of its body, its tail slicing the air as Rain and Robert fought to avoid it at the front of the boat. Opposite her, Seb was wrestling with his camera - either to protect it or to record the desperate thrashing shape - Celeste couldn't tell.

Peter threw himself over the outboard motor, battling to steer the boat away from the side of the ship.

Celeste found herself staring into the mouth of the creature. It was as long as she was, and deep, shining blue-black. A tapering tube of solid muscle. The triangular head was half sliced through, hanging by a strand of skin. Celeste could see the severed white cartilage surrounded by a ring of red meat. And yet by some dark miracle, the body still fought them. The mouth still gasped and clamped and tore at everything it touched.

She grabbed the side of the boat, fighting to stay on board as Peter turned the throttle and they bounced away. The dying shark was in a frenzy now, but it was stuck, somehow wedged between the floor and the seats. Its mouth was tearing at the rubber floats. Its tail smashing at the floor and at Robert and Rain at the front of the boat. At any moment, it could puncture the dinghy or catapult one of them overboard.

There was only one chance.

Celeste reached down into the bottom of the boat, put both arms around the squirming body and lifted. It was heavy. So heavy and so thick, she had to hug it close to her own body as she lifted and twisted it. She felt its skin against her face. Rough like sandpaper. The elongated head hanging limply, its mouth still gulping. It clamped, fixing itself to her jacket at the shoulder, tearing through it. She wrestled the body around, turning herself until she was half-standing, half-kneeling on the seat at the edge of the bouncing boat. With one final lunge, she pushed the shark away from her, and over the side. The moment it hit the water, the boat's speed dragged it away, its head and body pulling its still shaking tail down into the water and back away behind the boat.

The five watched as the dark blue body wove its way, snakelike, along the surface for a moment, before disappearing beneath. Nobody spoke until they had rounded the prow of the fishing vessel and started to head back down the other side towards the net at the back.

Celeste felt her stomach clench. A sick, physical anger. "How can we stop this?" she hissed.

"We can't," said Peter. "About seventy-five million sharks die this way every year. Three quarters of the population is gone." He spoke with the dry, tourist-guide tone of someone who had repeated the figures a hundred times to a hundred audiences. The information tripped off his tongue in a practiced rhythm as though the words meant nothing to him, but his eyes told a different story. He stared directly at her, anger coming off him like heat.

"So what are we here for? What do we do?" she said.

Peter slowed the boat at the stern of the vessel, following along the line of buoys which kept the long net afloat. The boys moved slowly, dragged slowly in by the huge winch on the ship.

"We're going to cut the nets," said Peter. He reached under his seat and handed her a knife.

"You in?"

16.

Celeste took the knife. It felt heavy in her hand.

"How do we cut the nets?" she said. She had a grim feeling she wouldn't like the answer.

Peter nodded at Robert who, without a second's hesitation, tipped himself backwards over the side of the boat and into the water. Celeste stared after him, as he bobbed to the surface, buoyed up by his cumbersome life-jacket. "What the hell are you doing?"

Next to her, Rain followed Robert into the water.

"You're not serious!" yelled Celeste. "There are sharks in there!" Rain righted herself, and then pushed back the hood of her now soaked waterproof.

"They won't hurt us," she said. "We're trying to save them."

"This is your big idea?" Celeste shouted at Peter. "You're going to get these idiots killed!"

"You're either in or you're out." said Peter. She looked disbelievingly at him, and then at the water where Robert was already powering away with an impressive front-crawl.

"Aren't we supposed to have wetsuits at least?" she said.

"Yeh," said Peter. "Shall we nip back and get them?" He glared at her. "I'm sorry! None of this is ideal. We just have to do what we can!"

"You're mad!" said Celeste. She stared at Peter, then at Seb. "I notice you're not going in the water."

"One has to have a record," said Seb, holding his camera up.

"For Christ's sake!" said Celeste.

"Nobody's forcing you," said Peter, "but I can't keep the boat here. We're a sitting target."

Celeste opened her mouth to ask what they were a target for, but she only got as far as drawing breath before she was hit from the side by a jet of icy water so strong it knocked her sideways. The spray soaked the boat in a second before it passed over them and out to sea.

"Water cannons," Peter yelled. "They're onto us."

Celeste turned. From the deck of the ship, a solid, white spray arced above them, powering into the ocean. Peter wrestled with the engine just as whoever was controlling the water cannon adjusted their aim and the beam of water swung back, towards the boat.

The engine roared into life. Peter opened the throttle and they jerked forward just as the water cannon hit Celeste square in the chest. She did not stand a chance. She felt the water hit. The world span. The rubber of the boat slid across her. A moment of nothing, and then she hit a wall of water, shoulder-first. An ice cold shock encased her body, squeezing inwards. Her vision went blue, then blurred white as the life jacket brought her to the surface.

She flailed, then wiped her eyes. Over to her left, Peter was gunning the inflatable hard, weaving, pursued by the beam of water from the ship.

"We'll draw them away!" he yelled. "Cut the net!" The little boat zig-zagged away, the water cannon spray following.

Celeste turned in the water. The initial shock of the cold was subsiding into a dull ache and she could feel her breathing starting to return to normal. She raised her hand, and realised with some surprise that she was still gripping the heavy knife. In front of her, a few metres away, an orange buoy the size of her torso washed up and down in the water. Robert was hanging onto a thick rope attached to the buoy, lifting it out of the water, while Rain hacked away at it with her knife. She wasn't making much headway.

"Over here!" Rain said, looking up at Celeste. "I can't get through it." Celeste turned back. The motorboat was two hundred metres away by now, throwing up huge fans of water as it swerved back and forth in the clear water between the fishing vessel and the Green Crusader. She could just make out Peter wrenching on the outboard. Seb, raising his camera, training it on the vessel, then on the nets as Peter fought to dodge the flailing stream of water.

The little craft bounced and banked as he brought it in closer to give Seb a better shot at the rising nets and the creatures snagged and dangling from them as they were hauled up towards the winch. The inflatable skidded underneath the net, close to the hull, and out towards the river of blood and the twisting bodies still being flung from the side of the ship. Seb was swinging his camera, but at that speed, it would be a miracle if he got anything other than a blurry smudge.

Whatever. Celeste had bigger problems. Peter wasn't coming back for her anytime soon and she was starting to feel rather exposed floating on her own in the open sea. She thought of what was in the water beneath her. Tangling nets, blood and sharks. It wasn't a good mix.

At least the other two, slicing at the ropes, had something to hang onto to stop themselves being carried away into the open sea. Against her better judgement, Celeste fought her way through the waves towards them.

"Don't tangle your feet," shouted Robert, still holding the strong thick rope that marked the top of the net. "Don't get caught like the fish."

Celeste did not need reminding. She half-swam, half-dragged herself through the water, but it was slow work. The life jacket was cumbersome around her, preventing her arms from swinging properly. Her clothes were against her too. Heavy with water, they weighed her down. She felt a sudden current against her, pulling her away and sideways back towards the Green Crusader. She put her head down into the water, and reached arm over arm, inching forwards against the swell.

Tiring now, Celeste felt the burn of salt on her lips. She raised her head to take a breath but felt a wave slap against her open mouth, water choking her. She coughed and floundered blindly, arms flailing. A second later, her left arm struck something solid.

The rope.

She grasped it, rough and fibrous, and felt herself jerk to a halt. Wrapping her arm around the rope to prevent herself drifting further, she grabbed it with her other hand, and steadied herself. She looked up. She had drifted further than she thought. Robert and Rain were a good ten metres in front of her.

Celeste shoved the knife into her belt and began to haul herself forward along the rope. Her hands too cold to grip properly by now, she held on by wrapping her wrists around the rope and then pulling with her shoulders. Arm over arm, she moved towards them.

Beneath her, she could feel the motion of the nets. The rushing of the current pulling her back. The vibration of the winch, far in front and high above, juddered through the rope as it slowly pulled them in. But there was another movement too. Sharp strikes, pulls, wobbles of the rope, and the net below it. The movement of unseen creatures fighting for their lives beneath and around her. Wound in the net as the sharks were, Celeste now felt she shared their strange sense. The sense by which they hunted. The sense of movement in the water.

Celeste tried to ignore the movement - the knowledge of what must be down there, just a few metres from her feet. She pulled herself on through the waves striking her face until she reached Robert and Rain. They were both struggling now. He, straining to hold the rope out of the water, gritting his teeth with the effort. She, hacking away at the wrist-thick twine with her heavy knife. She was fighting hard, her thin knuckles white with effort and cold, but she was getting nowhere. The rope was a monster. Frayed and salt hardened, it was actually a dozen strands of rope, woven together like the plaited hair of an ancient sea-faring Rapunzel.

Rain's hacking had cut through a couple of the individual ropes, and splayed out some more into a mess of even thinner strands, but she was tiring now, and becoming weaker and weaker.

"Here," said Celeste, pulling herself level with the other two, and dragging her own knife from her belt. "Let me try."

Rain nodded, and put the rope onto her shoulder, hefting it higher out of the water so that Celeste could reach up and get some purchase on it. Celeste turned her knife so that the serrated edge was against the rope and began to saw at it.

It turned out to be tougher than she had thought. She had to press the knife down into the rope with all her weight, as she cut, and with her legs treading water in her heavy clothes, and her other hand holding the buoy to stop herself floating away, it was impossible to get any real purchase on it. She was getting nowhere.

Eventually, she found that if she hooked her heavy boots into the net under the surface, she could effectively stand up on it, and put her whole weight on the knife. One by one, the strands snapped through, and the rope began to come apart.

Rain and Robert were exhausted, but Celeste was impressed at how dedicated they were, struggling on, using the last of their energy to keep the rope high enough out of the water for her to slice at it. Below the water line, the rest of the net was made of thinner rope, single strands of nylon weave. She looked over towards the fishing vessel, and the net stretching diagonally up out of the water towards the winch. The top rope was the net's backbone. If she could get through that, she was pretty sure the rest of the net would not hold when it was pulled out of the water, and the whole structure would tear through.

But they were getting perilously close by now. As she sliced away at the rope, she had been ignoring their movement in the water. The fishing ship had been inching the net further and further in towards itself. Now they were only a few metres from the point where the rope curved up out of the water.

And there was something else. Robert saw it first. Looking out towards the river of blood, his mouth fell open. He pointed.

Celeste saw his expression, and turned. Something was forcing its way against the current, along the deep red stain. Attracted by the blood. By the vibration. By the unmistakable movement of distress in the water. A fin. Tall, grey. An un-injured shark. A huge one. Snaking its way down the river of blood and directly towards them. The fin slowly sank beneath the waves and vanished. The three stared at each other.

"Don't move," she said. "They hunt by..." She didn't have time to finish the sentence before the water two metres in front of them exploded. The huge, grey, and white body of what could only be a great white shark, mouth wide, erupted from the water, netting stretched across its head.

The rope was hauled out of the water with such a force that Rain and Robert were thrown out into the ocean away from the net.

Celeste was less lucky. The rope she was cutting flew over her head, and down, trapping her between it and the water. At the same time, she felt her foot slip through the net below her, and the nylon line slide up to grip around her thigh. She was stuck fast, pinned to the water, her life-jacket forcing her up into a loop of netting while the rope on top of her forced her head down under the water.

She turned, caught and tangled. Opening her eyes, she could see nothing but blue and white foam and feel nothing but the stinging of salt and the strands of net tight over her head. She pushed up just far enough to take a breath before the weight forced her down again. She tried again, but this time, the net was too tight. Panicking, she strained her neck and shoulders, but she could not lift her mouth out of the water. She felt her heart thumping, her lungs straining. She had just seconds left.

If only she could dive down, she might be able to free herself. She tried, but she was fighting the buoyancy of her life-jacket, forcing her upwards against the net. There was just one chance. She brought her knife up between her chest and neck, and sliced sideways across her shoulder. She felt something break, and pulled the knife down to her waist, slicing again through the straps of the life-jacket, feeling it release. Celeste wriggled herself out of her life-jacket, immediately feeling the pull of the net around her legs hauling her downwards into the depths.

She allowed herself to go with it, until she was under the rope and then grabbed it and hauled her head up out of the water on the other side. She gasped, and panted, gripping onto the frayed half-cut rope. Her legs were still trapped but at least she could breathe.

Two metres away, the great white shark was trapped in the rising net. Half in, half out of the water, it thrashed with a wild, intensity. It turned over and over, wrapping itself more and more tightly in the net, and pulling Celeste ever towards it.

They were both caught now, and the winch was hauling them both up the side of the boat towards the deck - the source of the blood river, twenty metres above.

17.

Celeste felt the rope tugging tight as she was pulled through the water. In front of her, the silver torpedo shape of the shark was rising impossibly out of the sea. Upside down, its tail caught fast, netting across its nose and one fin, it peeled its head backwards, its rows of triangular teeth bared to pink gums and opening in a white chasm of a mouth that seemed to lead backwards and upwards into eternity.

But she was following the monster. She felt herself rising, feet first out of the water next to it as the net was dragged on and upwards, the sloping angle of the net swinging her closer to the creature's jaws as she rose.

Something in her brain clicked, and her panic started to rise. The ways this could end played out in her head as she felt the net tighten around her legs as they rose out of the water. Either she would drown, held upside down, head in the water, or the angle of the net would swing her straight into the great white's jaws. If she survived both of those fates, the winch would carry her all the way up to the deck of the ship, and deposit her amongst all the other writhing carcusses awaiting industrial butchery.

She held her breath, her head twisted under the water, blood rushing. The dizzying loss of control. Struggling and failing to haul herself up as the net dug into her leg, she couldn't raise her head above the water. There was nothing she could do but force the fear back into her belly, and wait, hanging limply, conserving oxygen in the frozen blackness while the water roared in her ears, and the winch did its work.

The pressure in her lungs rose. The urge to breath grew stronger and stronger. Her stomach clenched, almost forcing her mouth open.

And suddenly she emerged. The water sank away, lapping at her hair and then dropping below her. She gulped a lung-full of spray filled air, choking on it immediately. The salt water which filled her nose sent her into a coughing fit.

Recovering, she found herself hanging upside down, beside her - almost at touching distance was the huge wall of flesh that was the white shark. The two of them, suspended, dripping from the line, struggling together, as centimetre by centimetre the winch lifted them up the stern of the boat towards the butchery deck. Beyond its gaping, gulping mouth, the sky-blue metal wall of the ship's stern got slowly closer.

She turned to face the shark. One solid, impossibly powerful muscle twisting and convulsing, driving that gaping mouth. Those teeth. For a moment it paused in its threshing, exhausted. Hanging, opening and closing its mouth, gulping, trying desperately to breathe. Its huge black eye level with hers, round and terrible. She couldn't help but stare into it. Searching - stupidly, she told herself - for some meaning, some readable emotion in the shark's eye.

Sad desperation. Uncomprehending panic. The lonely fury of a trapped predator. All her own imagination, she knew. She pushed the feelings from her mind. She was doing nothing but projecting her own feelings onto a fish. Just because they were both caught in the net it did not make them companions. In the water, the shark would kill her without a thought. Even here, it would twist its body and engulf her given the chance. This was not, she told herself, a meeting of minds. She was as incapable of understanding the shark as it was of understanding her. The only thing they could and should share was a lack of pity for each other. They each had their own problems.

And yet... She stared, cold, upside down and dripping, for a long, long second until she could see the shape reflected in its eyes. The shape of her - knife still clutched in her fist - raised as if to strike.

Of course, the knife! She had been unaware she was still holding onto it.

She looked down. The water was three metres below her now, and she could see Peter's inflatable as Seb hauled Rain and Robert up into it. At least they'd got out.

Grabbing the thin lattice of nylon strands, she dragged her body upwards until she could grasp the thick rope backbone of the net. She twisted herself around until she could reach the point where she had cut almost through the rope, and slipped the knife underneath it. The rope was taut now, its few remaining strands held guitar-string tight as the weight of the remaining net hung from it. She sawed away back and forth with the knife, pulling it towards herself as hard as she could and feeling the strands snap one by one under the blade.

A final yank and the rope snapped directly above Celeste's foot. The effect was instant. Its backbone gone, the remaining thin lattice of the net could not hold its own weight. It tore open, unzipping from top to bottom, the remainder falling back into the water. Celeste felt a sharp sting as the strands holding her leg pinged apart, leaving her free, but still hanging on to the remnant of the net which, now no longer held taut by the weight of the net in the water swung back, hanging from the winch.

Celeste clung to the rope as she and the shark swung back, slamming into the stern of the ship. She felt a sudden, jarring pain and let go, tumbling down and crashing into the water below.

She went under, and started kicking immediately towards the surface, realising only in that second that without her life-jacket, her clothes were impossibly heavy. She battled towards the light above her, but she didn't seem to be moving.

Suddenly, her flailing hand caught onto something. Another hand. She pulled herself up, and her head broke the surface.

Peter. Reaching over the side of the boat into the water. She scrambled up, pulling herself into the inflatable. Gasping for air.

"I didn't think you were going to make it," said Peter.

"Well, I did. No thanks to you!" said Celeste. The other two were already sitting in the boat. Holding onto the seats. Grim, scared expressions on their faces.

"Sit down," said Peter. "We've got to go!"

From above her, Celeste heard a hollow clang. She looked up. Above her, the shark had thrashed back into life. Its mouth open, it was slamming itself again and again into the metal wall of the boat, powerful and pitiful. That round, grey eye found its way back into her mind. She could not leave the shark there to die. She just couldn't do it. The tattered net hung down below it into the water like a step ladder. Peter grabbed her shoulder and spun her back towards him.

"There's nothing you can do," he said. "We have to go right now!" Celeste punched him square in the face and he staggered back, sitting down hard beside the outboard, clutching his nose. She turned back, grabbed the ladder of rope and climbed, almost running up it towards the gaping, thrashing mouth.

The shark was well tangled in the net around its jaws, gills and front fin but the shark could probably work itself free given time. The tail was another matter. Several strands of netting had looped around it half a dozen times as it turned and spun to try to free itself, and now it was this mess of nylon that the animal was dangling from as it was hauled up towards the deck.

If she could only cut that away, it would be free.

A part of Celeste realised that what she was doing was stupid beyond belief. A part of her cursed herself with every step up the netting. But she knew herself far too well to believe reason or rational thought, or even self-interest would stop her now. She shook her head to clear her mind, and focussed on what her gut had told her she was going to do.

Above her, the shark was still thrashing and writhing, snapping and gulping, but there was no other way. Her path to the tail would take her right past the huge jaws. She stuck the knife in her belt, and climbed, hand over hand, legs pounding up towards the fish. Her hands were icy numb. Her legs aching as she hauled what felt like her own bodyweight in waterlogged clothing up the swinging shred of netting. Below her, Peter, Rain and Robert were yelling at her. Seb was taking pictures. She ignored them.

The shark's head was swinging back and forth. Its eyes were not black now. They were white - the eyeballs rolled back into the head to protect them during a strike. She could see its teeth bared, as though tearing at prey. Behind them, the white gill flaps hung open, strangely delicate, vulnerable, the ropes cutting into them.

She paused just out of reach, then as the huge head twisted away from her, she scrambled past, her own head and torso passing in front of the eye just before the head swung back. She felt something hit her leg, and instinctively she kicked out. Her booted foot hit something soft.

Celeste just had time to realise that she had kicked inside the animal's mouth before it jolted away again and she was able to drag herself past the head and up towards the tangle of netting that held the shark's tail.

By now, the boat below them looked tiny. The three figures watching from inside in gobsmacked silence. Above, the winch was just a couple of metres away. She and the shark were almost level with the deck now, and she could see fishermen, yellow waterproofs ankle-deep in blood, long gutting knives in their hands, watching open-mouthed as she pulled out her own knife and started to hack away at the nylon netting holding the Great White.

She only had a few seconds, but the rope came away easily, breaking strand by strand as she hooked the knife between the creature's flesh and the net, and yanked it away.

Below her, the shark was thrashing with renewed vigour, battling to free itself. Just a few strands of netting remained. She jammed her knife in where the tail-fin joined the body, drawing blood as she hooked the last of the strands, and she yanked backwards as hard as she could.

Suddenly, they were both in freefall.

She could hear nothing. See nothing but the side of the ship rushing by. It felt like she was falling forever.

Then came the explosion as the shark hit the water behind her. Half a second later, she felt the jarring impact as she landed, back-first into the sea. It hurt. She felt like her head and shoulders had been smacked by something metal, but, because of the angle she hit the water, when it closed over her head this time, it was only for a second. She threw her arms outwards, and righted herself immediately, shaking her head to clear it, and looking around her.

The shark was motionless in the water, floating, fin rising out. A little netting still wrapped around it, but free. It was maybe ten metres from her. She spun around in the water. Peter was skidding the boat around in a circle. Seb, Robert and Rain were yelling and pointing. Whether they were shouting at Peter or at her, she couldn't tell.

It hardly mattered. The stunned shark twitched in the water, then its tail slowly started to sway from side to side. Under the water, Celeste could see the huge shadow of the head turning towards her. It didn't matter how fast Peter was or how skilfully he piloted the little craft. The shark was going to get to her first.

She faced it. Watched the fin pivot to aim directly at her, and the bow wave ripple towards her as the Great White picked up speed. The fin sank slowly until it vanished just a couple of metres in front of her. She shut her eyes and braced for its impact.

Something brushed the underside of her boot, and then there was nothing. She opened her eyes. Looked around. The sea was flat and empty save for the fishing vessel, the Green Crusader, and Peter's little dinghy bouncing towards her across the water.

18.

"Don't say anything!" said Celeste as Peter, Robert and Rain pulled her aboard, and they started back towards the Green Crusader. "Just don't say anything!"

Nobody did, but she thought Peter may have smiled under his fist as he wiped a little blood from his nose. He'd won, Celeste realised, and he knew it. Despite herself, she had bought into his crusade. She watched him steer the boat in. Little droplets of water clung to his hair. One day she was going to have to work out how she felt about him. He didn't look at her.

A second later, the boat's radio crackled into life. Peter picked it up and called into it: "We're on our way"

"You need to move fast!" said a voice on the other end. It was Josh "Is all - kicking off here."

Celeste shaded her eyes against the sun and looked up at the Green Crusader. A few crew members - Mum and Dad among them - were watching anxiously over the railings as the dinghy bounced back towards them. The rest had gone. She looked up to the ship's bridge. There seemed to be some kind of commotion on the steps leading up to it. A crowd of people were crushed together on the stairs, but the sun was in her eyes and the boat veered in under the curving hull before she could get a good look.

Josh already had the crane out. The straps were dangling into the sea, and Peter guided the boat in. Celeste grabbed one strap as it passed, and clipped it into her side off the boat. Peter and Robert attached the rest, they pulled tight, and Celeste felt the dinghy rock, and then swing free as it was lifted out of the water. Hanging in mid-air, they began to rise.

Suddenly, the little boat dropped about half a metre, swinging outwards and twisting like a fairground ride. Celeste felt her stomach swoop and she gripped the side of the boat. She looked up. The winch above them lurched, sending them twisting again. The five in the boat slid across the benches, grabbing onto anything they could to prevent themselves being tossed overboard as they swung back towards the hull.

"What the hell was that?" said Celeste. The five stared at each other, then up at the arm of the crane.

But it wasn't the crane that was moving. It was the Green Crusader itself that had juddered into motion. The ship tilted as its direction changed, and it started to pick up speed. Peter groped for the radio under his seat.

"What the hell is going on?" he yelled. The only reply was static, but the crane jerked into motion again. "Hang on!" said Peter. Celeste grabbed two of the straps holding the dinghy to the crane. They were the only secure things to hold onto in the boat, but her frozen hands couldn't grip. As she was tipped, sliding towards the edge, she wrapped her forearms around the straps so that they bound her, almost hanging, to the boat. It jerked and swung upwards, sending the others, sliding about in the bottom of the boat in front of her in a bundle of soaked waterproofs.

As they reached the level of the deck, Celeste could see Josh fighting the controls of the crane, desperately trying to bring them in and land them on the moving, tipping deck of the Green Crusader. She watched, tied to the boat by both arms as he brought them swinging in, grazing the safety, railings and causing the dinghy to pivot through ninety degrees and back again in what felt like half a sickening second. Peter had grabbed onto a bench and hauled himself up onto his knees by now, and Josh started to lower them towards the cargo deck. The others were still struggling in the bottom of the boat.

They were still a metre above the deck, when Celeste saw Peter's mouth swing open. His eyes were darting between the gaggle of angry looking crew-members crowding the stairs up to the bridge, and the fishing vessel, just a few hundred metres away.

"Oh, no!" he said. "Dad, you bloody idiot!" Peter hauled himself, hand over hand up the straps until he was standing in the boat, swaying as though on a huge swing.

"What is it?" said Celeste.

Peter almost threw himself over the side of the dinghy, dropping onto the metal deck.

"He's going to ram it!" he said.

"What?" Celeste fought to untangle her arms from the straps, and tried to follow Peter. She put her hand on the rounded float of the dinghy's side and swung her leg over it, but the crane, or the boat, or the entire ship suddenly shifted and her frozen hand slipped. She tumbled sideways over the edge, and fell awkwardly onto the deck, jarring her shoulder in a way she would feel for days.

By the time Celeste had scrambled to her feet, Peter had made it to the steps and was forcing his way up, shoving people out of the way. She tried to follow, but two figures were blocking her way.

"Are you OK, darling?" Mum grabbed her around the shoulders in a hug of pure, joyful relief. She tried to fight free, but there were too many layers of clothing. She tried to speak, but her mother was crushing the breath from her lungs.

"We saw what you did," Dad was saying over Mum's shoulder. "What were you thinking?" He shook his head in disbelief, but Celeste wasn't watching him. Her eyes were fixed on the huge fishing vessel as it swung into view, now directly in front of the Green Crusader. Their ship had completed its turn in the water, and now faced its adversary head on.

Celeste felt the throb of the engines under her feet change. Their vibrations deepened, strengthened. The pitch dipped like a car changing gear, and then started to rise. She felt them beginning to move.

On the steps, the bewildered crew were staring at each other as Peter rattled the handle of the bridge door, then, finding it locked, he hammered on the window with his fist. There was no response.

Celeste tore herself free of her mother's grasp. Behind her, Josh and the rest of the dinghy crew had reached her.

"It's the captain. He's going to ram the fishing boat," said Celeste. "We have to stop him."

"He'll kill us all!" yelled Josh. "Is psycho-crazy!"

Peter shaded his eyes and stared through the bridge window above her, shook his head, then looked out to sea where the crew on board the fishing boat could be seen running up towards their own bridge, clearly suspecting what was about to happen. The water behind the fishing boat began to churn as its own engines fired up.

Celeste saw him turn and almost throw himself down the steps towards her.

"With me!" he shouted as he sprinted past. Celeste followed.

"Where?" she said.

"We have to get to the engine room!" said Peter, hurling himself across the deck, and down towards the lower deck.

19.

"**W**hat do we do?" said Celeste as they all burst into the engine room. The engines were running at full power by now. The noise and the heat were overpowering. Peter put his hands to his head, staring from one piece of equipment to the next. He seemed unsure of what to do.

"Can't we just unplug the engines?" said Seb.

Josh shook his head.

"Not so simple," he said. "He just restart them."

"Then can we steer it from here? Can we turn the ship?" said Rain.

Peter ran his fingers through his hair. Desperation obvious in his face. "Even if we could, the other ship is moving. We might be steering into it," he said. "Anyway, it's all controlled from the bridge."

"Then we do no good here!" said Josh. "We need to be on deck - in lifeboats."

"No," said Peter. "There must be a way."

"We hit any second," said Josh. "Engine room is worst place. We all drown down here!" There was real panic in his eyes.

"Ok - cool it!" said Peter, "they're electric engines, and the controls are electric too. But they're powered by a diesel generator. We need to stop that, and then prevent the backup from kicking in."

"Will take too long," said Josh. "Is procedure."

"Can't we just pull it? Like a fuse box?" said Seb. Peter shook his head again.

"It could cause too much damage. We might never get it started again."

"If we don't do it, we'll just sink!" said Celeste.

Peter stared for a second, the sound of the engine rose even higher and Celeste felt their speed increase even further.

"OK," said Peter. "Josh, disable the backup. It's the control panel in the corner." Josh ran over to a grey box in the corner and flipped it open. Peter turned to a screen behind him, and scrolled through some menus. A number appeared, reducing slowly. "Celeste: when the load hits 100 Kw, you need to press the breaker - there." He pointed to a metal cabinet adorned with a "danger of death" sticker. She pulled it open. A confusing network of wires, fuses and boxes faced her.

"Which one?" she said.

"Now! Do it now!" yelled Peter." Celeste scanned the box in front of her. Which was the breaker? She reached out, and yanked the biggest lever in front of her.

There was a bang, and instant, total blackness. The pitch of the engines dropped as they wound down slowly into silence. The chugging of the generator continued, its own pitch slowly reducing too as it idled. Celeste felt the ship lose its momentum, but only a little.

"Have we stopped?" it was Rain's voice in in the darkness.

"No," said Peter. "We're still moving, we just have to hope we slow enough for the other ship to get out of the way."

Celeste stood in the silence, her hand still on the circuit breaker. There, at the bottom of the ship, she could almost feel the cold weight of the ocean around and above them. Her clothes, still soaked with its water, clung to her heavily. She imagined the collision, the sharp jolt in the darkness. The folding and tearing of the metal hull. The route from where she now stood, through the door up the stairs, along the corridor, through another set of doors, and up yet more stairs to the open deck. It seemed an awfully long way. She pictured making the run now. In the dark, the cabins around them turning as the ship listed. The corridor filling with water. She doubted she'd make it. She doubted any of them would. Nobody spoke. A long moment passed.

Nothing.

"Are we OK?" it was Rain's voice again but Peter didn't answer until it almost seemed the sound had been swallowed by the darkness.

"I think so," he said, eventually. "But he's not going to be happy when he gets down here."

"He won't get in unless we let him," said Josh. There was the unmistakable clang of the metal door being closed and bolted. "We decide what happens next."

"Well, then I suggest we hurry," said Seb. He flicked on the screen of his camera. Its dim light bobbed through the engine room to the chairs where Celeste had first met the group. They all sat down.

"We can't let your Dad captain the ship," said Celeste. "He's a madman."

"You don't know him," said Peter. "He's not mad - he's angry, obsessed, desperate - but he's not mad."

"Desperate why?" said Rain. Peter looked down, and said nothing.

"He could have killed us all," said Celeste. After everything that had happened, she suddenly felt the anger welling up inside her. "He could have killed you! Doesn't he even care?"

"Yes, he cares!" said Peter. "It's just - more complicated than that."

"How?" said Celeste. "If he'd rammed that ship then even if we survived it, even if we made it to South America, that would be the end! No more saving sharks. No more protests. No more dumb concerts. His ship would be finished!"

Peter glared at her. "Haven't you even looked at the state of this ship? It's finished already!" he said. "We've been getting your parents to paint the rust in the hope we can make it through the Panama Canal without being impounded, but wherever this ship docks, it'll never leave. This is the only life he knows, and it's over, and he knows it."

"So he wants to go out in a blaze of glory - is that it?" said Celeste. "And if he takes us with him, so be it?"

Peter stared at the camera screen, leaning over it as though it were a campfire. He looked back up at her. In his eyes, the cold blue square was reflected. "Don't tell me you've never been that angry," he said, "because I saw you today."

"How can you defend him?" she said. "He hit you!"

"So did you," said Peter.

"The engines are a mess," said Josh. "You and I - we keep them running. Without you, we'd be drifting within a day. He cannot sail on his own."

"And I can't navigate it without him," said Peter. "He's run this ship for thirty years. Nobody else on board knows anything."

"So he needs us and we need him?" said Celeste.

Peter nodded.

"Can you stop him trying to sink us?"

"I think so," said Peter. "By the time we get moving again, the other ship will be gone. Now we've cut the net, their trip's over. We've done about $100k of damage to their operation. Might even have put them out of business. He won't want to chase them down."

"That's good to know," said Celeste.

113

"What we have to decide," said Peter, "is what to do with the net."

"What do you mean?" said Seb.

"There's about eight kilometres of it left in the water, I reckon," said Peter.

"So?" said Seb.

"Discarded fishing nets are a big deal," said Peter. "If it stays in the sea, it'll become a ghost-net. It'll keep drifting - catching - for years. Decades."

"Then we have to pull it up." said Rain. "We can't leave it there."

Josh rounded on her. "We're behind already," he said, simply. "We leave it."

"We can't," said Rain. "What about all the sharks?"

"Huh," said josh. "Not just shark. A net like that will catch turtle, dolphin, whale maybe."

"So we have no choice," said Rain. Celeste could see her eyes in the dim light. They were filling up again.

"I don't know," said Peter. "We should lift it, but we've lost so much time."

"If we leave it, everything in those nets dies," said Josh. His voice dropped lower. "If we bring it on board, then we own it. It all still dies, but now we have to kill it ourselves, you understand?" He paused. "I can do that. Done it before," he said. "It is hard work and every one is different. Some of them struggle. Some of them just let you do it. Some die right away. Some you hack and hack and they twitch for hours after. Look at me and tell me you can do it. I don't think so." He stared across the screen, its dim light casting shadows up from under his chin to the outline of his dark hoodie. Celeste thought he looked like death.

114

Opposite him, Rain's shoulders were starting to shake. Her eyes were wide, and dripping tears.

Suddenly, there was a rap on the door. A hollow, metal clang.

"Open up!" it was the captain.

"I'll talk to him," said Peter. He stood up, and moved towards the door. Celeste stood to follow, but Peter shook his head.

"This is all on me," he said. "You stay out of it." He unbolted the door, silhouetted for a moment in bright, shaking torchlight, and slipped out, leaving them in the darkness.

20.

By the time the lights came back on, it was night-time and Celeste had got dried and changed and watched the fishing vessel grow smaller and smaller, its bright lights winking out as it vanished over the horizon. Peter had worked on the generator, patching up the damage the sudden shutdown had done, with his father standing over him with a lamp. The pair had refused her help, working in almost complete silence. It had seemed the two had nothing to say to each other or to anyone else, so she had eventually left them to it. However, by the time they emerged, and the captain walked up to the bridge, started the engines and brought the Green Crusader back onto her old course, it was clear something had changed between them.

As they left the long line of orange buoys that marked the remnant of the shark-net in the water, Celeste stood with Peter at the rear of the ship, looking out. She recognised his expression. He had won against his father - changed their relationship - but he had said things that could not be unsaid. There was damage on both sides. Celeste had been there.

They watched the receding reflection of the moon on the sea above the net. Whatever was dying down there now was beyond help - a casualty of the settlement between Peter and his father. The sooner it was out of sight, the better.

For the adults on board, the return of light and power was like a quick-erase switch. In a single second, they all seemed to forget that they were in a broken ship, captained by a madman who had just risked all their lives, that they had just seen their children perform the most reckless stunt in a shark-infested ocean and then sabotage their vessel. All that seemed to matter was that the lights were on and the ship was moving. The adults, including Celeste's parents, were bizarrely in an

116

even better mood than they had been before any of this had happened, and switched straight from being dazed observers, wandering the decks, into party-goers.

Robert's father, Maurice started it. The moment the lights burst back on, the long, slow rising notes of his double bass creaked like a triumphant whale from the mess, filling the ship, and summoning the adults to him. Pachebel's Canon in D again. Celeste was beginning to think he knew nothing else.

By the time she and Peter made it to the mess, the party was in full swing. Reheated soup was being doled out while the old battle between Robert's dad and Rain's folk-rock parents flared up again.

This time, though, the mood had shifted and Celeste watched as the crew began to tap, and clap, and eventually break out into isolated rashes of dancing and singing. Maurice's slow sawing at the double base faded into the background, and he eventually gave up and sat at a table opposite his instrument.

Maurice was an odd sort of man, when you looked at him. When he had something to occupy his hands - a piece of the ship's engineering, or his musical instrument, he seemed to spring to a jagged sort of life. But the moment his hands were empty, he became silent, uncomfortable, almost invisible.

Rain and Seb walked in with Robert just behind them. The moment he spotted his father, Celeste could see the boy become instantly uncomfortable too. Robert didn't seem to know what to do with his hands until Celeste gave him a bowl of soup and he cupped them around it . The three joined Peter and Celeste on what had, from the start of the journey, been designated as "the kids' table."

A few minutes later, Josh edged in, concealing a large bottle of Tequila.

"Where did that come from?" said Rain. Josh seemed cagey until Peter grinned and pushed his soup-cup over to Josh, saying; "Come on - Dad won't miss it." Josh refilled all the group's soup with generous slugs of the stolen alcohol. Celeste looked down into hers. The soup and alcohol refused to mix, turning the soup into a churning cloudy pond in which lentils and tomato skins occasionally surfaced. She put it to her lips. it tasted strong and strange, but it felt more wholesome and more warming than either of its ingredients did individually. The group stuck with it all evening.

After a couple of bowls, Peter drained his soup. "I think you can all be proud of yourselves today," he said.

"Is this what it's like then -" said Celeste, "for you?"

"No," said Peter, "sometimes it's dangerous." He paused. "Seriously, we did good."

"We cut one net," said Celeste, "and nearly got ourselves sunk."

"Or eaten," added Josh, raising his glass - Josh hadn't bothered with the soup. He was drinking his Tequila straight. "Don't forget your little stunt, Shark Girl."

"Don't call me that," said Celeste. As if anyone was ever going to call her anything else again. "Seriously, they'll go home, get new nets and start again."

"Nets are expensive - so are crews," said Peter. "We've cost them a lot of money. But the real prize is the photos." He nodded at Seb's camera, lying on the table.

"That boat was all over the place," said Celeste. "Even if you were a professional photographer, you wouldn't have got anything."

"I'm not a photographer," said Seb. "I'm a lens-based visual artist."

Celeste shrugged. "Let's see then," she said. Seb flicked his viewscreen out and the group crowded round while he started to scroll through his pictures.

They were extraordinary. They told the whole story, from the launch of the little dinghy through to Celeste's reckless climb to cut the great white free of the net. The sight of herself hanging there, her body dwarfed by the shark's streamlined shape made her catch her breath. What had she been playing at?

But what really took her breath away was the images. Not just sharp. Not just clear. But terrifyingly beautiful. Moving. They seemed almost like painted pictures. In one, the river of blood rolled horizontally across the frame, beyond it the dark shape of the fishing ship's hull glowering slightly out of focus. In the foreground, a little shark's pointed head, white and black eye oversized, wide and staring, rose out of the water, a gash where its fin had been. In another, a fisherman on the deck looked down directly into the lens, his weathered face bewildered at the protestors below him.

There was the rear of the ship, net half-hauled in, full of sharks hanging in it silhouetted against the sky. Above them, the refracted arc of the water-cannon had inscribed a rainbow. There was Rain in that moment before they dived into the water, clutching the knife. Her face rimmed with waterproof hood, vulnerable as ever, but resolved.

And there was Celeste herself, standing on the net as though on a tightrope. Long knife in her hand, the shark's tail beside her. She was almost at the level of the ship's deck. The sea so far below. The next shot was of her and the shark again, tumbling this time, towards the ocean. Its body had curved towards her, as though swimming. Hers too was curved towards its tail so that they appeared to be frozen in

119

mid-air chase - it following her, her following it, round and round together.

"That one's tolerable," said Seb. "Given a little touching up, it might even make the portfolio."

"I don't like being in photos," said Celeste. But maybe those two images could be exceptions. "What do you mean the pictures are the real prize?" she said.

"Our job out here is to document environmental crimes," he said. "As long as we've got a record, maybe one day we'll be able to show people what's happening. That's how things change."

"What do you do with the photos?" said Celeste.

"We have an archive," said Peter, "on our website." Celeste stared at him in disbelief.

"That's it?" she said. She pulled out her phone, and loaded up the site. "This website?" she said. Suddenly, she was waving her phone in his face. "This piece of crap?" The site looked a mess - a huge, sprawling list of unreadable links overlaid on an eye-strainingly lurid green background.

"Yes," said Peter. "What's wrong with it?"

"You don't go online much, do you?" she said. "It's hopeless. Half the links don't work. There's no video. Look at this!" She pulled up a page. Three pixelated photos, all different sizes, were jammed together. It was impossible to see what was happening in any of them. Over the top of the images, white text was jumbled and dislocated.

"So," said Peter. "That's what the Internet looks like."

"Yeah," said Celeste. "In 1992. It's not even optimised for phones."

Peter shrugged. "It's up there. That's what's important." he said.

"No," said Celeste. "What's important is that people see it. Have you even checked your metrics?" Peter looked confused. Celeste pulled up another tab and drew down some figures. She held up the phone to show Peter a bar chart.

"I can't see anything," he said. "What am I looking at?"

"Hits on your homepage," said Celeste. "And you can't see anything because nobody is clicking on it. You have literally no followers. No views. No wonder you're running out of money."

"You can earn money on the Internet?" said Peter.

Celeste just stared back at him, mouth open. "Oh, my god," she said.

Peter looked back, blankly.

"Data," she said suddenly.

"What?"

"If you do go to the jungle - and I still think it's mad - but if you do go, you don't just need to come back with photos. You need data." she said. "You need to hack into their computer and you need to bring back the data - the files that link everything Zoila is doing right up to Drier and PetroMoto. That's the only way any of this will be worth anything."

"I'm not really clued into the whole cyberspace thing," said Peter.

"No kidding," said Celeste. "Listen to me. When I hacked the school, it got on the national news, all the papers. Everywhere - and that was nothing - just a prank. This stuff you've got here," she waved her hand at Seb's camera - "this is dynamite! If I were running this, you'd have blanket coverage, you'd be going viral on Facebook, Instagram, Twitter, Youtube, and I'd watermark every image so you could get metrics on every view and share. I'd set up an untraceable

121

anonymous bitcoin wallet so people could donate instantly through it. I'd link it to an ad-serve account taking money for advertising so you got a drip-feed of cash per view, then I'd have a masked, black-hat auto-viewing network to bump the views and likes until you hit a million views per day, and then organic traffic would take care of the rest. Then I'd sell - not give - but SELL the best pictures to the papers through a fake account on a stock photo service. You'd be famous, but anonymous. You'd be everywhere but invisible. You'd have global reach, and global funding."

Peter didn't speak for a long time. Then he turned to her, his gaze, intense. Serious.

"And are you?" he said, slowly. Quietly.

"Am I what?"

"Are you going to run it for us?" said Peter. "Are you in?"

Celeste took a breath. What she'd said, she'd said without thinking. An instant reaction, exploding out of her, she had barely registered that she had said it out loud. Now he was calling her on it.

"I guess I am," she said. "Only -" She paused. "I don't need to be recognised. We have to blur our faces."

Suddenly, they became aware of a tall figure standing over them. Celeste looked up. Maurice. Stooping, gangling.

"Robert," he said. "I didn't know you could..." He faded out for a second, groping for a word to describe what he'd seen his son do in the sea that afternoon. "... swim." he said eventually.

"I am in the county team," said Robert. "I have nine medals. Five bronze, four silver."

"I didn't know," Maurice repeated.

Robert shrugged. "You weren't there." Celeste couldn't tell what his voice was trying to convey. Anger or regret. Boredom or care. He could have meant just about anything or could just have been a statement of fact. Maurice tightened his lips. His eyebrows raised in an equally unreadable gesture.

"Fair point," he said. "Yer Mum didn't want me to be."

"I've been living on my own for a year," said Robert.

"Look," said Maurice, "I'm tryin' now, ain't I? Can we try to start again?" He tried a smile.

"I know you're trying." Again, he could have meant anything.

"Thought this trip'd help us - you know - clear the air. Bond." He shifted from one foot to the other, and shoved his hands deep into the pockets of his pantaloons. Robert nodded, hunching his shoulders.

"I've changed a lot since you left" said Robert. "I know I used to get angry. It must have been hard for you too."

Maurice seemed about to say something, then changed his mind. "You want a hot chocolate?" he said.

"Why? Are we out of beer?" said Robert.

Maurice grinned, and shuffled off to get him a drink. Robert got up and followed, sitting opposite his father at a table in the corner. Neither seemed to want to speak first, so they just sat there.

Josh emptied his glass and refilled it. He looked over at the pair for a moment.

"Robert's better off without him," he said.

"He's his father," said Peter.

"A man is not a man if he follows his father around." said Josh.

"The man is a waster,"

Josh drank his Tequila in one gulp, then shook his head. "I know about fathers - he's no better than mine," he said. "No better than yours either." He shook his head again, then stood up suddenly. "You're on your own. We all are." He turned, leaving the bottle on the table, and walked, slightly swaying to the door leading down towards the cabins.

"What's got into him?" said Seb. "My Dad didn't have much time for me - you don't see me whining about it."

"Your Dad left you in a private boarding school," said Peter. "His left him in the sea. It's different."

Seb shrugged and turned to Rain who was sitting beside him, scanning through the photos, pausing every time she found one of herself. "You're good." she said. "Why don't you ever take pictures of me dancing?"

Seb shrugged. "Dancing is pretending," he said. "Only reality interests me."

"I think you don't understand dancing," said Rain. "Come on!" She dragged him to his feet and off to the front of the mess where a group were already dancing. She started to twirl and spin, her skirt and hair flying out around her. Her bare feet tapping the floor in perfect time to the imperfect beat her father was strumming out on his guitar, but her arms and head swinging a little too strongly, dizzied by the alcohol. She swayed a little, then staggered. Seb caught her in his arms. They laughed. Looked at each other and were suddenly kissing.

Celeste looked away from the floor, accidentally caught Peters eye, and looked down at her murky Tequila soup. Some people made all that stuff look so easy. Either that or some people made it look really hard.

"I'm going to turn in," she said. "I've got to sort out your website tomorrow." She hadn't meant it to sound quite so much as though she were blaming him for the state of it but Peter nodded. She got up from the table, a little unsteady. Either the sea had got choppy or the tequila soup had been stronger than she thought. She headed for the door.

"Celeste," said Peter.

She looked back.

"You did good today," he said. "A bit crazy, but good. Only next time, maybe don't hit me, OK?"

"Then don't get in my way," said Celeste.

Peter smiled. "Goodnight, Shark Girl," he said. She walked out without looking back, but she felt herself grinning.

21.

Celeste woke up feeling about as bad as she could ever remember having felt. The room spun above her, while underneath, the ship was pitching and swooping, its engines vibrating through the metal frame of her bed and deep into her body.

Her head pounded. Her mouth felt dry and sticky. Tequila soup. The thought made her want to throw up. But it was more than that. Piece by piece, her muffled brain fed her back the previous day. She had been in the sea. She could still taste the mouthfuls of salty water, sucking every drop of moisture from her lips. Parching her throat.

She tried flexing her fingers. They ached, but not as much as her calf muscles. Her thighs. The muscles in her stomach. Her arms. Celeste had pushed herself hard, and now she felt it.

But it was more than even that. She had been cold. Wet. The chill had entered her body and left her shaking and sick. Her half-waking brain struggled to separate the illness from the tiredness from the hangover. She needed to know the extent of each, but it was impossible. There was just too much wrong with her body to pull apart the sticky threads of bad feeling.

She raised her head to look out of her tiny porthole. Outside the sea was rough and the sky dark grey. Part of the swaying she felt in her stomach was the real movement of the ship, but it was impossible to tell which part. Today was a bad day to be sick.

It was a couple of hours before Celeste managed to fight her way back to the mess. She was driven by thirst more than hunger, but water felt wrong as it hit the mess of her stomach, and so she grabbed the plate of fried food offered to her by the cheery, teetotal, Rose, taking it over to a quiet corner to devour it.

The beans, hash brown, mushrooms and egg should have been exactly the wrong thing for her, but somehow, the moment she started eating, Celeste felt a little better. Well enough, at least, to raise her head and look at the rest of the crew shuffling, white-faced around the room. With the exception of Rose, everyone was suffering from sea-sickness, or a hangover, or both. People stared into whatever food or drink they thought might be able to bring them back from the dead, and held grimly onto their tipping seats. Celeste scowled at them from her corner. She had no sympathy. They looked as bad as she did, but they had only been drunk. None of them had rescued a great white.

She took another plate of breakfast, stumbled back to her cabin with it, flipped open her laptop and focussed on the screen. She had work to do.

She pulled up the Green Crusader's website. It looked no better on the laptop than it had on her phone. It was going to take days to shape it into something usable, but she had promised Peter, and at least it was something she felt pretty comfortable doing. The other stuff she had promised Peter in her Tequila fuelled state would be more difficult. She was going to need a clear head, and the help of the dark web. She must have sounded pretty cocky last night. She had over-promised, but for some reason was determined to deliver for him. She decided not to think about why.

First things first though. Back in Milton Highbury the police must, by now, have put two and two together, and realised that it was Celeste who took down the school. The thought of it hung about in the back of her mind like an unopened letter. Just because she didn't know what was happening didn't make it any less of a threat. If things had gone well, Celeste and her family could lay low for a few months, and then swing back to pick up their things. if they had gone badly, they would never be able to set foot in their home country ever again.

It didn't take her long to find what she was looking for.

The police had indeed linked Celeste's family's disappearance to the cyber-attack. However, thanks to Mum's lack of organisation and Dad's paranoia - in particular, his mistrust of banks - combined with the fact that they had only been resident in the town for a few weeks before the attack, it had proved impossible to put a name or a face to any member of the family. The house had been rented in cash. The electricity was on a pay meter and all their other official documents were still registered to their previous address. They had made no local friends, and had no ties in the town.

When they had left, Mum had grabbed clothes and food. Dad had ignored such practicalities and instead swept the house clean of anything that might identify them. In an age where information was everywhere, and everything left a data-trail, he had done exceptionally well. Well enough that the authorities' search of the place had hit a brick wall, and police had become convinced it had been a professional job.

Now, as Celeste searched the news archives, she found herself represented not just as a shadowy hacker, but as part of some dark taskforce of spies. The fantasy had escalated to the point where the family - known only now as Unit X - were being linked to the secret services of foriegn powers. The home secretary had been quoted in an interview as suggesting the Russian government were involved. Although why the Kremlin would want to attack a school in South East England nobody seemed to know.

Celeste closed the tab on her laptop, her mind spinning. On the one hand, nobody was pursuing the family right now. On the other, the whole thing had been blown out of all proportion. If she were ever recognised, or the police were ever to discover her identity, there would be big, big trouble. According to the police, she was a fugitive, a criminal, and probably also a spy.

One thing was clear. She couldn't tell Dad. With every day he spent tinkering with the mechanics of the Green Crusader, Dad's mental state was getting better and better. He was focussed and sane. He rarely even mentioned drones or shadow organisations now. It was not a good time to let him know he was wanted by MI5.

Celeste flicked over to the utter horrorshow that was the Green Crusader's website. Just looking at it felt like her brain was bleeding. There were no frames, no banners, just a mess of different-sized fonts fighting for attention against a lurid background of oversaturated photos. Words ran into each other, pages of text scrolled on down into irrelevance, links went nowhere. What was worse, there was no social media. None. No Twitter feed. No Insta. Not even a comments section. Everything, she decided, would have to go.

The website was password protected of course. She considered asking Peter what the password was on the off-chance he or his father knew it, but her head was banging and the thought of trying to track him down and having that conversation felt like a major undertaking. After the second helping of breakfast she felt like she could just about type, but if she stood up, she would probably be sick.

It took her all of three tries to break into the site. Someone must have thought they were being so clever. The password turned out to be "GreenCrusader2". Using '2' instead of '1' as the obligatory number in the password, thought Celeste. Clearly she was up against top-level cyber security now.

She downloaded the whole site just in case there was anything worth using. She scanned through the files. A few text documents. A few badly scanned magazine articles and poorly taken photos. But they told the story of the Green Crusader well enough. The ship had been one man's vision right from the start and it looked like Peter's father had been quite a revolutionary in his day.

Newspaper cuttings from the 1970s showed him with piercing eyes and horrendous dress sense which would have placed him right at the forefront of fashion. His hair was long and full, and the pictures showed him hand in hand with celebrities and pop stars. In one image, he was shaking hands with a young-looking David Attenborough. In another, he was scaling the cooling tower of a nuclear power plant, trailing a huge banner.

For a while, it appeared, he was a figurehead for the global fight for the planet, and when the drug-fuelled lifestyles of the most well-known of the flower-power generation finally started to catch up with them in the mid-1970s, the Green Crusader's bank account benefited from a number of generous bequests. Peter's father moved quickly to purchase the ship and fit it out with the best technology 1978 could offer.

Then came the big split. The rest of the environmental protest groups went one way, focussing on the kind of touchy-feely stunts and protests that brought worldwide support, and funding from rich and reputable trusts and foundations. The Green Crusader went the other, taking up lost causes, and dirty jobs. While the softer campaign groups protested outside parliament and published scientific research into global warming, the Green Crusader took on seal-clubbing expeditions in hand-to hand combat on the ice flows and put themselves between whalers and their prey. It was tough. It was dangerous. And for a lot of supporters it was just too strong to stomach.

Celeste scrolled on through the archive until she came across the first picture of Peter himself. Taken on the deck, the sun shining through the ship's communications tower created a glow that almost obscured the two figures in the foreground. Peter, aged about nine, a huge unruly mop of hair on his head, was grinning from ear to ear. His father's arm was around him, his own smile broad and easy. It was hard to believe it was the same man.

What had gone wrong, Celeste wondered.

In any case, it was pretty clear that things had started to go downhill around the time of the photo. For the last ten years or so, the Green Crusader had been running itself down. The website had fallen into disrepair, and with it, the international reputation of its captain and crew, the level of donations and eventually, inevitably, the fabric of the ship itself.

Peter might be disinterested in the ship's online profile, but he was wrong to think it didn't matter. If the Green Crusader were to stay afloat, then more urgently than a coat of paint or an overhaul of its engine, it needed a virtual presence.

Rather than try to revamp what was already there, Celeste decided to start from scratch. A basic site that didn't mention the Green Crusader by name, but which showcased the best of Seb's photos in a form that the press could purchase. The point here was the story of their encounter with the illegal shark-fishers, and the upcoming story of whatever happened when they reached the rainforest. Anything else could be added later.

Everything needed to be anonymous. If her family were linked to the attack on the school, and traced to the ship, then they wouldn't be safe anywhere. But all the emails and social media accounts needed a username. Her fingers hovered over the keyboard. She needed something instantly recognisable.

She thought back to last night. What Peter had called after her as she left the mess hall. It was meant as a joke, but it felt oddly right. She filled out the online forms as @sharkgirl, and with that name, she registered a free email, a Twitter handle and facebook and Instagram accounts. All basic stuff.

She ran everything through an anonymous VPN. The same high-level encryption anyone in China or Iran would use if they wanted to sidestep their country's security services.

With that done, she set about creating a basic website. Blank pages with titles for now. Once she got Seb's photos from him, she'd be able to quickly fit them into the site, and they'd be up and running.

Before she could do that though, she needed some deeper level work. Work she couldn't do herself. She needed help. There were, she knew, two types of coders in the world. White-hat coders - who did everything by the book, obeyed the rules the search engines set up, and tried to do whatever it was they wanted to do through legitimate means. And then there was the other type. The black-hat coders. If you were a black-hat, there were no rules. If you saw a weakness in security, you exploited it. If you found a way to play Youtube's search engine so it always listed your videos at the top, or fake a social media profile so it automatically generated friends, or likes, or follows, then you did it. If you found a backdoor into somebody else's website then that was fair game. If you didn't, then one could always be made.

What Celeste needed now was a black hat guru. Luckily, there was someone. @thelogician had shown up in her feeds pretty much the moment she'd first started poking about in the black-hat forums at the age of twelve. Every time she asked a dumb question, or came up with a clever idea, @thelogician had replied almost immediately with helpful advice, answers, new hacking challenges. She had never asked anything about @thelogician - never even knew if they were male or female, but still, she felt she knew them. If Celeste had ever had a teacher in the ways of the dark web, it was @thelogician.

She tapped his name into a forum, and within five minutes a reply came back:

@thelogician: **You've made a pretty mess.**

Celeste: **What do you mean?**

@thelogician: **The school. That was you, right?**

Celeste: **How do you know?**

@thelogician: **it had your fingerprints all over it. What do you need?**

Celeste: **I need to make my image posts instantly popular. I need an automatic untraceable advertising revenue generator in cryptocurrency.**

@thelogician: **(shrug) Doesn't everyone?**

Celeste: **It's important.**

@thelogician: **You finally found something to fight for? OK, I'll help out. What do you want me to do?**

22.

Zoila Chavez Marched across the compound. Her boots squelched on deep black-stained, viscous mud. Things were going well, and that made the jungle an even more horrible place to work than it had been before. The stink of oil was an acid in the air, and the deep sound of the burnoff - the roaring flame at the top of the tower in the centre of the compound - was a constant underscore to the chirping of insects and birds and the growling and clanging of the vehicles. Day and night, the place was deafening.

Oil seemed to get everywhere. On her boots. In her clothes. In her office. In her bed. Smudges of thick black contaminated every piece of paperwork, and fine droplets of it condensed on every flat surface, a fine spray which seemed to come from everywhere and coat everything in a thin dirty film. The air stank of it. Her skin was oily with it. Her food tasted of it. When she had arrived, she had disliked the jungle. Now she hated it with every fibre of her being. The sooner she was out of the place, the better. It could all burn for all she cared.

She sealed herself into her office, flipped open her rugged looking laptop and wiped the oil from the screen with a dirty cloth. The video-call sprung into life immediately and the face of Lincoln Drier appeared. He was dressed in a sharp, clean suit. Behind him a window looking out high above the Dallas skyline.

"Every day you're costing us money," said Drier without a pause for an introduction. "I want good news, right now."

Zoila fought the urge to punch the screen. Instead, she silently tapped a button just below Drier's line of vision. A tiny red dot on the screen indicated she was recording the call. Zoila's Insurance.

"Things are tough out here," she said. "There are operational difficulties."

"You know how many rigs my company runs?" said Drier. He leaned back, pausing as though waiting for an answer, but she knew he was not expecting one. "Two hundred," he said. "Two hundred and then some. We have interests in seventy countries. I know what it takes to bring a barrel of oil to market."

"So do I, but -"

"Do you, though?" said Drier. "Because to date your field - your whole country has produced - let me just check the figures..." Drier rifled pointlessly through a sheaf of papers on his desk. Zoila watched him, he knew the answer as well as she did. "Ah, yes," he said eventually. "Damn all! Remind me why I'm paying you and your little tinpot outfit." Zoila paused. No point playing softball.

"You're paying me," she said, "because as we both know your 200-and-then-some rigs are drying up fast. Last year you bought 20% fewer barrels to market than the year before, and though nobody but you has seen this year's figures, I'm going to bet from the look on your face that they're even worse." She smiled. "You need my little tinpot outfit as much as we need you, because the Amazon is a big place, and the signs are -"

"I've seen the reports." said Drier. "But I don't sell reports. I sell oil. What about your security issue - your little problem with the natives?"

"There's a village just downstream. They're no threat. Not anymore, "Zoila thought about the boy with the monkey on his shoulder. Since she'd shot his companion, nobody had seen anything from any of the tribe. "I... discouraged them."

"I need you in full production asap, and I need you expanding."

"We've got a problem with disposal of waste," said Zoila. "The more we pump the more waste there is. We're burying it in pits right now, but we don't have the capacity to keep up if we increase production."

"Funny, 'cos my map says you got 5.5 million square kilometres of empty jungle," said Drier.

"There are regulations." She was getting tired of his sarcasm.

"The regulations are your problem." said Drier, "Pump it in the river."

"That's drinking water for the village," said Zoila.

Drier looked at her as if she was talking a different language. "Do they have guns?" he said. "In fact, no, scrub that question. Do they have more guns than the security team you've got sitting round pickin' their butts?"

Zoila paused. "What are you saying?" She knew exactly what he was saying, but he was going to have to say it.

Drier obliged. "Kill them," he said. "Kill them all. If you don't have the stomach for this work, I've got people who have."

"Understood, sir," said Zoila.

"Good," said Drier, "and put nothing on the paperwork. Nothing ties this to me. Got it?"

Zoila nodded. Her eyes flicked to the red recording dot in the corner of the screen. She hoped it would never come to it, but if he ever tried to drop her in it, he'd be going down too. He wasn't as clever as he thought.

"And you'd better be ready with that first boatload of oil. The moment that first oil comes out of the jungle is a big public relations hit for us. I'm gonna have press and TV on the quayside watching. When that first shipment comes down the river I'm gonna be ridin' that boat."

"You're coming here?" said Zoila. "I thought you were doing your announcement from the port!"

"I ain't missin' this!" said Drier. "This is a feel-good story for the whole damn company. I wanna be drivin' that boat myself! When I announce Amazon oil to the world my share price is gonna spike!"

"Of course, sir," said Zoila.

"Good. Now, get comfortable," said Drier. "If your reports about how much oil is down there are right, you'll be living in that jungle for the next twenty years." The screen went blank. Zoila collapsed back in her seat. That was what he thought. She'd tolerate this stinking place just long enough to secure her investment. After that - well, Drier's office above the Dallas Skyline was more her kind of place.

But for now, she had problems. Drier, coming here. She hadn't dare tell him that they were way behind in filling that first shipment. The boat was waiting to take the oil down to the port, but it was only half full. If Drier was expecting to actually visit the drill for his PR stunt then she would have to take action.

She pulled the walkie-talkie from her hip and spoke into it.

"Samuel, get here now," she said. "We need to up production by 15% - so get a team laying pipes down to the river." she paused. "And we have to deal with our native problem too. They've just got inconvenient."

23.

Celeste's illness had subsided by the following morning, dropping from an overwhelming nausea to a dull ache somewhere behind her eyes, but it provided her with a good cover for spending the next few days locked in her cabin setting up the social media campaign. Linked Twitter, Facebook, YouTube and Instagram accounts waiting to promote Seb's pictures.

Meanwhile, when Celeste did emerge, she noticed that things on board were settling back into their own comfortable and uncomfortable patterns. Mum was getting increasingly close to Rose and Annette who, apart from complaining at having mislaid various items of jewelry, seemed happy spending their days sanding and painting the ship. Dad was burying himself in searching out and cataloguing blockages in the ship's pipework. Peter and his father went about their work almost entirely without reference to each other. When they passed on the deck, they nodded, but that was the extent of their interaction. Their relationship had been changed forever when Peter and Celeste had cut the engines, and now the captain seemed even more broken than before.

Robert and Maurice were making stumbling, mostly silent attempts to build a relationship through handing each other spanners in the noisy engine room, and coffees in the mess, but after being absent for so much of his life, Robert confided to Celeste that he was finding his father's sudden constant presence tough to take. He wanted to get to know his Dad, he told Celeste, but this was too much. Too fast. They had time. Robert begged Celeste for a job that would keep him off the decks for a while, and she eventually set him to work drafting a series of tweets, captions and updates ready for when they launched their site. He turned out to have a writing style that was simple and to the point. Just what the website needed.

Celeste rarely saw Seb and Rain, and never saw them apart. When they weren't hiding out together in his cabin, they hung around the decks together, staring out to sea, or sat in the mess, heads almost touching as they exchanged intimate and earnest conversations over steaming coffee. They seemed to have formed a bubble which no-one else was welcome to enter, but Celeste had reached the point where she could go no further without him, so she steeled herself and barged between them as they stood watching the sunset one evening.

"I need your photos," she said. Seb stared blankly at her. "From the fishing boat," she added.

"Oh, yes, of course," said Seb vaguely. He appeared to be staring straight at her, smiling, as though he were staring through her, trying to catch a glimpse of Rain behind her. "Be my guest."

"Well?" said Celeste. "Where's your memory card?"

"Right- they're in my cabin, plastic box next to my camera," he said. Behind her, Rain's hand fumbled its way along the railing to meet and clasp Seb's. Celeste left them to it and headed for the cabins.

Seb's cabin was the third on the left. None of the doors had locks on them. She pushed it open. Sebastian had been a private school boarder all his life and he was no stranger, by the looks of things, to cramped accommodation and military-style discipline. The cabin was meticulously neat. His clothes, laid out and folded. His camera equipment arranged on a shelf as though placed there for effect. His shoes lined up on the floor. His bed had been made, the sheet folded over the blanket and smoothed down as though prepared by a valet. Honestly, thought Celeste. Who made his bed? Her sheets were left where they landed when she fell out.

The memory card was next to the camera as promised. She pocketed it and left the room.

Just as she was closing the door, Josh emerged from a cabin at the end of the corridor. The moment he caught her eye, he looked instantly guilty.

"That's Rose and Annette's cabin," said Celeste. "What were you doing in there?"

"That's Seb's - why you in there?" he said. He stuck his hand deep into his pocket, but not before she noticed something shining in his fist.

"Were you stealing from them?" she said.

He nodded at the door to Seb's cabin. "You'll get caught if you take anything from there. Too tidy." He looked back at the cabin he'd just left. "This place is a mess."

"I wasn't taking anything," said Celeste.

"Me neither," said Josh. He turned to leave.

"These people saved your life."

Josh shrugged. "You can't fool me," he said. "You are not stupid. You and me are the same."

"You're stupid, if you think nobody's going to notice you stealing from their cabins," said Celeste.

Josh looked away. "It's not like anybody's got anything on this ship anyway. They're hippies. Sharing the world and all that."

"You never been to my town," said Josh. "To me, you all rich. He's got his camera," said Josh, nodding towards Seb's cabin. "You've got your laptop."

"Touch it and you're dead," said Celeste. Josh put his hands up in mock surrender. "Leave my parents' room alone too." She paused. "What's with you?" she said.

"Nothing is with me," said Josh. "Nobody owes me nothing, and I don't owe them."

"What are you doing here, then?" said Celeste. "Why join the group?" Josh tilted his head to one side.

"Where I come from, if you want to survive, you follow the money," he said.

"Is that what you do?" said Celeste.

"No work in my town, but the fishermen have a little money, so me and my Dad, we follow the fishermen. Whalers have more money than fishermen not much more, but some, so I follow the whalers."

"And the whalers left you to die," said Celeste.

"So what?" said Josh. "The whales are their money - they followed the money. It's what I would have done."

"And the people on this ship?"

"They act poor, but they're rich enough to pay for their trip. This is a holiday for them!"

"So you don't believe in any of this?" said Celeste.

"Don't pretend you do. You're tough, like me. We're just the same," said Josh.

Celeste walked right up to him, until she was staring straight into his hoodie. "I don't believe you," she said. "You could have left the ship in England. Plenty of money there. More than South America. You could just sit it out, and wait to dock. Instead you've bought into Peter's gang. Why do that if you don't care?"

Josh shifted his head. His eyes narrowed. His face seemed to tighten as he stared at her for a long moment. "There's money in oil," he said. "Real money." he paused. "Peter wants to check the place out. I do too."

"What? Do you think they have stacks of cash lying around waiting to be stolen?" said Celeste. "Or are you looking for a job? Or what?"

"I don't know," said Josh, "I go where the money is, then I make my decision. Just like you." Celeste searched his face. He looked older.

"You're nothing like me," she said. "And if you steal anything on this ship, people will find out."

She turned and walked back to her cabin, leaving him standing in the corridor.

24.

Celeste dumped Seb's photos wholesale onto her drive. They were neatly organised into folders by date so she opened those from the day of their attack on the fishing boat and flipped through them one by one.

They looked even better on the laptop screen than they had on the camera's tiny display. They were crisper, stronger, more brutal. The frozen droplets of foam and water and blood hung in the air in strings like streamers at a parade. The shapes of fins and boats and buoys were sliced and framed by ropes and nets. The sharp halted moments of expression in the faces of Rain, Celeste and Peter told a story of pain and effort, determination and anger. They were perfect.

It was a shame that they had to go.

Nobody had put a face to Celeste back home and nobody had connected the family who fled the town to the Green Crusader. If Seb's photos hit the media in the way she thought they would, she couldn't risk somebody from Milton Highbury spotting them and identifying her. In fact it was vital that everyone associated with the Sharkgirl hashtag remained safely anonymous.

To take his action shots, Seb had set his camera to burst mode - capturing sequences of dozens of images each time he pressed the shutter.

She imported the pictures into her image editor, selected just the faces and darkened them until the detail was lost and the figures' hair surrounded black vacuums that seemed to sink back into the space behind the screen as though Celeste and her group were dark ghosts, then she sequenced them, so that each image became an animated GIF - a constantly repeating snapshot a few seconds in length. There were shots of sharks writhing in the blood-red water.

The arc of the water cannon spiraling towards the camera. But the most impressive GIF by far was the shot of Celeste herself, freeing the great white from the net. Two bursts of images showed her climbing past its jaws as it twisted to attempt to grab her, and then, a few seconds later, cutting the last few strands of netting holding both of them in place, and tumbling in slow motion beside the shark into the water.

Defacing the pictures by removing the faces felt, to Celeste, like vandalism. But she was hardly a stranger to vandalism. Destruction was, she was becoming aware, the chief way in which she expressed her emotions. Anyway, there was no choice. She had to admit that shots of her idiotic performance in the shark net were iconic, and compelling. Instinct told her that they would play well on Twitter and Facebook and that, whatever she felt about her own actions, was the point of all this.

Before she changed her mind, she uploaded the GIFs to the @sharkgirl Twitter account and Facebook pages, and linked them to a longer slideshow on Youtube containing more pictures and Robert's text telling the story of what happened. With that done, she signed up to allow advertisers to put their own ads next to the youtube video which would make a few tenths of a cent every time a viewer clicked on one of the ads. She then set up her own separate advertising which would take any money the Youtube video made, and use it to promote the original GIFs on Facebook and Twitter.

The idea was that if anyone did watch the video, and it started to generate a few pennies in advertising, then that money would be automatically ploughed back into getting more people to watch. Celeste discovered that she could choose to advertise the GIFs on Facebook to people with specific interests, and she had spent enough time hanging around festivals with her parents to know exactly what their environmentalist friends talked about, what bands they listened to and how they used social media.

Building a profile to target her advertising was easy, and with that done, she sent links to The Logician. Whatever black-hat techniques could help get those first few views and likes that would seed the whole process, The Logician would be able to set them in motion.

As usual, The reply came within a few seconds.

@thelogician **I will send these to my network.**

Did The Logician ever sleep, she wondered.

Celeste: **What do you want in return?**

@thelogician: **Consider it a favour. I can see from these images that you took a considerable risk. May I ask why?"**

Celeste's fingers hovered over the keyboard.

Celeste: **Don't know.**

@thelogician: **I understand.**

Celeste was about to reply that she doubted anyone could understand, but at that moment she spotted something on the screen. She had been idly clicking through the other folders on Seb's camera card, and had opened a file from a few days earlier.

On the screen was something that brought her up short. She flicked through the other images. There was another, and another. She checked the pictures from the previous days, over and over again, different contexts. Different compositions, but the same subject. What was he playing at? She started to feel the anger build inside her.

Suddenly the cabin door flew open and Robert's head appeared around it.

"Doesn't anyone knock on this ship?" yelled Celeste.

"Sorry - I," He was visibly embarrassed. "It's just we've spotted -"

Celeste snapped her laptop closed and slipped it under her arm. "What?" she said, angrily. "What have you spotted?"

"Land."

25.

Land was a thin, low line, a dark bump on the horizon slowly gaining definition as Celeste followed Robert to the ship's bow where the rest of the crew were already gathered. She quickly saw where Rain and Seb were standing, hand in hand. She would speak to Seb, but not right now. This wasn't the time. Instead, she watched with the others as the landscape grew, slowly surrounding them.

Huge ships started to speckle the horizon all around, and then became denser as they closed in around, all facing inwards as though they were sentinels keeping guard over some far-off event, somewhere directly in front of the Green Crusader. Blocky container boats, hung low in the water, loaded with coloured boxes, like skyscrapers laid down on their sides. Some were moving, slowly gliding inwards. Others just hovered, waiting for a signal.

Two pencil-thin towers rose in front of them, and grew into a huge bridge spanning the entrance to the canal. Little tugs and sailboats started to appear, criss-crossing in front of them, like shoals of fish, darting back and forth in front of the ship, playing in their bow waves.

Celeste dug her hands deep into her pockets. After so many days of open, featureless horizons, this crowding sent prickles up and down her back. It felt confusing, oppressive. The deck, too, felt flooded with people. She suddenly longed for the certainty of the empty sea again.

Peter appeared beside her. She forced the feeling back.

"What happens now?" she said. Beyond the bridge, the sides of the canal started to close in fast. A little official-looking boat guided them in, blasting a trail of black smoke from its funnel, as a scattering of white, square, blue-roofed buildings appeared in front of them and grew slowly to form a concrete dock. The Green Crusader slowed to a stop beside the dock. The little boat came alongside.

"Now, a pilot comes on board to take us through the canal to the Pacific," he said.

"We're not allowed to do it ourselves?" said Celeste.

Peter shook his head.

"Your Dad won't like that."

"He's got no choice," said Peter. "The canal is so congested they can't just have anyone piloting ships through it. Only their own pilots are allowed." He paused, looking back down the gangway, where a serious-looking man was marching up towards the bridge. He was dressed in a blue long-sleeved shirt over which he wore a white T-shirt with an embroidered insignia.

"Will it be OK?" said Celeste.

"As long as he thinks the boat is seaworthy," said Peter, "and all our papers are in order."

"And are they?"

"Mostly," said Peter. "My Dad still has a few friends in Panama." He shifted slightly. "Although he's got far more enemies," he added. "Maybe we'd better just make sure."

Celeste followed Peter up to the bridge. Half-way up the stairs, she looked back and noticed another little tender coming alongside. On it, four men wearing dark jackets and shades stood, waiting to board. The man at the front was the only one she could see clearly. He wore a black, wide-brimmed hat and carried a long black case. His face was like tanned leather and deeply creased with lines that looked like late nights rather than hard work.

They looked strangely out of place on the deck of the little boat, but just as she stepped through the door into the bridge and lost sight of them, she noticed her Dad at the front of the boat point back, and the whole crew started babbling excitedly.

She ignored them and closed the door.

On the bridge, a conversation was going on in Spanish between the captain and the pilot. It was unmistakably an argument. The pilot stepped towards the wheel. The captain's voice, gruff, uncompromising made him step back, protesting. Peter stepped between them, a stream of Spanish sounded odd coming from his mouth. For the first time, it occurred to Celeste that English might not be Peter's first language. His strange, stateless accent began to make sense to her as he calmed his father, placated the pilot, subtly shifted the position of both until the scowling captain was standing at the back of the room, while the pilot took the wheel and started guiding the ship forward between the two concrete banks.

She watched the pilot's face, as he glanced over the ship's controls. Dirty, rusty. Half broken. He looked as though he had been on a lot of bridges and was used to them looking a lot better. Before his eyes reached the broken computer screen with the old monitor taped to the top of it, Peter shot her a warning glance, and she stepped in front of it, blocking the man's view. She grinned broadly. When he looked away, she slipped off her coat and draped it casually over the console, covering the most badly wrecked set of controls.

The man didn't seem impressed. He turned to Peter, and spoke in English this time:

"I get you through the gate, then I want to see the ship," he said.

Peter nodded. "Of course," he said. Peter turned to Celeste. "Meeting on the cargo deck now." He smiled a tight smile, and stepped off the bridge.

26.

One moment, the children - those who were not sick from the black poison in the water - were playing around the fire, where cassava was roasting and the women wrapped fish in bijao leaves, the rows of packages tightly pinned, ready for the fire. A second later, men were swarming the village, running, yelling.

Eena was in the big, thatched shack at the edge of the village. He was tending to the very sick. The ones who could not come out to eat. He had brought them water from the river. Taking it from up-stream of the pipe helped a little, but the river was slow-flowing and the rainbow film had spread way up stream as though the newcomers had pierced the earth and now its blood was bubbling up with poison everywhere. It was getting worse, and Eena had been trying to convince the elders to abandon the village - move on up the river. But they were slow to leave their home, and now there were too many sick. It was too late to move. He fed them the sick water in the dark of the shack.

Suddenly, men appeared in the doorway. They shouted, and when the sick, too weak to respond, merely struggled to turn their heads towards the voices, the men grabbed them, hauled them towards the door, and flung them out into the bright sunlight. Eena shrank back into the shadows, hid himself by pressing himself backwards into the untidy thatch or the shack walls, so that he became part of them. The monkey dropped from his shoulders, scampered out to the safety of the trees. Eena watched as the men emptied the building. Even old Maowa, lying hovering on the edge of death, was torn out of her bed and thrown into the light.

Eena could hear their shouts from outside mixed with the yells of the elders, still trying to negotiate, and the crying of the children. Filled with terror, he crept to the doorway and peered out. The whole tribe was gathered, pressed together, beside the fire. The men, surrounding them, hard-faced, still shouting. And then suddenly it began. The men raised their weapons. Eena put his hand to his mouth to stifle his own shout.

The rattling explosive sound, The men and women falling. The children too. After the first few fell, the rest started to run in confusion, fleeing, screaming, cut down as they scrambled for the doorways of the huts or the darkness of the forest. Eena watched it all in silence.

The men were efficient. When everyone had fallen, they went from body to body, checking for life, and pointing their weapons again into the bodies. Wherever someone was not quite dead, another burst of sound silenced them.

Finally, when it was all done, Eena prayed that they would leave, but instead they started to check the shacks again. One by one, the men entered the buildings to check for anyone hiding there. They got closer and closer to where Eena was hiding.

He knew he had to run. He waited until the men were checking a shack on the other side of the village, and threw himself through the doorway and out across the village.

He got half-way before the shout went up. The explosion of fire burst in the air. He felt the stinging pain in his leg, but somehow, he kept on running, diving forward until he felt his body break out of the clearing and into the enclosing jungle.

He dodged to the left where he knew the downhill slope towards the river would help him move faster, but the uneven ground was harder on his leg than he had thought it would be. Behind him, the men were following. Uninjured, he could have outrun them easily, but his leg was bleeding, dragging. He felt its power draining as though half-asleep. His leg was no longer a part of him from the knee down to the ground. And behind him, the crushing boots of the men, their shouts. The splintering cracks of their weapons grew louder.

When he realised he couldn't outrun them, he thought of the trees first. If he could climb, he could hide while the men ran past. But no. His bleeding leg would give him away, leave a smeared trail all the way up the trunk, and sitting in a tree, he would be an easy target. Instead he took the only choice he had. He ran down towards the river, where the ground dropped rapidly away down the side of the mountain. He skirted along the edge of the drop. They were nearly upon him now, but beside him, the jungle was so thick, and the slope so extreme, that they would never be able to follow.

He turned abruptly, and felt the ground vanish. His heel hit the ground again. He took one step, trying to balance, but his injured leg buckled under him. He tipped, over and over. The trunk of a tree hit him square in the chest, knocking the wind out of him, but not stopping his fall. The ground was getting steeper and steeper until it was almost a cliff. He felt himself buffeted by leaves, ferns, tree branches. Falling, no longer able to separate the pain in his leg from the pain in his chest. His stomach swooping from the roar in his ears. It was one all-consuming storm around him. It enclosed him closer and closer, until suddenly, it was gone and he was falling free of the jungle.

Another moment and he felt the thick, wet impact of his body on the oily water. The freedom from gravity. The tugging slime of water weeds below and around him. He pushed for the surface, but when he broke through, it felt as though he were still underwater. A thick coating covered his mouth and nose. He put his hands to his mouth and eyes to scrape them clear and allow him to breathe and see again. They came away coated in black oil. The water was slick with it, and it plastered his head and body as he floated, concealed. He fought the urge to push the disgusting substance from his body, and waited, still and almost submerged like a camen until the shouts of the men died away, and he could crawl to the bank.

27.

From the aft cargo deck, Celeste had a good view of the huge metal gates closing behind them like a set of prison doors. The massive hull of the cruise liner they were forced to share the lock with rose up out of the water in front of them, glistening and white, crested with row upon row of lighted windows. It looked like a spaceship.

The water level dropped until it seemed as though they were in a deep pit. The walls of the lock rose high on either side, casting a shadow over the whole deck. The gates lay behind, and the cruise liner was almost touching distance in front of the ship.

"I'm going to get Rain, Seb and Robert," said Peter. "You get Josh." Peter walked off towards the front of the ship.

Celeste stood for a moment and watched the wet concrete walls rise, then she looked around. Josh had been at the front with the others, watching the approach of land, but now the crowd had vanished. In fact, there seemed to be nobody left on deck but Celeste.

It must have something to do with the four new arrivals she'd seen boarding just before the gates closed. If they weren't on deck, they'd be in the mess.

She crossed the gangway and opened the metal door.

Of course. The band. With all her focus on the website and Peter's group, Celeste had almost forgotten that the adults had a plan of their own. The Pale Riders, the legendary super-group of the 1970s wich Celeste knew well from grainy Youtube clips and Dad's small, but constantly replayed CD collection, were now standing in the mess, surrounded by a frothing, buzzing crowd.

The lead singer, Harry Tense, stood, signing autographs, clearly enjoying the limelight. Behind him, Vin West, the bassist, clutched his guitar case, and across the room, Dave Costa, keyboard player and the band's songwriter shuffled uncomfortably. It was their rivalry over a supermodel socialite (whose name Celeste could not remember) that had caused the band to split 30 years ago, and the two had famously not spoken since.

At the back of the room, the drummer, Bill Fury, lounged in a pile of cylindrical carry cases, a cup of coffee balanced on a box next to him. He clearly preferred luggage to furniture. Fury had barely made it out of the 1970s after drug-fulled incidents wrecked several concerts and left Fury himself close to death. Even now, a roll-up cigarette was pinched between his thumb and forefinger.

Celeste glanced over to her parents, clinging to each other like starstruck teenagers. With role models like the Pale Riders, it was surprising Mum and Dad were as well-adjusted as they were.

Celeste wasn't surprised to see her parents fawning over the group, and she was even less surprised that the rest of the adult crew were doing the same. Dad had, after all, described the group as the "Masters of Rock". Although to Celeste they looked more like elderly gangsters.

What really surprised her was Josh. He was dashing back and forth between Costa and Fury, carrying cases and coffee. They had only been on the ship for five minutes, and Josh was already behaving like the band's personal roadie.

"Meeting," said Celeste. "On deck, now."

Josh shook his head. "I'm busy," he said.

"What are you doing?" said Celeste.

Josh nodded over towards Harry Tense. "Like I said, follow the money," he said.

Celeste left him to it, and returned to the deck where Peter was waiting with Rain. Robert was just behind them.

"Josh isn't coming," said Celeste. "He's too busy looking after the band."

Peter shot her a puzzled look. "We have to work together," he said. "If this pilot decides the ship is unfit, we'll be turned back. That's another three weeks going around South America - even if the ship isn't impounded, we'll miss the deadline. The crossing will take ten hours. We have to make sure he's kept busy the whole time. After that we have one night's sailing and tomorrow evening is the concert. That's when we slip off the ship and go find the drilling camp. Any questions?"

"I've got one," said Celeste. She flipped open her laptop, and held it open. The screen faded in from black. On it, a photo taken by Seb a few days earlier. It showed a sunset over the prow of the ship. Celeste herself was front and centre of the image, staring out over the sea. "What the hell is this?"

"What?" said Seb.

"It's lovely," said Rain, nudging Seb. Smiling. Celeste pressed the arrow key. The image faded and another shot appeared.

"And this?" she said. The photo was of the mess. It was a long exposure. The chaos of people eating on the run had turned into a dark, coloured blur, but in the centre, Celeste was frozen, face lit by the blue glow of her phone. "And this?" She clicked. The image changed: Celeste again, this time, a close-up, profile, hair wet stuck to her face as she walked determinedly down the gangway.

156

She clicked the button again and again. Other crew-members were in shot, but always off-centre, out of focus. Celeste was there every time. Celeste, oil on her face in the engine room. Celeste, stretching to tie the straps onto the crane. There was even one image taken along the corridor between the cabins just as Celeste was crossing, mid-step between the showers and her cabin. She was wrapped in a towel.

As Celeste carried on flicking through, Rain's smile fell. She unhooked her arm from Seb's and stared at him.

Seb affected a dismissive wave. "I'm an artist," he said.

"Don't give me that, you've been following me around, taking photos of me," said Celeste.

Seb's mouth fell open. He seemed genuinely surprised at her reaction. "I'm interested in trying to visualise conflict through images." He said. "When I see conflict I'm drawn to capturing it. You have a lot of conflict" Celeste glared at him.

"Damn right!" she said. She yanked the memory card out of her computer and threw it at Seb. It skidded across the deck. He scrambled on the ground to pick it up.

Rain looked down at him. "How could you?" she said, eyes filling with tears. "You never photograph me!" She turned, spinning her flowery skirt around her, and marched off. Seb looked as though he was about to answer, but instead, grabbed his memory card and set off after Rain.

"Don't take pictures of people without asking them!" Celeste shouted after him. She could feel her face flushing. Pointless tears prickled behind her eyes. A stupid reaction. She used her anger to force them back.

"What did you have to do that for?" said Peter.

"You saw what he did!"

"But what about the team?" said Peter.

"You're going to take his side?" said Celeste. She turned to Robert who stared, from one to the other.

"Are you all right, Celeste?" said Robert. She blinked at him. Neither of them had a clue.

"Fine!" said Celeste. She snapped her laptop closed and walked off. Behind her, Peter was shouting at her to wait. She ignored him.

28.

Celeste planned to stay in her cabin for the rest of the day. For the rest of the voyage if she could. It wasn't what Seb had done that bothered her so much, but Peter and Robert's reaction. As though it were her fault for causing a scene - for breaking up his precious team. She was angry with Seb for taking the pictures but she was angry with Peter too for siding with him. She was angry with Robert and Rain for being so witless, and she was angry with Josh for abandoning all of them to hang around the band.

Most of all, Celeste was angry with herself for being angry. For caring at all, one way or another, what any of these people thought. She had never needed other people's approval before. Why was she so bothered now? It didn't make sense.

It was the ship, she decided - being forced so close together for so long had distorted her feelings. That was what it was. If she'd been back on land, she'd have just walked away and thought no more about any of them - or, even better, she'd have just punched Seb in his stupid entitled face and the family would have left town. Life before had been so much easier.

She felt the ship start to move. The concrete walls outside her porthole vanished to reveal the wide expanse of water beyond, and thick trees set back from the bank, but the journey was a short one. The Green Crusader crept towards the bank, out of the way of other vessels and came to a halt, its engines silenced. Curiosity overcoming her need to escape human contact, Celeste left her cabin and went up to find out what was happening.

They had escaped from the dark pit of the lock and now sat now on the massive Gatun Lake, almost an inland sea in itself. On deck, however, another darkness had crept over the whole ship. The huge, shining space-ship of a liner which had shared their prison gave a deep, low blast on its horn and slid away to join the other ships passing like floating cities, but the Green Crusader was going nowhere.

The pilot's suspicions about the ship's seaworthiness had hardened, and now he was actively looking for problems. He fought his way around the ship, tapping gauges and poking his fingers into rusty pipework, shaking his head at every fault he spotted.

Celeste could see that the crew was doing its best, flocking and bustling around him, harassing him, distracting him from the worst features of the ship by standing in front of them, pointing out where fresh repairs had been done. The captain was at the front, angrily barracking him while Peter fought to stay between them, remaining practical and level while the pilot shook his head and blew great sighs through pursed lips.

Celeste kept her distance. The protests were getting them nowhere. The pilot was dogged and uncompromising. Eventually, out on the cargo deck, followed by a crowd of babbling crew-members, he held up his hands for silence. Celeste didn't need to understand Spanish. The man's body language said it all.

Celeste turned and walked back to the front of the ship, leaving the crew to their pointless arguments. It was over, and nothing they could do would change the pilot's mind. Slowly, the crew drifted away, back to the mess, or to their cabins. The ship drifted in silence through the afternoon while Celeste looked out at the scrubby banks and untidy box-buildings and back at the slow queue of vessels passing on the wider lake.

Peter's gang were in no better mood. Seb was nowhere to be seen. Rain moped around the deck, occasionally throwing dramatic glares in Celeste's direction. Josh was sticking with the band - obviously he saw them as his best chance to jump ship and improve his own life. She could hardly blame him for that.

Robert went from one group member to another, pestering, following them around, talking in his earnest, relentlessly friendly way to each in turn. It was Robert Celeste felt most sorry for. The group and their mission might have been a fantasy, but for Robert it was more than that. He had bought into the whole thing like it was part of his soul.

Celeste picked a spot at the back of the boat, and kept out of the way. It didn't matter anyway. The whole thing could go to hell now for all she cared. She looked out towards the shore. If the ship was grounded here they had no money to get back to England. Still, this was as good a place as any for she and her parents to start a new life. There were palm trees. There were buildings. Square, white boxes. It looked a bit shabby and a bit basic and of course, she couldn't speak the language, but she didn't talk much to strangers anyway. Not being able to understand them was actually a less painful prospect.

Robert joined her by the railings, leaning over and smiling up at her.

"Hello, Celeste," he said.

"Hello, Robert," she sighed. She wasn't in the mood. "How come you're always happy?"

"I'm not," said Robert. "Not always. Are you still coming to the jungle?"

"Nobody's going, Robert. It's not going to happen," she explained. "The ship is being turned back."

"No, it isn't," said Robert.

"It's over. I'm sorry." Celeste felt hotness in her eyes, and a hard lump in her throat. She realised as she spoke that she was telling the truth. She really was sorry it was over. Not for him. Not for Peter, but for herself. Robert wasn't the only one who had come to care about the mission. She put a hand on Robert's shoulder. His smile didn't falter.

"It's ok," he said. "I fixed that." As he spoke, Celeste felt the old vibration starting up under her feet. The engines were running again. The ship started, very slowly to move forward.

"What?" said Celeste.

"I fixed it," said Robert.

"How?"

"I gave the pilot money," said Robert.

"You bribed the pilot?" Celeste felt a laugh push its way out of her chest. "But where did you get money?"

"I got it from Josh," said Robert. Celeste grappled with the idea. It wasn't possible. But all the time, she could feel the ship accelerating, swinging back out towards the centre of the lake where the huge boats were passing in long lines.

"But Josh hasn't got any money!" said Celeste.

"He got it from the band."

"Josh persuaded the band to give him money, and then gave it to you to bribe the pilot?" said Celeste. It made no sense. "Why?"

Robert didn't seem to understand. "So that we can go to the drill," he said, as though it was obvious.

"Josh doesn't care about the Amazon - Josh is only interested in money," said Celeste.

"That's what he said," said Robert, "so I showed him the bitcoin wallet."

"What are you talking about?" said Celeste. She grabbed her phone, and flicked it on. The Logician had done his job better than she could have imagined. The screen lit up with the last thing she'd been working on - the Twitter account she'd just been setting up. She had notifications. Hundreds of them.

She scrolled through the first twenty or so, thumbing the screen faster and faster as message after message, sharing and tweeting about the #sharkgirl hashtag, spun past. She switched to Youtube and stared at the screen. Her montage of Seb's photos and video clips played, one shocking image after another, but Celeste wasn't looking at the video. Her eyes were focussed on the counter below it. It read 6,345,221 views. She gasped, looked up at Robert, still grinning, and then clicked back to Twitter. In the time it had taken to glance at youtube, the meme of Celeste cutting the Great White free had been shared another twenty-six times.

Celeste flipped quickly to Instagram, to Tumblr to Facebook. #Sharkgirl was trending on every social media site. Her memes were exploding out across the world. Millions of clicks, and every one generated a few fractions of a penny in advertising money in untraceable cryptocurrency, feeding directly into promotion building the audience even further as the memes were liked and shared again and again and again.

Just in the last hour, the equivalent of hundreds of pounds was building up in the Sharkgirl advertising account - accumulating faster than the automated advertising could spend it. Celeste stared at the screen. No wonder Josh had suddenly become a convert to the cause.

She turned to Robert. "And you convinced the official pilot to take a bribe in order to let us through in an unseaworthy ship?"

Robert nodded.

"You're lucky he didn't arrest you!"

"I'm not a threat. Nobody is scared of me," said Robert, smiling up at her, his face the picture of innocence. "It means I can say anything to anyone without getting into trouble. Everyone has a superpower. That's mine."

The ship was turning now, joining the convoy of giant container ships and cruise liners, buzzed and harried by tugs and yachts and other little vessels. Celeste watched as a container ship passed close by. A patchwork wall of lorry-sized metal squares in orange, blue, red and white formed a wall beside them rising high above, like the zoomed-in pixels of some massive scrambled image.

"What's my superpower?" she said.

"Pretending you don't care," said Robert.

Celeste laughed, despite herself. "It doesn't matter anyway," she said. "Rain hates Seb now. Both of them hate me - and Peter thinks it's my fault! You can't fix that, can you?"

Robert tilted his head to one side. "I don't know," he said. "Maybe. That depends on you."

"What do you mean?" said Celeste.

"Peter still likes you. Rain starts crying every time she talks about the rainforest, so she'll be happy if we go there," said Robert.

"And what about Seb?"

"He likes you too," said Robert.

"I don't know how to explain it to you," said Celeste. "It's the wrong kind of like."

"He wants to talk to you," said Robert.

"I'm not apologising," said Celeste.

"Ok," said Robert. "But will you promise not to hit him?"

"No," she said. Robert smiled and walked off. She watched him go. How did he do that?

29.

Celeste remained on deck until the distant edges of the lake closed in and the scattered white buildings petered out. Her eyes flicked between the endless green of the jungle either side of the canal, and the increasingly bizarre virtual landscape of her phone.

Every time she looked down, her own faceless image, stared back up. Copied, posted, reposted, tweeted, captioned, liked, disliked, followed, commented on. As she watched herself fall from the net beside the shark once again, a stream of little yellow astonished emojis popped and bobbed. It was a strange feeling that gripped her in the stomach. A surge of power - she had done this. She *was* this. She had created and launched something that was spreading like a contagion. It was a feeling that overpowered and pumped through her. And yet at the same time, there was another feeling. An equal and opposite force. She was powerless. Out of control. Her own image. Her own confused, reckless, impetuous decision to risk her life for a fish was now out of her control. Owned and shared by the world. Her own secret self was a toy to be thrown around the Internet, caricatured, joked about. Judged. It was the same feeling she got when she discovered Seb's pictures of her, only this time she had done it to herself.

When it became unbearable and she looked away from her phone, and out across the rolling jungle, the after-image of her screen remained, superimposed on her retina. The black pit of her own missing face, framed by her hood, hung over the jungle as it scrolled slowly by her.

Celeste could feel it. She was becoming something. She wasn't sure what. She didn't know if she liked it or hated it, craved it or feared it. But whatever it was, it was coming, that black, faceless figure was her whether she liked it or not.

166

Eventually the sun dipped and the lights of the cruise ships winked on like stars locked to the water. The night was warm, and Celeste stayed on deck, looking out until Seb eventually came and stood beside her.

"One feels one may have overstepped the mark," he said rather stiffly. "As a boarder in a boy's school," he said, looking in the direction of her gaze rather than at Celeste herself, "one comes away with certain gaps in one's understanding of the world."

"Is this supposed to be an apology?" said Celeste. Seb's expression suggested he was either struggling with a difficult concept, or had acute toothache.

"A gap year is supposed to broaden one's outlook," he said. "What I'm trying to say is before I got on this ship, met Rain - my experience of girls - I'd never -"

"You'd never what?" She almost laughed. Why was he telling her this?

"Good Lord, no! Not that!" he said. "I mean I'd never met one! - I mean obviously, one sees them, speaks occasionally. But they - you - they were never a part of one's milieu - you have to understand."

"Why, Seb?" said Celeste. "Why do I have to understand?"

He hung his head, shifted from foot to foot. "I know I always look confident," said Seb. "That's school - my school at least. Confidence, certainty - it's how you survive there - you know?"

"No kidding," said Celeste. "That's supposed to be an excuse?"

"Doesn't mean a thing on the inside. You know?" She did know. She knew exactly. "What I'm saying is I don't know what to do with girls," he said. He shrugged, "Don't even know if I like them."

"You mean you prefer boys?"

"No!" said Seb. Then he added "I don't know."

Celeste felt herself laugh. It was involuntary. "You're hopeless!" she said.

"Probably." Seb hung his head.

"You like Rain?"

"Yes, I do!" he said. He was pulling the toothache face again. "So much... But she expresses such - feeling. One finds it difficult to know how to respond."

"You've got that right," said Celeste.

He paused. "I meant what I said, you know. I photograph you because you're interesting. I photograph the ship too. The broken parts - if that makes any sense."

She laughed.

"I'm just saying not everyone is as experienced as you are."

Celeste blinked at him. By her reckoning, Seb was at least one relationship ahead of her. Why did he think she knew anything he didn't?

He faced her, his eyes almost pleading. "I'm just asking you to let me work it out without hating me. Can you do that?"

"Depends," she said. "Can you stop being an arsehole? Can you promise to stop taking photographs of me?"

He looked at her for a long time, then out across the water.

"Honestly, I don't know." he said, eventually. "I know you think I'm pretentious, but I am serious about my art. I'm a boy, but I'm an artist first. You get that?"

"No, I do not!" said Celeste. "You need permission to take someone's photo."

"You think I should have asked the shark fishermen's permission? You think the pictures would have been better if I had?" he said.

"It's not the same," said Celeste.

"Why not?"

"Because you're my friend!" She stopped, mid breath, clamped her mouth shut, but the words had already come out. She was frozen now, mind reeling back, scanning to find the last time she had used the word 'friend' to describe anyone. It had been maybe ten years.

She turned away, avoiding his eyes, but on the other side of her, Peter was already standing there. She jumped.

"So," said Peter, "are we back on?"

"I am," said Seb from behind her.

Peter tilted his head, waiting for her answer. His expression was blank, but his eyes pinned hers. She bit her lip.

"I guess so," she said.

30.

Drier stepped out of his cabin and headed up to the deck of the oil tanker, now moored at the quayside, towering over the little Columbian Port town. As he stepped outside for the first time, he thought the blast of heat was from some air-conditioning unit on the deck, but it wasn't. It was the reflected heat of the sun, coming straight up off the metal deck like someone was pointing a hairdryer in his face.

He felt the soles of his brand new hand-made Italian shoes sticking as they started to melt to the metal, the sweat seeping into the fabric of his silver-grey tailored suit. When this trip was over, the entire outfit would have to go in the garbage. The company might be on the ropes, but it didn't do to let it look that way - even in a tin-pot little country like this, you had to walk the walk. The predictions for the company's other wells were dire, and if the shareholders got wind of that before they'd secured the rainforest wells, things could go bad very fast, but providing Zoila did her job, and the press conference went well, the company - and Drier himself - would come out of this richer than ever. There was a private island in the Bahamas with his name on it.

Drier crossed to the little stage platform and smiled a broad smile as he stepped up behind a perspex lectern, and greeted the assembled photographers and reporters. He glanced down at his speech - a new era, blah, blah, blah, clean, environmentally-friendly extraction, blah, blah, latest technology, blah blah.

The PR people had crammed it with all the best buzzwords, and given it the perfect tone to prepare the press for the main event. His black helicopter was already running up its engines on the other side of the deck, waiting to take him into the jungle, and when he returned, riding that first precious boatload of Amazon oil, they'd have the perfect photo to go with his quotes.

He waited for silence, and opened his mouth to speak.

At that moment, the deafening foghorn of another ship drowned out all sound. Drier spun around in time to see another ship - The Green Crusader steaming into the river mouth passing right alongside his tanker. A banner unfurled along the entire side of the ship reading "SAVE THE AMAZON". Drier felt his shoulders drop. That damn ship again, he thought.

In an instant, the press turned, ran to the side, and started taking photographs of the newcomer. Drier was left standing on his own behind his lectern. His PR team appeared in seconds, bundling him off the stage.

"Why didn't I know about this?" he demanded as he was hurried into his waiting helicopter. Somebody was going to lose their job. What a mess!

There was a slight bounce, and the helicopter lifted off, tipping sideways as it swooped off across the scruffy port town. Drier looked down. The press were still fussing around the Green Crusader.

He ordered the pilot to swing round and do a low pass over the Green Crusader's deck, so he could get a better look. The vessel was in a much worse state than it had been when he'd last seen it. When its crew had scaled his oil rig in the Gulf Of Mexico to hang their pointless banners. Much worse than when its unstable captain had followed his oil exploration vessel around the Arctic, trying to stop them making their tests. Now, the boat seemed more like a wreck that had been dumped in the river mouth than anything capable of challenging him. He hovered next to its deck and watched through expensive sunglasses. He smiled.

They'd made a scene, as they always did, but it would make no difference. Drier had all his ducks in a row on this one. He had the locals on side. He had the government on side. He'd get the press back by morning, and nobody was going to stop buying oil. The Green Crusader's presence was an annoyance. Nothing more.

And it lifted his heart to see the mess the ship was in. To someone who had been in business as long as he had, it was obvious. The Green Crusader was out of cash. And just as he was about to open the biggest drilling operation in history. Despite the disruption of his press conference, this was a good day.

He grinned down at the crew scurrying about on the ship's deck. They seemed to be in the middle of building some kind of stage. Whatever it was about, it didn't matter.

A teenage girl was standing at the back railing, looking up at his helicopter. He gave her a dismissive wave, and signalled the pilot to take them up away from the ship.

They circled around and over the little port town - another typical hopeless run-down dump. You got to see a lot of them in his line of work. All over the world. South America, Africa, Russia, the Middle East. Some were hot, some were cold. But they were all the same. Caught half-way between a past that no longer worked, and a future they didn't understand.

The inhabitants would be delighted when the news came out about the oil finds. The filthy poor in their little shacks would be thumbing through their out-of-date glossy magazines, and eyeing the fashions of New York and the skyscrapers of Dubai, and imagining that soon their little town would be awash with oil money.

Not if Drier could help it. The next wave of automation was coming and his Research and Development team would see to it that the Amazon's oil wells were the most automated in history. Mechanised rigs, self-driving transporters. There would be few jobs for the locals this time. Still, the fantasy suited him well enough right now. Being welcomed by the locals made it much easier to get in and get set up. Once the wells were set up, the town - the whole country could all go to hell.

The helicopter twisted in the air as it approached the river mouth. The pilot followed the line of the river out of town. Below them, the forest canopy blurred in an unbroken green carpet unchanging. A landscape which stretched to the horizon to either side. Drier knew it extended well beyond what he could see. An infinite landscape of forest. Millions of square kilometres. The idea that the few tiny pinpricks of drilling he planned could possibly have a significant effect on this forest was plainly absurd.

A hundred drilling rigs - a thousand or ten thousand for that matter - would be swallowed up in the vastness of the Amazon. The protestors were fools - and selfish fools at that. There was plenty of room for drilling rigs and trees in their precious forest. Drier despised them and their hopeless sentimental attachment to places they wouldn't even bother visiting, and wouldn't survive five minutes in if they did.

He flicked open a tablet. On it his own GPS position was marked as a red, dot on a green map whose only feature was the murky river whose line they were following. He clicked, and a series of icons appeared, spread across the map. Little black balloon markings showing other places where

Zoila's team, spreading out from their test-site, had discovered traces of oil. Potential new drilling sites peppered the green map. Each one hundreds of millions of dollars in potential revenue. Of course they would need access. Roads, refining plants. And of course, dump sites for the toxic residue of the mining process. But that could all be managed. It was somebody else's problem. Zoila's problem to be specific.

31.

"We'll slip away at midday," said Peter.

Rose and Annette had been dispatched to the shore after their noisy photobombing of the press conference, to pick up fresh ingredients from the market, and the group were now gathered in the mess, stuffing themselves with a hearty brunch of avocado, black beans and plantains. The ship's menu had become a repetitive stream of dried pulses and rice, so this breakfast marked an exotic change and felt to Celeste like a good preparation for the day's adventure into the jungle. It was still a dumb idea. Still probably pointless. Still risky for any number of reasons. And she still wasn't convinced that the team was up to it.

But there was something writhing in Celeste's guts. A growing excitement that had kept her turning all night. A thrill at doing something secret and dangerous and subversive. That same thrill she had felt sitting in the library taking down the school. Only this time, it was different. This time she was doing something right. And this time, she was sharing it. Sharing it with Rain - even though she still kept shooting theatrically evil glances at Celeste every time she even looked at Seb. Sharing it with Josh - though his motives were unclear to say the least. With Robert - who was grinning and chatting like it was just another day, barely aware, apparently of the seriousness of what they were doing. With Seb - who kept fingering his camera and refusing to meet her eyes. Most of all, with Peter. Peter who didn't give up on her when she walked out that first morning. Peter who concocted this whole madness, and seemed so determined to see it through. She watched him eat, shovelling black beans into his mouth like coal into the engine of a steam train. His eyes were clear, focused. As though behind them was just one thought.

"Why midday?" said Celeste.

"That's when the final sound-check is," said Peter. "After that, they'll all be busy until the concert starts and then nobody will care where we are. We'll be back before morning. Nobody will know anything until we show them the photos."

"How do you know they'll be busy?"

Peter paused, fork half-way to his mouth. "I put all the audio cables in the wrong boxes," he said. "By the time they sort them out, they'll be two hours behind."

Up on deck, Celeste watched the stage taking shape. The scaffolding, speakers and amps which had been borrowed and stored in the hold for the journey were now being unpacked and assembled by the confused, but eager crew. A giant screen was being assembled. Nobody had a clue what they were doing, but nobody cared. They were all grinning. Dad and Maurice, burying themselves in cabling up the speaker system, relishing the mess of lost and misplaced wires. For them, it was like a puzzle. Mum, Rose and Annette with Rain's parents running up and down ladders, fixing lights while the rest of the crew scuttled about, bolting scaffolding poles together, discovering they were in the wrong place, and then unbolting them again to re-fix somewhere else.

Normally, Celeste would have been dismissive of their efforts. Frustrated with their incompetence. Bored by their worthy cheerfulness. But not today. Today she felt different. Her parents and their friends were idiots, of course, but they too were on their own team mission under the heat of the sun. Doing something they, at least, thought was worthwhile, and doing it together.

After today, who knew what would happen - where they would go, what they would do. But as she watched them from the back of the boat, Celeste felt, for the first time in a long while, that things might just be OK.

A second later, Peter, Seb and Rain appeared, with Josh and Robert right behind them. Everyone was dressed in dark clothes, and hoodies - even Rain. Celeste tried not to register her surprise. She didn't think Rain owned anything that wasn't covered in flowers and sequins.

"We need to get the inflatable into the water without anyone seeing," said Peter. "Celeste, you get in the boat and I'll lower you into the water. Everyone else needs to make sure nobody sees. Once you're down there, keep the boat close, and we'll climb down the ladder after you. Got it?"

"Why do you want me in the boat first?" said Celeste.

"If any of the crew catches you doing something stupid, they're less likely to try to stop you," said Peter.

"Why?"

Peter grinned. "Because you're scary," he said, "and because you do stupid stuff all the time."

Celeste held her breath as she sat in the little inflatable waiting for Peter to drop her into the sea. Where the crane was positioned, it couldn't be seen from the main stage area, now almost complete. Most of the crew had retired to the mess for lunch, but Maurice and Dad were still running around from one box to another searching for missing pieces of wiring.

Celeste couldn't see whether anyone was coming, but she could see the back of Robert, posted halfway along the gangway, and Josh, keeping guard on the entrance to the cargo deck. First one, then the other turned and gave her the thumbs up signal that there was nobody coming, and Celeste signalled to Peter, at the controls of the crane. The lines went taut, and then the boat jerked up off the deck. If anyone caught them now, the game would be up.

It seemed to take Peter forever to swing the crane out over the side of the ship, and start to lower her down towards the sea. Just as Celeste's eye level dropped almost below the deck, she saw Josh turn suddenly from his guard post, and wave frantically. Someone was coming!

Celeste signalled to Peter. He wrestled with the controls, and the crane jerked and swung, first down, then up, then back down again. The little boat rocked in the air, and Celeste gripped the side. He couldn't operate the controls quickly enough to get her back on deck.

"Drop me!" she shouted, waving at him. "Drop me!" He stared at her for a second, hands wavering over the controls, then he looked up and away towards the deck. He made his decision. She saw his hands punch the control panel, and suddenly, the winch above her went lose. She felt the boat drop.

For a single, stretched moment, she and the boat were in freefall. She felt her stomach wrenched away from her as the side of the ship rushed past. The breath was squeezed from her lungs as she plummeted towards the sea.

A second later, she felt the boat under her hit the ocean as though it were a solid sheet of metal. She slammed into the boat's side, shoulder first. Felt her head wrenched sideways, impacting with the rubber floats so that she bounced back up into the air before smashing down again into the wooden boards at the bottom of the inflatable. It hit her knees. Her elbows. Her shoulder again. A sickening pain.

There would be bruises later, but for now, she lifted her head, shook it to clear her mind, and looked back up at the deck. For a long time, there was nothing, then Peter's head appeared over the railings. He grinned and gave the thumbs up.

She fumbled with the straps, releasing them, and the crane arm above her swung back into place. Beside it, a wire rope ladder rolled over the railings, and Celeste grabbed the end, holding the inflatable close to it while Peter and the others clambered down to join her.

32.

"Get out of it!" said Celeste as Peter reached over to try to take the inflatable's tiller. "You think I'm letting you drive after the way you worked that crane."

Peter laughed. "Suit yourself," he said. "By the way, you're not the driver, you're the captain."

"I like that," she said, and she took the boat away from The Green Crusader, hugging the shoreline where all the other little fishing boats were moored up to avoid being spotted from the ship's decks.

After the thrill of the escape from The Green Crusader, the crew were all grinning broadly. Even Josh was smiling like a naughty kid under his hoodie. As Celeste took them over the brown water, and away from the wide estuary with its bustling shoreline, the settlements died out very quickly to be replaced by fields of planted farmland, and then, without warning, by wild forest trees, their exposed roots, gripping into slick mud.

The banks started to close as little rivers branched off the main route, and snaked away into the jungle. The change from wide open estuary to dark, overhung river, from ramshackle human habitation to dense jungle was abrupt and brought with it a complete change in mood. The group was suddenly silent. Suddenly thoughtful. They sat back in the boat, eyes focussed on the thick walls of green on both sides.

There were new sounds too. A thick wall of insect noise inhabited every frequency from the high whine of mosquitos to the low, spluttering engines of giant beetles. Sounds that could have been insects or birdsong. Sounds that could have been big cats or monkeys or frogs. They created a texture as dense and as lush as the thicket of leaves and branches rising from either bank.

180

Celeste kept her hand on the tiller, its vibration numbing her fingers as she ploughed a straight course down the centre of the river. The sound of the outboard sank into the background of the jungle, so that it could have been nothing more than a swarm of bugs keeping pace with them as they chugged down the river.

Once, she saw a log floating in the water, and almost took the boat straight over it before it twisted in the water, and the jaws of a huge camen pivoted open just a metre from the boat, revealing a cavernous pink mouth, before snapping shut and vanishing beneath them.

Once, they rounded a corner and surprised a flock of twenty or so macaws perched together in a tree. A scream of cries and a shocking burst of red and blue wings exploded towards them across the river, as they all cowered into the boat, then all sat bolt upright, staring after the birds as they evaporated into the trees on the other side.

The jungle looked and sounded and felt and smelled unlike anything Celeste had ever experienced before. It was an alien world, and it set her every sense on edge. As though it were watching, waiting to swallow her up. She felt the sweat trickle down the inside of her hoodie, down the back of her neck, down from her armpit to her wrist.

The dark thick clothes they all wore were not the right ones for this world, but they would make it easier to remain unseen while they were photographing the drilling, and easier to edit later to remove their faces and turn them into the anonymous shadows they had to become.

Only Rain seemed unintimidated by the place. She was silenced just as the others were. Awed just as they were, but there was something in the way she reacted, pulling her hoodie back, and staring, left and right, up and down, eyes stretched as though pinned open in wonder. Looking, listening, feeling, drinking it in. To everyone else, the jungle might have been an alien world. But to Celeste it seemed that Rain had come home. When the boat was suddenly and inexplicably enclosed for a shimmering moment by a swarm of sapphire blue butterflies, she simply raised her arms and let the creatures settle all over her, eyes alight, a huge joyful smile spreading across her face. As Seb fumbled for his camera, Rain turned to Celeste, her eyes huge and innocent. Her exaggerated caricature of hate, forgotten, now replaced by an exaggerated caricature of ecstatic love. She laughed, and Celeste felt herself laughing back. Rain's apparent parodies of emotion, Celeste realised, were not an act. She felt every one of them right down to the depths of her heart. What must it be to live like that? It was hard not to be jealous.

As the butterflies lifted like a sheet blown in the wind, wafting back down river, Celeste had to remind herself that the jungle would kill Rain as quickly as it would kill the rest of them.

The butterflies had broken the silence in the boat. Any tension between Celeste and Rain was carried with them as they floated away. Seb too was lighter. Whatever had been keeping him from taking photos had been freed and he now spun back and forth in the boat, zooming, focusing and clicking at everything around them. He even snapped off a couple of shots in Celeste's direction. She felt slightly uncomfortable, frozen in place in front of his lens, but she forced back the feeling, and didn't stop him.

After a couple of hours, a series of little islands in the centre of the river signalled a messy fork as the flow divided. To the left, it kept flowing straight on. To the right, it swerved and bent out of sight in front of them.

"Which way now?" said Celeste.

Peter frowned, "Let's try the left one," he said.

"Try the left one?" said Celeste. "This place is a labyrinth! Please tell me you've got a map!"

"I'm not used to this kind of river system," said Peter. "It's close to the bank is all I know."

"You're an idiot," said Celeste. She remembered the satellite map she'd downloaded when she'd searched up the oil plant. The river breaking up into a web of hairline waterways like veins feeding the jungle. "Take the tiller," she said. She handed over control of the boat and pulled out her phone.

"Your phone won't work out here," said Seb. "No data in the jungle."

"No," said Celeste, "but the GPS should, and if we're very lucky…"

She flicked the phone on, and loaded up her maps app. "I sent myself a copy of the map and set it to local caching," she said.

"Meaning?" said Peter.

"Meaning it ought to have stored the satellite photo for faster loading later." She tapped the phone. Their position appeared as a red dot. All around it, the screen was a blank grey.

"What's the matter?" said Peter.

"This phone is pretty full," said Celeste. "When the memory gets clogged up - which is pretty much all the time - the cached maps are the first things the operating system deletes to save space." She pinched the screen, zooming out. "Yes!" Now, the screen was filling in. Pale green for the jungle. Blue traces for the river. The scale wasn't great, and she had to squint at the screen to see where the river forked, but at least it was something. "Ok!" she said. "Take the right fork."

Peter opened the throttle and the boat bumped its way down past the scattered islands until they joined to form a single wall of jungle either side of them.

33.

In front of Drier's helicopter, the flame of gas being burned off the drilling rig had appeared over the trees, and the mud-churned raw patch of the little site's compound opened up. Drier had seen a lot of drill sites in his time. The ones back in Texas were shining and well-ordered. Out here, where regulations were paper thin, and where nobody was going to be able to check anyway, the rules, such as they were, could easily be ignored. As the helicopter descended, Drier could see that the place was little more than a toxic waste tip. Zoila might be an amateur, but she was taking full advantage of the lax local regulations. If she played her cards right she'd be working in this jungle her whole life. If not, there were plenty of others waiting to take her place.

The helicopter touched down and Drier stepped out, putting his new shoes straight into black, oily mud. He could almost feel the calf's leather perishing as the chemicals ate into them. Zoila strode out of her tin hut and grasped his hand.

"I do hope everything is going to plan," he said.

"Of course." She sounded a little nervous, as well she might. Tonight was make or break.

"The boat - is it ready?" She nodded.

A thick set-man, driving a jeep, took them down the rough churned road to the water's edge. A jetty had been fastened together out of scaffolding and wood. Once production got going, they'd need something a lot bigger. Proper roads. A loading bay. Warehousing. But this would do for now. Tonight, they needed to get something - anything - out of the jungle to show the shareholders that their investment was a good one. This business was about two things: It was about oil, and it was about rumours. Right now, he knew the oil was there, but it was the rumours that were killing him. If Zoila let him down tonight, the stock would crash. The banks would call in their loans. He would be finished. No smart suits. No private helicopters. Everything he owned would be taken away, and he'd be lucky to escape jail once the tax inspectors had finished poking around in his company. But that wouldn't happen. The moment he was photographed floating out of the jungle standing astride a boat-load of barrels, he'd be a hero - a god - to the money markets. The cash would start to flow again and this whole enterprise could really take off.

He could see Zoila scrutinising his expression.

"It's all temporary," she said, "but it'll do the job." She gestured to the end of the jetty. A long, low bunkering vessel was indeed moored there. It looked little more than a giant metal rowing boat, some fifteen metres in length, laden, and low in the water. Piled high with barrels. The kind of boat used to supply bigger ships moored offshore. It wasn't pretty, but she was right. It would do. The Green Crusader could make all the noise they wanted to. It wouldn't make a shred of difference.

"What about the natives?" said Drier.

"Dealt with," she said without hesitation.

"Ok," he said. "Your office now. We need to go through the figures…." He trailed off. Behind her, just away from the river, where the track met the trees, he could see a dark shape. A man. No, a boy. Naked. Red marks painted across his chest. On his shoulder sat a tiny monkey. The boy was motionless. Almost invisible. He stared straight at Drier. Black eyes, still. Zoila spotted Drier's expression, and turned. For a second, her head blocked his view of the boy.

"What is it?" she said. He stepped to the side, to regain his line of sight, but the figure had vanished. Maybe it was never there. He stared for a second.

"Nothing," he said. "Your office."

34.

They followed the river for hours more. It turned and divided. It was met by other streams, and many more led away from it. At times, the river turned back and coiled so much that it seemed they must be heading back on themselves, and with no landmarks but endless trees, Celeste could easily see how travelers could be lost forever here. At times the map was confusing, so complicated was the network, but always, Celeste and Peter found a way through. They knew that the drillers planned to take their initial loads out by boat, so they could reject the tiny, overhung tributaries where no decent sized boat could pass.

Eventually, the river slowed and widened and they could see a little further. They glimpsed the high walls of mountains either side where the trees sloped up from their valley. The red dot on Celeste's map was getting closer and closer to the marker showing their destination until it seemed they were almost on top of each other.

"We're close," said Celeste. "It must be around here somewhere."

"How close?" said Peter.

"No way to tell," said Celeste, "It's not like in a city. The satellite coverage is weak out here. GPS could be off by hundreds of metres."

Suddenly, Rain was staring out of the boat. "Look at the water," she said.

Celeste looked. It seemed to be just water. Rain leant over the side, pulling her sleeves up and putting her hand slowly down towards the river just as she had done when they had followed the shark fishers.

"Don't!" said Seb, "There could be camen - piranhas - anything in there!"

188

Rain ignored him and reached down, sinking her hand into the flowing river. This time, when she pulled it out, it was black, like a glove that reached to her elbow. She looked disgusted.

"Oil!" she said, grimacing. "The river is black." Now that she said it, Celeste could see. A thick dark film formed a swirling trail out from around the bend in the river in front of them. On its surface, a ragged rainbow of violet, yellow and orange shifted as they moved through it.

Rain wiped her arm on the side of the boat, trying to use the rope ties to get the worst of the oil off. It smeared and stained. "Look!" she said.

Ahead of them, a shape struggled in the water. A wing flapped uselessly against the surface. A macaw had come down to the water's edge to drink and become stuck in the oil, then dragged out into the river. Its once bright reds and blues and greens were replaced by a jet black coat, utterly smooth and shining across its body, but ruffled and tangled at its wings into a matted, dull mess. Its eye stared round and wild out of the slick, blinking. Beyond the bird, the silver bellies of a dozen upturned fish floated with the current.

They passed the struggling creature. It was too far gone to help, but they all stared after it.

As they approached the bend in the river, something in the trees caught Celeste's eye. The shock of a human face, staring out of the jungle. She jumped. It was a boy. Maybe her own age. Just his bare chest and face visible. A little monkey sitting on his shoulder. Black hair, hanging straight down around his face. No expression. The boy did not move. He just watched, looking at the boat, she supposed, but he seemed to be staring only at Celeste. She felt a prickle at the back of her neck.

She opened her mouth to tell the others, but by the time the shock had subsided enough for her to form the words, Peter had taken the little craft around the bend in the river, and the boy was out of sight.

Suddenly, Peter wrenched the tiller, and the inflatable veered around, sending up a fan of oily water, and crashed into the overhanging trees at the side of the river, showering all of them in leaves. Peter cut the engines.

"What is it?" said Celeste. Peter pointed through a gap in the branches. Further down the river, a wide pipe emerged from the trees, and overhung the water. From it, filthy viscous silt poured almost constantly into the river, bobbing up and spreading out to form the slick they had encountered further up the river. Beyond the pipe, a long, low boat was moored against a scaffolding pier. It was loaded with barrels.

"I guess we're here," said Celeste. "How close do we need to get?"

Seb put the camera to his eye, and shot off a couple of photos. "Very close," he said.

"I guess we follow the pipe, then," said Celeste. "Come on."

35.

Celeste grabbed the thin branches above her head, and together, the group dragged the boat into the bank until they could clamber out onto the mud, and tie the inflatable up to a tree. Together they hooked down some branches and pulled them across to hide the boat as best they could. They stood back, looking at the bright orange rubber floats. It was a bad job.

The boat was only a few metres from the pipe, and a few more from the jetty. The boat wouldn't be obvious, but neither was it well hidden.

"We need to camouflage it better than this," said Celeste. "This boat is our only way back."

Peter shook his head. "We don't have time," he said. "We have to get back before the concert ends."

"I'll stay here," said Josh. "Somebody has to look after it."

"What are you going to do if it's spotted?" said Celeste.

"I can look after myself," said Josh. Celeste didn't doubt it. He'd already shown her that much.

"Great," said Robert. "See you later! Which way shall we go?" He turned towards the jungle.

"We need pictures of that pipe," said Peter. He gestured towards the pipe spewing black gunge into the river. "It's evidence."

"Wait!" said Celeste. She looked around at the group. Peter, Robert, Seb and Rain looked back. "You're happy to leave him with our only way out of here?"

"What's your problem?" said Josh.

"I caught him stealing from Annette and Rose's room," said Celeste.

"I was just getting something for them," he said. "They asked me to."

"'Follow the money.' That's what you said, isn't it?" said Celeste. "Is that what you're doing here? How do we know you won't just leave us all here, and go back to the ship? You could tell people whatever you wanted, and then just clear out the money from the advertising account. How do we know you won't turn us in to the miners? They'd probably pay you!"

"I had not thought of that," said Josh. "Perhaps I could."

Celeste rounded on the others. "Do you trust him?" she said. There was a long pause.

"Come on," said Peter at last. "We don't have time for this." He set off towards the pipe, followed by Rain, Seb and Robert. Celeste hesitated.

"You'd better go with them," said Josh. "Is bad place to get lost."

The waterside plants were lush and thick, and the ground soft. By the time Celeste made it down to where the pipe overhung the river, Seb was already lying on top of it, trying to get a shot that included both the stinking liquid erupting from it and the vast swirl of black, coiling out into the river. The end of the pipe had been roughly hacked where it met the water, and had been half-heartedly buried in a little earth. Below it, black sludge was already building up and spreading out into a puddle of black mud that stank of tar and oil. Clearly a rush job.

"This is completely illegal," said Peter. "It's poisoning this whole section of river."

Rain said nothing, but her face darkened. Suddenly, she pulled out her diver's knife and hacked through a handful of ferns. She wadded them up into a tight ball, pulled back her arm and wedged the handful shoulder deep into the pipe. Gritting her teeth, she grabbed another handful, and almost hurled it into the pipe, inches from Seb's face.

"What are you doing?" said Seb, scrambling off the pipe.

"This is for the parrot!" said Rain, grabbing another handful. Celeste remembered the oil-covered bird flapping pathetically as the current rolled it away from their boat.

Seb started snapping away as Rain worked frantically, eyes blazing with rage as she punched fist after fist of compacted leaves into the pipe. She pulled her filthy arm out, grabbed another handful and rammed it deep into the pipe, grunting with the effort, her face overtaken with fury. The flow slowed to a trickle.

"It's ok, it's blocked now," said Robert. He put a hand on her shoulder. Rain ignored him, and kept jamming leaves and rocks into the pipe, using a thick stick to crush her makeshift plug down deeper and deeper. There was oil and blood on her knuckles now where she had scraped them on the walls of the pipe.

Seb grabbed her hands. "Stop now," he said. "It's done."

She glared at him for a second, then calmed a little.

"We must do what we came to do. Once we get the pictures out, we can force them to stop. OK?"

"You've got a lot of faith in the legal system here," said Celeste.

"We've got a chance," said Peter. "As long as we keep our heads."

Seb was holding Rain's hands now, wiping the blood and oil from them. She was shaking, but her fists opened slowly.

"OK?" he said.

She nodded, paused, then suddenly broke away from his hands, striding up the path cut through the jungle by whoever laid the pipe. "Let's get on with it then. This must lead back to the compound, right?"

Celeste followed, the others behind her, as they picked their way in silence up along the rough channel through the undergrowth.

36.

The pipe ran along the leaves of the forest floor like a thick and dirty snake. As she walked beside it, it brushed against Celeste's leg and she could feel the black blood coursing thickly through its body. It would be backing up now, filling with the liquid. She wondered how long Rain's block would last. It didn't matter - for her it had been the action, not the result that mattered. Celeste got that at least. She might have more in common with the blonde hippy than she'd thought.

"Remember, we're just here to take pictures," said Peter from behind.

"I know what we're here for," said Rain, not turning around.

She marched a few paces in front of Celeste. Head down. Fists clenched, raw and bloody, black-stained.

"And files," said Celeste. She turned in time to see Peter shrug. He didn't have a clue how important data was. Seb's photos would get them attention, but without files that showed the company was corrupt - deliberately breaking the rules - everything would quickly be brushed under the carpet. A few local workers would be blamed for any "accidents" and the company itself would go on opening new mines.

She clutched her phone, and looked around her. The channel carved through the jungle by the pipe created an easy path to follow. Rough-cut and freshly-splintered wood formed a tunnel through which the group could walk, but it was an illusion. Beyond it, the jungle was thick with vertical stems and filled in by layers of feathery fern leaves at every height. Anything could be in there. Above, the canopy closed over them, blotting out the sky. It felt claustrophobic. Dangerous. Poisonous spiders lived in and amongst the trees. Deadly snakes. Jaguars. Celeste had stopped her research after she had read about a small selection of the jungle's dangers. What was the point in knowing more? They weren't intending to hang around, and, where they were going, there were worse dangers than animals. If they were discovered by the miners... Well they were a long way from help, and nobody even knew they were missing.

Up ahead, Rain stopped abruptly, and signalled behind her. She dived off the path and into the undergrowth. Celeste followed without thinking, and the others did the same behind her. She felt the wet leaves close around her as she turned and crouched close to the soft ground. She froze, holding her breath and peering back through a tiny gap in the leaf cover.

A moment later, three men, tanned and enclosed in orange boiler suits, appeared following the pipe's pathway down towards the river. They were talking loudly over each other in Spanish, laughing. The first two men held a pickaxe and a wrench. The third swaggered into Celeste's view. At his hip, just centimetres from her face, he held a sub-machine gun. Through her leafy shroud, she could see the tiny metal spike of the barre, the dull blocky shine of the gun's body. The man's hand was dirty, grit ground into the thumb. It rested loosely on the top of the gun. She could see his bitten fingernails which were close enough to touch if she reached out a hand.

She detected a movement on the leaf in front of her. A brown shape crawling. She refocused her eyes. An ant. About the size of her fingernail. Its wide jaws twitching open and closed. Open and closed. Behind it was another, and another. The whole plant was crawling with them.

A dawning recognition crawled into Celeste's mind. Army ants! They could be all over her by now.

She saw the ant in front of her drop. Felt it land on the back of her hand. A sharp sting. Instantly, instinctively, she shook her hand to dislodge it. In front of her, the man with the gun tensed suddenly. The other two silenced their laughing. She held her breath, feeling as though her whole body were crawling, expecting more bites at any second.

The man with the gun swung it left and right. From where she was crouching, his hip and the gun was all she could see of him. His hand had shifted now to the trigger. She tensed. If he spotted her, she would have to make her move first. In her head, she planned it. Stepping out, pushing the gun up and backwards, kicking, punching. After that... She didn't know.

She clenched her fist and waited for the moment.

After what seemed like forever, the man took his finger off the trigger, waved his companions on, and they continued on their way down towards the river.

Celeste waited for a few agonising seconds until she was sure they had gone, then emerged from the ferns, shaking her arms, brushing her body down. Ants rained from her hoodie, her trousers. The others followed.

"They have guns," said Seb.

"What did you expect?" said Celeste. "This isn't a game." She looked at Rain. "They've probably detected the blockage in the pipe," she said. "Let's hope they don't realise it was deliberate, otherwise we're dead."

Seb swallowed. "We should go back," he said. Rain stared at him. Seb looked back down the path towards the river, and then up into the jungle. "One accepts a certain degree of danger, but-"

"But what?" said Rain. The fire returning to her eyes. "If you want to go, then go. Just, leave your camera!"

197

Seb gripped his camera harder. "Simply making the point," he said.

"What?" said Rain. "What point?"

"We know nothing of what's up there. We have no clue as to how many of them there are," said Seb.

"That's why we're going," said Rain, her teeth clenched.

"We should re-group and reassess," said Seb. "There's no rule of law out here. They could do anything they wanted to us - nobody would ever know."

"Let's keep it together," said Peter. "Whatever we do, we all need to agree on it. This is a democracy. I vote we came here to do a job, so we do it and go." he stuck his hand in the air.

Celeste looked back and forth between Rain and Seb as they stared at each other. Her fuming with rage and determination. Him suddenly uncertain and scared. Both completely ignoring Peter.

"We don't have time for this," said Celeste. She turned and walked past Rain and up along the pipe. When she looked back, she saw that Rain and Robert were following her. Peter shifted uncomfortably, not wanting to abandon Seb, then eventually followed the other three.

Left standing in the path, Seb threw his arms up. "Fine!" he said, "but I take no responsibility if we're all dead by morning."

"Ok," said Rain. "I promise not to blame you."

37.

There was no fence between the jungle and the compound beyond. The trees simply ended in a churned clearing of yellow-brown mud, and the pipe continued out into the open man-made clearing. Getting in wasn't going to be a problem.

Celeste signaled to the others and they pushed off the path to crouch amongst the last layer of trees where they could observe the compound without being easily seen. If getting in was going to be easy, doing so without being spotted would be harder.

The compound was a hive of activity. In the centre, the tall metal framework of the drill rose up. The roaring of the burning gas at the top formed an undertone to the buzz of the insects. Clustered around the drill, an untidy village of metal porta-cabins had been arranged. Yellow, white and blue, they were minimal and generic. They could have been barracks, offices, or housings for machinery. Men in orange overalls shuffled around and between the industrial pipework and corrugated metal huts.

To the right, an un-tarmacked courtyard surrounded by heaps of storage barrels, and filthy forklifts and digging machines where more boiler-suited men tended the vehicles, shifted barrels, or just stood around smoking and talking.

To the left, there were the pits, three swimming-pool sized rectangular ponds, each filled with a different shade of thick liquid. The furthest was a dark yellow brown. The closest, ink black, and overflowing, seeping down into the jungle beside it. Caterpillar trails of black led from the pits to a huge tip - a repository of broken machines, food waste, building materials and punctured, leaking barrels.

All around the edges of the compound were the guards. Men in green overalls, carrying guns, identical to the one they'd already seen. There seemed to be dozens of them. Labour was obviously cheap around here. Most of the men seemed pretty bored. Standing, looking disinterestedly out into the jungle. Watching the work-parties with half-hearted sullen looks.

"Why so many guards, I wonder?" said Peter. "It looks like they're expecting trouble."

"Animals, maybe?" said Rain. "There are jaguars here."

"I don't know," said Celeste. "If I were worried about animals, I'd have guards with rifles, not machine guns." The men were all over the compound. They weren't paying much attention, but that would soon change if the little group got sloppy and was spotted.

Peter pulled a branch aside and peered into the compound. "This doesn't change anything," he said. "We're here to gather evidence. Nothing else. Seb's pictures of the waste pits, and Celeste's hacking thing."

Celeste rolled her eyes. He had no clue. "I need to patch into their WiFi and download as much as I can onto my phone."

"Ok, go on then," said Peter.

"What?" said Celeste.

"Do your thing," said Peter.

"You don't get it. If I could do it from here, I could do it from England," said Celeste. "I have to get in there - find the router. Get the password." Peter's face dropped.

"Well, where is the router?"

Celeste gestured to the compound's mess of steel buildings. "Take your pick," she said. "It could be anywhere."

"That's not very helpful," said Peter.

Celeste turned back to the compound. Half-way up the drill, a satellite dish had been bolted to the scaffold framework. Wires looped down from it. She followed them down until they vanished behind a yellow corrugated shed of a building.

"It could be there," she said.

"Could be?" said Peter.

"I can't be sure."

"Great," said Peter. "What about you, Seb? Please tell me you can get your shots from here."

Seb looked into his viewfinder, aiming the camera through trees at the steaming pit of tar. He played with the focus and zoom, then withdrew the camera, twisted the lens off, placing it in his shoulder bag, and pulling out another, much longer lens.

While he clicked it into place, and fiddled with the settings, Celeste looked back to the courtyard. Half hidden behind the nest of buildings was an object she thought she recognised.

"Give me that," she said, taking Seb's camera, and aiming it. Using the long zoom, she scanned the buildings until she located it and brought it into focus.

"What is it?" said Peter.

She was right. The long, black tailplane of the helicopter which had buzzed the Green Crusader that morning. That figured, she thought. That guy she'd seen in the back, with his sharp suit looked like a city type. He certainly didn't belong in a tiny little fishing town.

"There's a helicopter in there. I saw it back at the ship," she said. She moved the camera down. Something was moving on the other side of the compound. A dirty jeep bounced into view, and lurched to a halt. Two figures got out. She focused and zoomed in.

"Jackpot!" she said.

"What?" said Peter

"Here," said Celeste handing the camera to Peter. "Look."

Peter put the camera to his eye. "Christ!" he said. "That's Lincoln Drier! I never thought he'd actually come into the jungle. This must be really important to him."

Celeste nodded. "And Zoila Chavez. He must be here for the PR stunt at the port. But if we get them both together and we can pin Drier to the abuses and there's no way out for either of them."

"We need pictures," said Seb. He took his camera back and aimed it at the two figures, shooting off a couple of images. Seb looked down at the screen of the camera.

"Damn it!" he said.

Celeste looked at the screen. Drier and the woman were both clear and in shot. "Looks OK to me," she said.

"No, it's rubbish," said Seb. "This is not evidence of anything. We need more. We need to tell a convincing story, and we can't get those images from here."

"What are you talking about?" said Celeste.

"I have to get in there," said Seb. "We need shots of the waste pits. The toxic dump. We need to show the real state of the place - and we need to show that Drier knows about it and has seen it all."

"Ok," said Celeste, "But that's no good without documents from their server to show a paper trail leading back to head office."

"You were all for giving up and going home back there," said Rain.

Seb rounded on her. "You think I'm scared?" he said.

"That's not what I meant," said Rain.

"Well I am scared!" said Seb, "But if we're going to do this, we have a duty to do it properly."

"Ok," said Celeste, "so we need two raiding parties. Seb and Robert, you need to go in and get the pictures. Peter and I will go and find the router."

Rain suddenly softened. She put a hand on Seb's arm. "You don't have to do this to prove anything to me," said Rain, slowly.

"I'm not," said Seb. "I'm doing it because I'm not some paparazzi." He stood up, put the camera over his shoulder. And straightened the strap. "I'm a lens-based artist."

"I'll come with you, then," she said.

"I hate to breakup your little love-in," said Celeste, "but you can't go with him. We need someone to distract them while we get in." Celeste nodded through the branches. Two of the guards were wandering dangerously close to where they were hiding. One of them absent-mindedly kicked at the exposed waste pipe as they laughed together, their machine guns swinging at their hips.

"There are about a dozen men with machine-guns!" said Seb. "What can she do? She's a girl."

Rain's eyes flared. "Just be ready!" she said. "Meet back here." She raised her hand, her knuckles still coated in drying blood and oil, pulled her hood up over her face, and turned and vanished into the forest, skirting around the outside of the compound.

"That was a dumb thing to say," said Celeste to Seb.

The group waited, scanning the edge of the compound, waiting for Rain to re-appear. After a couple of minutes, Celeste spotted a shape in the trees at the right hand side, between the stack of empty barrels and the row of earth-movers.

"There she is," she said. "Give me the camera."

Celeste looked through the viewfinder. She watched as Rain sprinted from the trees to a forklift truck parked up at the edge of the forest, ducking down behind it for cover. A few seconds later, her head reappeared from behind the forklift. She waited for a few seconds, checking the compound, but nobody seemed to have spotted her. The forklift truck itself was a scratched yellow cube with bulbous thick-treaded tyres. On top, an exposed driver's cab was perched. It was parked side-on at the edge of the compound, its forks slightly raised. What was Rain planning? Celeste hoped it wouldn't be anything too dangerous. If Rain were seen, the guards would certainly chase her, and she might stand a chance of losing them in the jungle, but it was a high-stakes game. She could easily be caught, even more easily be unable to find her way back to the meeting place, or get herself hit by a stray bullet. Even if she got away, the guards would be on edge. They'd know something was up and they'd be looking out for trouble.

But as she watched, Celeste saw Rain's hand reach out behind the truck, and pick up a rock from the muddy ground. She checked nobody was looking again, and reached up, jamming the rock into the floor of the forklift - just where the driver's feet would have been. Celeste pulled the camera away from her eyes and pushed it back into Seb's hands.

"I know what she's doing," she said. "She's jammed the foot pedal. Get ready!"

She squinted across the compound. She could just see Rain's arm reach up to start the engine of the truck, and, as it juddered into life, she slunk back into the cover of the trees.

The forklift started to roll slowly forward.

"Wait for it," said Celeste. The truck gathered speed, bouncing and lurching over the rough ground. Nobody spotted it until it crashed straight into the stack of empty barrels, toppling them. Sending cascading metal barrels clanging to the ground and rolling out across the compound like skittles.

The shout went up instantly. Guards and workers from all over the site dropped what they were doing and ran to intercept the rolling barrels. Meanwhile, the truck trundled forward, its path altered by its collision with the barrels so that it was now closing in on the black helicopter.

Three men were running along side it fighting each other for the chance to climb into the cab and steer the machine away from the helicopter. It was now or never.

"Go!" said Celeste.

She broke from the trees, Peter right behind her, and sprinted for the cluster of buildings crowded around the drill. It was a good hundred metres of wide open ground, and there was not a scrap of cover. In seconds of leaving the jungle, she realised she had misjudged the texture of the ground. What looked like solid earth was just a crust of dried mud. Her foot cracked through it instantly and started to sink. She got three steps before her forward momentum started to pitch her forwards, and she staggered, regained her balance, then twisted her foot sideways, lunging, rolling and spinning forwards. She stuck her arm out, still holding her phone, and felt it crunch into the ground as she spun over and over, sprawling to the floor.

Behind her, Peter skidded sideways to avoid her and tripped as well, landing face first in the mud at her side. She raised her head, shook herself, and looked over towards the forklift. Two of the guards had regained the driving seat but were wrestling with each other and the wheel - one dragging it to the left, the other wrenching it to the right. A third guard dived out of the way as the truck rolled towards the helicopter. Barrels were still rolling, and workmen were chasing them across the courtyard. Nobody had spotted the group yet.

She felt Peter's hand on her back, hauling her up, and she scrambled to her feet, throwing herself forwards, just about sensing that Peter was doing the same beside her. The two staggered, half skidding, half falling through the mud and across the open earth until they hit the cover of the yellow tin building. Its metal wall was hot against Celeste's back as she flattened herself against it, Peter behind her, just in time to see Robert and Seb reach the cover of the rubbish tip on the other side of the compound.

Celeste and Peter sat, backs against the wall in the narrow gap between the yellow building and the blue one opposite it, panting, unable to speak. She gingerly pulled up the hand containing her phone, and turned the screen to face her. It was caked in mud. She brushed the screen carefully clean. Apart from the crack it had sustained on her way aboard the Green Crusader, it seemed undamaged. She put her thumb on the 'on' button. Nothing.

Peter stared. "What is it?" he whispered.

She pressed it again, harder. Felt the grating of grit and the slick, sticky slide of mud wedged into the button. And, thankfully, a second later, the familiar buzz of the phone waking. The blue glow of the screen showing up the smears on its surface.

"It's ok."

Across the compound, Robert looked back, and gave the thumbs-up signal.

38.

Celeste swiped across the grimy surface of her phone to open up her settings, and waited for them to load. The WiFi icon flashed, searching... searching... She hadn't told Peter, but it was quite possible that there simply was no WiFi signal, that all the IT on site was linked by old-fashioned wired connections. That was the way she'd have done it. Wires were faster and more reliable than WiFi. They were also more secure. If there was no WiFi, then she was stuffed. The whole mission was stuffed.

"What is it?" said Peter.

"Nothing," said Celeste, staring intently at the screen. She bit her lip and waited.

A tiny icon winked into life. WiFi.

"Got it!" she said. "It's a strong signal, so we're close."

She got to her feet and edged towards the corner of the yellow building. "Keep a lookout!" she said, shifting carefully around the corner towards the door. The building seemed to have been made from a modified shipping container. Next to the door, a single, small window had been cut into the side.

Peter's head appeared beside hers around the corner. She felt his body behind her. "Fine," he said. "What do you want me to do if someone comes?"

"I don't know," she said. "Knock on the wall or something."

"Well, be careful." She felt his hand on her shoulder, fought her instinct to push it free, and avoided his eyes as she slipped around the corner.   Edging along towards the window, she could still feel the imprint of his hand. She glanced back. He was watching her go, but the moment she caught his eye, he looked away. For that second, Celeste saw something. Felt something she couldn't ignore. Whatever was between them would have to be dealt with sooner or later, but the thought scared her more than the jungle or the men with guns.

Later definitely.

She was now in a thin metal passage between two corrugated buildings. A metre or so from her yellow one was a blue container. Its door faced the door to the yellow shed, but it was set into an entirely windowless corrugated wall. The yellow box's window was just a metre away from her. Anyone inside wouldn't have much of a view of anything but the blue metal wall opposite. Still, she supposed, nobody was here for the view.

She crept forward until she was level with the window. If she could get a look inside, she might be able to see if there were any signs of electronics. She shaded her eyes and looked inside. A rough curtain had been draped across the window. She put her eye to the glass where there was a gap in the fabric.

Beds.

Just rows of bunks. As her eyes adjusted, she realised there were men sleeping in each. Shift workers. The rig must be running twenty-four hours a day. While one shift worked, the rest slept. She ducked back down. They were unlikely to keep the communications technology in their dorms. Still, it had to be close.

The blue shed opposite beckoned. It looked like the door had no lock on it, but there was no window either.

She signalled to Peter that she was going to try the door. His eyes widened. He shook his head. There was no way for her to know what or who was in the building. Just walking in was way too risky. She turned away from him and dodged across to the door, twisting the handle and pulling it open in one movement. No point wasting time. She stepped inside.

The room was empty and dark. No windows. Just racks and rows of red and green LED dots like stars in a too-well-ordered sky. The grey black glow of a blank computer screen cast a desk in a dim light. She shut the door to cut off the sound of the jungle, and the noise of cooling fans replaced it immediately.

Celeste felt along the wall until she found the light switch and turned it on. The IT room was pretty much at the same level as the rest of the site. Messy, grimy and patched together in a hurry. There was one screen. One keyboard. A cabinet of rack-mounted computers. Each one presumably a vital part of the drilling operation. Her fingers instinctively reached out towards the keyboard. She tapped it and the screen glowed blue. It filled with a list of settings and icons. She pulled down the menu. Scrolled through them. Drill settings. Cooling systems. Alarms. Hard drives full of data. The damage she could do in here with just ten minutes.

But she didn't have ten minutes. Or even five. She could be discovered at any second and then it would all be over. She had just one job and she needed to get it done and get out. She looked up and down the rack of flashing lights. No router there. She looked under the desk. Nothing. She pulled the screen away from the wall. Nothing behind there either.

But it must be here. There was a gap between the rack cabinet and the wall. It was just wide enough for her to edge her way to the back where she could examine the explosion of wires that erupted out of the shadowy back of the cabinet, linking the stack of machines, powering them, leading to and from them.

Celeste pulled out her phone and turned on the torch, focussing it on the back of one of the racked machines. Then she found what she was looking for. A yellow network cable, looping out of the machine, and joining cables from each computer, bound together with cable ties into a wrist-thick rope of networking wires. She followed them down until they vanished behind the desk. She got down on her hands and knees on the hot metal floor, and followed the wires as they emerged and lead down.

Her heart sank. The wires lead through a hole into a sealed metal box. The router must be in there. Even if the password was, by some miracle, written on the router box, it had been screwed into the structure of the building with six screws. Without a toolbox - at least a screwdriver - there was no way she was going to be able to get to it. Even if she found one, it would take maybe a minute to undo each screw, a couple of minutes to find and write down the number. She didn't have that kind of time.

Suddenly, the door flew open. She threw herself under the desk, desperately trying to hide. It was hopeless. Her legs were sticking out. The light was on.

"Got it?" It was Peter. His head appeared in the doorway. She clambered out, shaking her head. "We've got to go now!" he said. "Someone's coming."

"We need that code!" said Celeste, "Otherwise it's all pointless."

"No time," said Peter. "Out now!" He vanished.

She looked desperately around the room, and was just about to dive for the door when she saw it. A yellow post-it note stuck to the corner of the monitor. A row of numbers and letters scrawled across it. It couldn't be. She snatched the note, and ran for the door, slamming it behind her as she leapt out into the light.

Peter grabbed her, hauling her to the edge of the building and around the corner, flattening her against the hot metal.

"Got it!" said Celeste.

"Shh!" whispered Peter. A second later, she heard voices. Two men talking. She heard a metallic scrape followed by a clang as the computer room door opened and closed again. He stuck his head around the corner. "That was too close," he said.

She held up the post-it note. "I got the code," she said.

"You sure that's it?" said Peter.

Celeste nodded, opened her phone and typed in the number. "Computer hacking, rule 1," she said. "Post it notes stuck to a computer screen are almost always passwords." She smiled as the icon on her screen went from grey to white. She was on the network.

"What now?" said Peter.

She flicked to her file download app, and did a search for drives. "Now I'm connected. I can download anything they've got on their server." Peter looked blankly at her. "I'm just going to copy anything that looks incriminating. We can look through it later."

"OK, good," said Peter. "How long do you need?"

"The closer we are, and the longer we stay here, the more I can get," she said without looking up from the screen. As she spoke, she was scanning through folders, flagging everything labeled as a document or a spreadsheet or a database for downloading to her phone. A progress bar appeared, crawling slowly across the screen. 1% done. 2%

done. Every file she added to the list slowed the movement of the progress bar.

"We can't stay here," said Peter. He kept glancing around the corner of the building, checking the way was clear. "Rain's distraction won't last long, and we've got to get out."

"Ok, said Celeste, "but there's something missing here. I've got loads of documents, but they're all about the running of the place. Technical stuff. Finances. Internal stuff."

"So?" said Peter. He was darting back and forth now, checking one side of the building and then the other. "We have to get out now!"

"So where are the emails?" she said. "We need to prove beyond doubt that the company - that Drier himself - signed off on the pollution. We need to prove he knew about the dumping and everything else, otherwise he can just sack a few local workers, and continue on. We need to tie him to a bigger crime if we're going to stand any chance of stopping this." Peter shrugged. "The emails must be here somewhere but -" she stopped suddenly, staring at the screen.

"What is it?"

"A locked drive!" she said. "A laptop with a locked drive. There must be a laptop somewhere on this site which is used only by Zoila. Everything we need will be on there. We have to find it!"

Peter shook his head. "No way," he said. We're getting out of here right now. Look!" He pointed. Through the gap between the two metal buildings, Celeste could just about see the rising framework of the tower. Through that, she could just about make out the far side of the compound, where the guards and workers were just re-stacking the last of the barrels and starting to wander back to their posts. Peter was right. They had to go now. She glanced down at her phone. 20% complete. It would have to do.

She nodded to him, and silently, they edged towards the corner of the computer building, dodged across to the yellow dorm building, and worked their way to the corner of that. From there, they could see back across the compound to the jungle. It seemed like an even longer run than it had on the way out.

"There's Rain," said Peter. Celeste squinted. The trees were almost dark, but she could see a darker shape amongst them. It was moving. Waving. As she watched, Rain threw back her hood and let her blonde hair free so that her head and face were clearly visible. She was frantically gesturing. Pointing over towards Celeste's right.

"We have to make a run for it," said Peter.

"Wait," said Celeste. Celeste turned to follow Rain's pointing finger. From where she was standing she could see Robert crouched by the stinking black pits. A few metres away, Seb was crouched, trying to get his angle. Neither of them had noticed it, but two of the guards, returning from the other side of the compound were wandering towards them, guns slung loosely around their hips.

Robert and Seb hadn't been spotted, but it was just a matter of seconds.

39.

Celeste watched as the guards wandered closer. Only a low fence and the side of the huge rubbish tip prevented Seb and Robert from being seen. They were oblivious. Seb repositioned Robert, gesturing for him to stand closer to the edge of the toxic pit, and circling around him to get the perfect angle. Celeste waved both hands frantically above her head, desperately trying to attract their attention, but the two were completely engrossed.

The guards were chatting. Laughing. Relaxed. The tall, skinny one was playing the fool, miming an attempt to catch a rolling barrel. He ran around his companion in an exaggerated, bow-legged gait. His stocky friend laughed. Clearly Rain's sabotage had been taken for an accident, and the guards were in no hurry, but every step took them closer to the rubbish tip and the pits, where Seb was arranging Robert like he was a model in Vogue magazine.

"We've got to help them!" said Peter. He stepped forward, out of the cover the buildings. Celeste caught the back of his hoodie and hauled him back.

"We can't," she hissed. "We'll be caught as well!"

"We have to do something," said Peter.

Celeste bent down, grabbed a stone from the floor and hurled it as hard as she could towards the pair. The rock plopped into the pit, causing a splash of black oil.

Robert and Seb looked up immediately, and spotted the guards. They dived for the cover of the rubbish tip, but just half a second too late. The skinny guard yelled, and grabbed his gun, pointing it right at Seb. Robert lunged forward, putting himself between Seb and the gun. He said something, but Celeste couldn't hear it. The stocky guard yelled back, and within seconds, every guard and worker in the place was running towards the rubbish dump.

Seb and Robert looked left and right. There was nowhere to go. No chance of escape. Seb slowly raised his hands, and Robert followed suit. They waited. A minute later, there were twenty sub-machine guns pointing at the pair.

Celeste put a hand on Peter's shoulder. "We can't do anything for them now," she said. "But us getting out is their only chance."

Peter nodded. In the trees, Celeste saw Rain put her hand to her mouth.

One of the guards, looking like their leader stepped forward. He was huge. Solid. Sloping, muscled shoulders below a bald head. His face was level, expressionless, as though he were too dumb to be surprised. He waved his gun at Robert and Seb and led them back across the compound, the other guards following in a disorganised gaggle.

Celeste and Peter drew back into the gap between the buildings. The only cover was a nest of pipework. It was a long way from being enough to hide them, but they crouched low amongst it anyway. It was hard to breathe. Celeste felt the pressure on her chest, pressing the hot humid air from her body as she fought the urge to make a break for the trees.

As the group passed close to their hiding place, Celeste and Peter cowered back into the pipework. It was still hot from the sun, and oily to the touch, but the guards were too preoccupied with their captives to notice the figures crouched in the shadows. For just a second, Seb glanced over to lock eyes with Celeste. He made a microscopic gesture down towards his hand, and she saw a movement as he dropped something tiny into the mud. The boots of the guards crunched over it unnoticed, but when they had passed, she saw it. A blue rectangle about the size of her fingernail, sticking out of the mud. She jogged Peter's arm.

"His memory card!" she whispered, pointing to the card, its row of gold contacts glinting in the last of the sun. "He's left us his photos. We have to get them."

"We've got to get them out," said Peter. The two watched as Seb and Robert were led towards a green hut over towards where the helicopter was parked. The rest of the guards were still following.

"Yes, but not now," said Celeste. "We have to get out while they're busy. This is our only chance."

Peter reluctantly nodded. The two crouched like sprinters and waited. The guard's leader knocked on the door of the green hut. It creaked open. Drier and the woman appeared in the doorway. She looked as mad as hell. He looked like he'd rather be anywhere but where he was. There was no doubt: Robert and Seb had given the pair a massive problem. Celeste couldn't help a smile despite the danger they were all in. If she had anything to do with it, things were going to get a lot worse for the oil prospector and her city boss before the night was over.

Seb glanced back through the crowd of guards at Celeste and Peter. He would know they were stuck, waiting for a chance to make a break for it. She saw his hand move to his camera, turn it so that the flashbulb was pointing at the big stupid guard.

A second later, the flash exploded. The big guard reeled backwards, a hand over his eyes. Seb used the moment to slip out of his grip and take a couple of running steps towards the other side of the courtyard, towards the helicopter.

For a moment there was chaos, the two bosses blinded, guards taken unawares, all turning to face Seb and away from Peter and Celeste. Celeste didn't need a second chance.

"Now!" she whispered. She fired herself from between the buildings, Peter a fraction of a second behind, her eyes fixed on the memory card in the mud in front of her. She reached down, scooped it up in one movement and the two fled towards the forest a hundred metres of open ground away.

To her left, a rattle of gunshot silenced the birdsong. She spun her head. The big security guard had let of a burst of fire just above Seb's head. Seb skidded to a halt, hands raised. His distraction had done its job. There was no need to get himself killed into the bargain.

Celeste didn't stop. She felt Peter next to her, sprinting, toppling forwards. The memory card in her hand was digging into her palm as she gripped her fist tight around it and forced herself to run for the trees.

"Get them!" A shout went up from somewhere to her left. She caught an American accent. It must have been Drier. More gunfire. The mud right in front of her exploded as a trail of bullets smacked into it. She skidded to her right, zig-zagging towards the trees. Beside her, Peter was doing the same.

Out of the corner of her eye, she could see the guards turning, falling over each other as they started to run towards her and Peter. She focussed on the trees. Only five metres now, until they reached the cover. Five more steps.

Five. The bullets zinged over her head.

Four. She could hear the running feet, the boots hitting the mud behind her.

Three. A look back, and one guard, a wiry sprinter, was ahead of his companions. He flew forward, only metres from them now, arm straight out in front of him.   Gun wavering, wobbling as he fired.

Two. Beside her, just in front, Peter dipped, grabbed a handful of earth and rocks, and hurled them into the man's eyes behind as he broke through the edge of the clearing and through the thick wall of green leaves. She heard a yell from behind, and the firing stopped for a second.

One. She was through. From the open yellow light of the compound, she plunged into the green darkness of the jungle. For a second, she was running blind, vines catching at her feet, leaves slapping her face and body. Then she could see Peter dodging and twisting a few metres ahead. Rain ran in front, leading him on through the trees. She followed, heedless of the fact that at any second, she could smash into a tree, or trip in the thick roots.

Behind her, she could hear the men. The guards were breaking through into the jungle. She snatched a look behind. They were slowing, their initial enthusiasm for the pursuit dampened by the dangers of the jungle. Caution was taking over. Instead of launching themselves into the thicket, they spread out. Took up positions. Took aim.

She leapt over a knotted thicket of twisted ferns, landing heavily on the other side just as the gunfire started. She dodged left, then right, just as a thick, dark green leaf the size of her body was suddenly sliced to pieces right in front of her face by the straffing of gunfire. Celeste instinctively ducked and the line of bullets rattled past her, splintering a tree.

She ran on through the terrifying storm of gunfire. It felt to Celeste like the jungle around her was alive, beating, tearing itself apart with the shredding supersonic rain. In the dense packed environment of the trees, every bullet hit something. Every one traced its course through the leaves and the trees and the hanging vines, each fragment of lead drawing its path through her sense of the space around her.

She was losing sight of Rain and Peter in front of her. Then glimpsing them again, diving towards them. Expecting.. her brain did a double-take as she ran. Expecting what? What did a bullet feel like? Was it a sting? A jolt? A shove in the back? The leaves scratched her. The branches buffeted her. Had she already been shot? Would she even know until the blood started to flow?

She forced herself forward, slowly becoming aware that the sound of gunfire was diminishing behind her. The splintering wood and tearing leaves were being left behind. The further she got from the camp, the wider the area the guards would have to search, and the more nervous they would become. Getting lost was a real danger here. If anyone strayed more than a couple of hundred metres into the jungle, there were no landmarks. No maps. They might never find their way back.

The gunfire behind her sputtered out into sporadic convulsions. Voices shouted to each other as they searched the forest. Her lungs were heaving. Her legs, tiring. She knew she was slowing.

Directionless now, following the half-seen shadows of Peter and Rain ahead of her, until the sounds of the men had faded completely.

In front of her, a fallen patch of forest broke the closeness of the forest and showed the sky. A rough clearing of shattered trees, their trunks still raw and broken, as if a bomb had landed there and scooped out the earth. But already, fresh growth was creeping in, covering the ground, and reaching up to the patch of sky in long fingers.

Rain and Peter had come to a stop, standing, motionless, breathing heavily in the clearing.

"You know we've got to go back, don't you?" said Celeste. Rain and Peter said nothing. "We can't just leave them in there!" She searched the pair for a response, but got nothing. The pair were just standing staring straight ahead. "What's wrong with you?" said Celeste. Peter's eyes flicked to Celeste, and then back to where they were both staring eyes fixed on a point in the trees somewhere over Celeste's left shoulder.

Celeste turned slowly, and for a second, she saw nothing but the forest. Slowly, her brain registered that there was something more amongst the leaves. It was as though her brain were assembling a jigsaw from the shapes of leaves and shadows.

40.

She saw the eyes first. Still and brown, they stared out. Human, but alien. The face. The hair, black, unstyled, hanging down as though dropped over the head. The body of a boy, maybe her age. Naked. Muscled arms, but thin. Too thin. Body striped with some deep red marking, faded now. On the boy's shoulder, sat a monkey, as motionless as its owner. Both radiating stillness, both staring back at Celeste, Peter and Rain.

It was the boy she had seen from the boat. In his right hand, he held a spear, as tall as he was, its blade pointing upward. The boy was leaning on it slightly, as if it were a walking stick, taking the weight of his right leg where Celeste could see an infected cut.

Celeste searched his eyes, but they didn't flicker. His expression was unreadable, as efficiently camouflaged as his body.   Fear,   anger,   judgement,   kindness,   sadness, understanding, confusion. Anything could have been running through the mind behind those eyes and she would never know until that spear he was clutching thudded into her chest.

"Back away slowly," said Peter without taking his eyes from the boy's. "These are uncontacted tribes. Their only experience of outsiders is the prospectors and the loggers." He took a step backwards. "Remember, this is his home. It's not ours."

The boy stared. His fingers shifted his grip on the spear, hand turning over so that his index finger pointed down the length of the shaft towards the ground. Fingers splaying slightly. The tiny change of grip turned the spear from a walking stick to a spring-loaded missile, but the boy did not even blink.

Celeste felt Rain moving beside her, stepping forward. The boy lifted his spear, brought it horizontally to his shoulder, the tip level with his ear, poised.

"What the hell are you doing?" Celeste hissed.

Rain smiled. She reached into her pocket. The boy brought his arm slowly back until the spear was pointing directly at Rain's heart. His shoulder and arm aligned now into perfect throwing position.

"You have to trust the forest," said Rain.

"Cut the hippy crap," said Celeste. "You'll get us all killed!"

Rain pulled her hand out of her pocket. She was holding a half-bar of chocolate, the ruffled foil peeled back to reveal a broken stub of pocket-weathered Galaxy. She held it out in front of her. The boy stared, spear hovering. Whatever he wanted, it didn't look like an offer of sweets was going to cover it.

"Get back!" Celeste hissed.

Rain didn't move. She stood her ground, arm out, chocolate held forward. Celeste tensed, glanced at Peter. In the long second that followed, that old, cold part of her brain kicked in, and emotionally, she abandoned Rain. This logical part calculated the odds, so mechanically that Celeste shocked herself. It decided that the moment the boy threw the spear into Rain, she would grab Peter and run. Rain had made her choice and Celeste would not be able to save her. By saving herself, however, she stood a chance - a slim one, but a chance - of saving Peter, Seb and Robert. Sacrifice one dumb, suicidal hippy to save three other people. It made sense. Celeste couldn't deny her own logic. She glanced toward the edge of the clearing and plotted her route through the shoots and fallen trees. Each step mapped itself in her mind and she tensed for the sprint.

A second later, she hated herself. Forced the escape plan and all its cold justifications down into the secret part of her brain where the worst of her lurked. Because what happened next made her realise she had misjudged Rain. She wasn't offering the chocolate to the boy.

The little monkey hopped lightly from the boy's shoulder, grabbed the spear, and used it as a branch to swing itself to the ground, pulling it downward so that its tip drooped harmlessly towards the forest floor. The monkey skipped over to Rain and took the chocolate, chewing the end, and sat, halfway between Rain and the boy, looking back and forth between them.

The boy pulled the spear back up to level it again, but the tension had been broken. The threat somehow diffused. Rain smiled again, looking up at the boy. He slowly stood upright, returning the spear to its position by his side, but his expression did not change.

The monkey tore the wrapping away from the chocolate with its teeth and reached a tiny hand into the foil to scoop out the remainder of the mashed and melted bar. It licked its fingers, then looked back at the boy and made a high-pitched screeching sound as if to signal to him.

Celeste saw the boy blink. His eyes shifted from Rain to Peter, then to her. It was the first movement she had seen in his face. She felt his eyes on her now and fought to meet his gaze with her own. She found herself looking away, and then being drawn back. Away and then back by his dreadful stare. As if it were impossible to either avoid or look directly into the boy's eyes. She told herself she was being stupid, but the feeling remained. As though the boy's black eyes were a

223

window into something dark and terrifying. As though he was asking a question she could not run from, and yet could not face.

He blinked again, and turned, slowly. The monkey left its spot and bounded back to his shoulder as he took three steps away from them, and back into the forest. He turned again, looking back at her, and then started to walk slowly away.

"He's leaving us," said Peter.

"No," said Celeste. She had no idea why. "He wants us to follow him."

41.

Eena walked on through the forest. He didn't look back. He didn't need to. He knew they were following. The three strangers made so much noise tramping through the jungle that he could have heard them on the other side of the valley.

He had watched them arrive, their noisy boat rattling down the river. Black shrouded figures hunched over. He had watched the girl block the poison pipe. Seen them creeping into the clearing, and then running back out, chased by the other outsiders.

He shouldn't trust them. They were strangers, just like the woman who had killed his brother. Just like the poisoners with their flying machines. But somehow these were not the same. Despite his fear. Despite the desperate grieving fury that felt like the only thing keeping him alive, Eena knew he had to trust these three enemies of his enemies. He had to because there was nothing else left to do.

He could feel the wound in his leg like a hot stone burning through him. He leaned heavily on his spear as he pushed himself forwards. It was getting worse. He knew he didn't have long. Old Maowa would have had herbs for him, a mixture pounded from leaves and berries that would have calmed the pain and stopped the infection spreading. But she was gone, and her secrets with her. His leg was past the point of healing now.

He lead them on. Forcing his leg, but forcing his heart as well. He did not want to go back there. The memories haunted him. But no choice. He had to do it. He had to show them.

Behind him, the girl who had fed the monkey, and the boy were talking in their strange babbling language. They

225

talked so much, these outsiders. The other girl walked just behind Eena. She was silent, but he could feel her there. From the moment he had seen her in the boat he had known she was their leader. There was a sort of strength about her. A kind of focus he recognised in the way she moved. The way she spoke. He didn't understand a word of her language, but he didn't need to. He heard her tone and that told him what he needed to know.

The woman who had killed his brother was the leader of the others. She had that same look. That same focus. The same way of being. Perhaps in their world all leaders were women.

The thought took him to the edge of the settlement. Home. He froze just before the clearing. A few more steps through the curtain of leaves and they would be there, but it felt as though an invisible wall were pushing him back. A soft, cold force that warned him away, made his body shake, his stomach turn. 'Do not return,' was the warning inside his head. 'Do not look at it again.'

But he had to.

The three outsiders had caught up, were waiting, watching him. Whatever he felt, it didn't matter. He had to show them. Eena gripped his spear, took a breath, and stepped through the curtain of leaves into the clearing. He felt the familiarity of the place, the thatched huts to the left and right, the black remains of the fire-pit, its smell of burned damp wood. The other smell. But he kept his eyes straight ahead, walked to the centre of the clearing. He turned back, stood straight and upright, pressed the blunt end of his spear down into the hard earth to anchor him, and relieve his wounded leg. Eena focussed his eyes on those of the girl as she stepped through - her followers behind her - into the clearing.

He watched her face change. The close-focussed concentration of picking her way through the jungle, of pushing aside one branch at a time, stepping over ferns and flowers and fallen vines made her slow to see. He watched her vision widen out slowly. She stumbled to a stop, eyes caught to the left and then the right, behind him. Around him where they lay. He watched her expression change. Focus, then confusion, her mind wrestling to understand the shapes. The realisation dawning, eyes widening, jaw falling. The horror flowering on her face like a pale orchid opening. He could see the shapes resolving themselves in her mind into known things. Bodies. Faces. Men, women. Children. Scattered.

Eena kept his eyes on her. He needed her to see. And she saw, but he did not need to see it again himself.

The girl stood without moving at the edge of the village, her eyes sweeping slowly. Narrowing. She looked back to Eena. Behind her, her companions' expressions turned to shock. The girl who had fed the monkey cried out. She put her hand to her face, shrinking in horror into the arms of the boy. The boy ran to the edges of Eena's vision. Knelt by the dead Eena would not look at. The boy said something Eena did not understand. The girl started to cry, forced it back and followed the boy. The two went between the slumped figures, bending over them. The girl pulled out a shining, flat stone-like object, aimed it at the figures, and it flashed. Eena supposed this was their grieving, or magic or some custom these strangers performed over the dead. It didn't much matter to Eena. Everyone he had ever known was lying there, and would be food for the jaguars whatever customs were performed. Everything was lost.

He fixed his eyes on their leader. She did not move. Did not examine the dead. Eena focussed on her eyes and watched the view sink into them. It was like watching two whirlpools, sucking everything they saw in and down. Absorbing it, compressing it, letting the fullness of it pour into her.

She blinked and pulled her eyes back to Eena's. They narrowed, and as he watched, a black-hot fire grew deep inside them, expanding, to consume their entirety. Her entirety. Anger. Heart-tearing, body shaking fury. He could see it in her. She understood. She nodded slowly to him. A promise.

The girl turned. Shouldered her bag. Her companion, the boy saw the change in her. Stood up. Ran to her side. Grabbed her shoulder. Spoke a few words. She shook her head. Spat some strange words back at him. The other girl joined them. Voices became louder. Hands were extended towards her - to restrain her, Eena thought. To persuade her. She pushed them away - shouted in pure fury. Her decision made. She turned and marched into the jungle, eyes blazing.

Her companions looked at each other in despair. The girl turned back to Eena, hovered for a moment, then they both left. Followed their leader back towards the camp of the death-bringers, leaving Eena alone in the village.

Certain people were demon vessels, Moawa always said. They held within them terrible powers that should never be unlocked. He had never understood what she had meant until he met the outsider girl.

Eena could see it in her eyes. Smell it on her skin. She held a demon and he had unlocked it. She would do what Eena could not, but he would be responsible. Whatever she did now was on him.

Good. The killers deserved bad magic.

The monkey hopped up onto his shoulder. As though to comfort him, its little hands reached in to pick something from his hair.

42.

Celeste could feel the blood pooling in the back of her brain. The pressure building. That old surge of adrenaline, flooding her with its power, making her function harder, faster. Sharper. More dangerously. That small, rational part of her that somehow held itself apart, watching her actions with terrifying ruthless logic, was awakening now. Cold and hard. Celeste did not, she realised, understand what others meant by "the heat of the moment". There was a heat. There was the moment. But for her, anger was not a red mist. Anger was clarity. That was what anger was for. An evolutionary device to drive better choices. Sure, she would regret her actions when she considered them later. But the truth was that she would be wrong then, and she was right now. She opened the floodgates in her head, and let it come.

"They're still out looking for us!" Peter was running to keep up, weaving his way between trees. Celeste just walked. Eyes forward. Head down. Phone clutched in her hand. Red and blue GPS dots blinking as they closed in on its location.

"Good," she said without looking at him. "There will be fewer of them guarding the camp." It was almost dark now, and she could feel the noises changing around them as the forest animals changed shifts, the day-birds quietening, the louder, more sinister sounds of the night, creeping in. Guttural croaks. Low hoots. Soft rustles. Uneven and sudden under the constant dance-beat of cicada wings.

"We're just here to gather information," said Peter. "We have to get Seb and Robert back, and take our evidence back to the ship. That's all."

"Fine!" she said. "You do that."

"What are you going to do?"

"I'm going to take the place out," said Celeste. She marched on, watching her cracked and smudged phone as the blue dot showing their position closed in on the red dot of the compound. Up ahead, she could see glimpses of electric light, and the flicker of the gas burning off at the top of the tower as it flitted in pinpricks through the forest canopy.

Peter stepped in front of her, forcing her to stop. She dodged to one side. He put a hand on her shoulder. "The closer we get, the more likely we are to be spotted."

"They wouldn't be dumb enough to leave the camp without torches," she spat through gritted teeth. "We'll see them before they see us."

"You can't go in there like this!" he said.

"If you think you can stop me then you obviously don't know me very well," she said. She glared at him. She did not push past him, but she felt the adrenaline pumping in her gut. The rage filling her.

He lowered his arm. "I don't!" he said. His eyes softened. "I can't stop you, but I don't want you to die."

"You were the one who got me into all this. You told me this meant something. That just talking about it wasn't good enough. If we just go home, we're no better than our hippy parents with their stupid concert. So was it all just talk, or did you mean what you said?"

"We have to think," he said. "Getting ourselves killed isn't going to help anyone. We need a plan."

She took the last few steps to the edge of the compound and crouched down. "I have a plan," she said. She peered through the branches. The place was on high alert. Spotlights scanned the edge of the jungle, casting fingers of blue-white light that reached in through the gaps between the trees, grasping and then withdrawing. A guard passed

231

suddenly, two metres in front of them, a torch stuck to the top of his gun with a winding of silver duct tape so that it illuminated wherever he pointed the weapon. He froze, swung his torch into the jungle so close that it blinded her. She tensed, ready to spring for him. Fingers in his eyes would be her opener. But the torch swung away. He hadn't spotted them. He walked on.

The guards were back from the hunt, and they were jumpy. That made things harder. They didn't need to run about in the jungle, firing at shadows, when they had Robert and Seb as hostages. They held all the cards, but they'd figured without Celeste.

She squinted into the dark. The helicopter was still there, lit only by the flickering flame from the burnoff above casting a weird orange light over the whole compound. That meant Drier would still be hanging around somewhere too. Good. She would send the place to hell, and he could go with it.

"My trick with the forklift won't work twice," said Rain. "There's no way in without being seen."

Celeste looked back to the huddle of tin buildings at the bottom of the drill scaffold. The one she'd seen Robert and Seb taken to had a single, small window. Light glowed out from behind a closed blind.

The door opened. Seb, and then Robert, were shoved through the yellow rectangle of the doorway. Celeste saw Robert stumble on the step. Seb caught his arm and helped him to his feet, as the doorway was filled with the shape of the huge, dumb security guard she had seen earlier leading the other men. He held a sub-machine gun like it was a toy in his huge hands, waved it at the two boys, and followed them towards the centre of the compound.

Behind him, Drier and Zoila emerged.

"What are they doing?" said Rain. The guard gestured for Robert and Seb to stop in the middle of the compound. They turned.

Celeste watched. A dark dread started to spread in the pit of her stomach. "This is for our benefit," she said. "They must know we'll be watching." Drier said something. Zoila nodded to the guard, who put a hand on Robert's shoulder, forcing him down onto his knees.

The guard walked slowly around Robert, looking out into the trees, then raised his gun into the air and fired off a few rounds straight up. The sound shattered into the jungle.

"We've got to do something!" said Rain. In the centre of the compound, the man brought his gun slowly down, holding it at arm's length, aiming it straight at Robert's head.

He paused, for a long second, then shouted, "Cinco!"

Another long pause, and then another shout: "Cuatro!"

Celeste felt Rain grip her arm. "We have to do something. He's counting down," said Rain "From five."

"We can't just walk in there," said Peter.

"That's exactly what we're going to do," said Celeste. "Tell me about that," she said, pointing up at the yellow flame burning in drifting sheets of fire at the top of the drill, as though an explosion were being extended over time.

"What?" said Peter. "We need a plan!"

"Tell me!" said Celeste.

He looked at her, bewildered. "It's used to burn off natural gas. Gas comes up with the oil. If they don't have the infrastructure to capture and sell it they just burn it off. It's a complete waste of resources. We don't have time for this!"

In the compound, the man's voice rang out again: "Tres!"

"What would happen if someone turned it off?" said Celeste.

"You can't be serious!" he said. "The gas would just build up and up - and eventually the whole place would blow!"

Celeste smiled. "That's what I thought," she said. She pulled out her phone. Swiped its screen. The wifi was still connected. "How long?"

Across the compound, Seb stepped forward, shouted some protest. The guard swung his gun towards him, and he froze, raising his hands above his head.

"I don't know. I'm not an oil engineer,." Peter said. "Seconds? Minutes?"

She pulled up an app and jabbed it with her finger. The screen flashed. A tiny image of the screen in the computer room appeared. "From here I can log straight in to the main computer as a console," she said. "I can control that computer just as if I were sitting at it." She pinched to zoom in, and pulled up a program. On the screen, sliders and gauges displayed the state of the gas pressure underground. They rose and fell. Numbers fluctuated, highlighted in green.

"Dos!" shouted the man in the compound.

"You can't do this!" said Peter. "It'll be a massive explosion. People could die."

She rounded on him. "Good!" she said. "You saw what I saw. And Robert and Seb will die too if we just sit here!"

"I'm with you," said Rain quietly beside her. "We do it. Whatever it takes."

"What about you, Peter?" said Celeste. She could see him wrestling with it.

"Uno!" shouted the man. Peter looked frantically from the compound to Celeste and back. He nodded.

She slid her finger across the screen, pulling the sliders one by one to maximum. Jabbing the buttons to disable the safety cutouts. Finally, she locked the screen, freezing out anyone who tried to take back control. High above them, the huge flame spluttered, then evaporated. The roar, a constant underscore so pervasive you forgot it was there, died suddenly, and the orange flame evaporated high above them, turning the orange-black of the compound into the deep, dark, blue-black of the jungle night.

The group around Robert reacted instantly. The guard stepped back, swinging his gun out into the darkness. Zoila and Drier looked up and around in confusion, then stared at each other for a stunned second.

"Just so you know," Celeste said, "I was going to do it anyway."

"I know," said Peter. "What now?"

43.

Celeste felt the crack and give of the compound's mud under her feet. She was running hard. All around her was panic and chaos, but in her own brain she felt that old strange stillness kick in.

A siren screamed and men poured out of the barracks where they were sleeping, grabbing at safety helmets, struggling into them as they ran. Some headed towards the machinery, to try to lock down the well. Some out towards the jungle, desperate to escape with their lives.

She was vaguely aware, as she ran, of a man tearing open the door of the computer room over to her left. She blanked him from her mind. It would take him a week to get back control if he even knew what she'd done.

She dodged as the guards fled in disarray around her. They would have no idea what was happening, but they would know a siren when they heard one, and the moment they saw the oil workers running in terror, they followed suit.

At the centre of it all, Zoila was yelling. Screaming orders. Who knew if anyone was listening. It didn't matter. Celeste had one objective and only one. Out of the corner of her eye to her right, she could see Peter and Rain heading for Seb and Robert. For them this was about rescue. For Celeste, it was about something else entirely. She veered off to the left, leaving them to it.

Just in front of her, Drier was standing still, looking left and then right. For a second, they locked eyes. She could see him calculating. Measuring the moment with the same icy detachment that had taken him to the top of his company. Risk and benefit running through his mind. Was there time to get the helicopter off the ground? Should he grab a hostage, or a gun? Who had to live and who had to die for Drier himself to benefit from this chaos. In that one second, Celeste could see it all flash across his face.

Drier was dangerous. Perhaps more now than ever, but he was not her objective. Not yet. She felt his eyes cutting though her, measuring her as she dodged around him, and pounded towards Zoila's office. What she needed was there. It had to be.

The door of the metal room was hanging open, and she didn't slow for it. She put a foot on the doorframe and crashed through, hitting a shelving unit on the far side, shoulder first. It hurt like she had been hit by a sledgehammer. The room shook. A sheaf of paper flowed out from the top shelf in a white blizzard that filled the room. Celeste waved the floating paper from her eyes. She focussed. It had to be here.

The place was a mess, but at the far side, a chair, a desk. A lamp pointing down, and in the centre, there it was. The laptop. She'd seen it on the WiFi. A ghost device. A disk drive, hidden. Blocked, and hovering at the edge of the network. And what it held could be deduced from what she hadn't seen. Everything on the open WiFi was operational data, how the place ran, technical stuff, schedules, timetables, worksheets. What was missing was why. The emails. The trail of responsibility. The blame that would lead from Drier back and back, down and down to the poisoned river and the bodies in the jungle.

The rugged, green laptop looked like it was military spec. Its thick screen surround, its shielded metal case, its impact-resistant blocky base, heavy and solid. It looked like it was built to survive land mines.

But as Celeste grabbed it and slammed the case shut, she couldn't help a smile. For all its protection, the device's designers couldn't defend it against the idiocy of its users. The string of alphanumeric characters scrawled on the yellow post-it note stuck to the back of the screen made it as vulnerable as a library terminal.

Around her, the paper was settling, the cries of running men dying away. The blood was still beating in her ears. She paused. Listened. There was something. The sirens were still wailing but it wasn't that. There was absence of noise too - no roaring from the flame above the compound, no thumping from the blades of the helicopter - Drier must have taken another way out, she realised - but it wasn't that either. Something in her mind was picking up an urgent sound. No, not a sound. A vibration. A rumbling, deep down beneath her feet, low and soft, but growing by the second. She wrenched the laptop from its socket and stuck it under her arm. She had to run. Now.

But as she turned, a shape filled the doorway. Shoulders as wide as the doorframe. A thick neck. A bald head craned down to fit into the room. Zoila's thug. The same man who had been ready to execute Robert. He still held the gun. This time, pointed at her stomach. She hoped the others had got away.

Celeste felt the ground starting to shake under her feet. What was left on the shelves was starting to vibrate. Something was coming from deep underground. Pressure, building, and with the burnoff shut down it had nowhere to go. Whatever would happen was seconds away and it was going to be bad.

"If you were clever, you'd be running," she said. The man stepped forward into the room with the lazy ease of someone who didn't understand the danger he was in. A stupid grin spread across his face.

Behind her, the lamp vibrated to the edge of the table, and tipped off, shattering on the floor. Negotiation over. She didn't have time for this. She needed to leave. Now. She had one second and one weapon.

She brought the metal cased laptop from under her arm, corner first, into the man's eye in a single movement. The gun went off in the same second, but she had been too quick, dodging sideways and towards him as she swung the laptop. She felt the impact of the computer against his face - soft resistance on the eye, then hard on the skull behind it. The man reeled backwards and she completed her 360 turn, ducking under his flailing arm and leaping out of the door, and pounding across the courtyard towards the jungle.

The ground was shaking now. An earthquake. Up ahead, the leaves of the trees shivered in the moonlight, shaken from their roots as though the jungle were alive. Angry. She veered left, heading for the carved channel between the trees where the waste pipe led down towards the river.

She got to the treeline's darkness, chest bursting, heart pumping, legs crashing so fast over blind black uneven ground that it felt like falling. She could sprawl at any second down into the thicket of tangling roots at her feet, but slowing now would be as deadly as tripping. The underground shifting was audible now. The growl of an impossible giant. A god waking, tearing off its bedsheets. An explosion already in motion while the jungle night waited for its impact.

Behind her, another gunshot rang out, and then something else. A second sound, dwarfing the gunshot, consuming it, bellowing over it like a tidal wave drowning out a snapping twig.

The jungle brightened to a blood-red instant dawn and beyond to the white hot harsh light of a camera's flashbulb. A second later she felt the wall of heat and the searing blast of the shockwave throw her forwards. Her feet ran against nothing, and as she flew through the canopy of the trees, leaves and twigs snatching at her. She felt herself hurled against their springing branches, catching her, slowing her, tearing at her.

In a moment it was over, and she was falling, again, the ground rushing up. Her hands flew out as she impacted into the soft, leavy mulch skidding through it, the debris in her eyes. The laptop was torn from her hands by the impact. It spun away, embedding itself beside the waste pipe a few metres away.

44.

For a beat Celeste lay still, stinging, twisted. Mouth down in something that tasted sweet and rotten. Hands, caught and forced backwards amongst roots. Pain messaging her brain from every part of her. Aching, stinging, bruising, pressure, and other, darker, unknown pains. The sensations of dangerous damage. But she could not allow them room. Not yet. It was not over.

She forced herself to struggle free. To sit up. To turn. Up the channel between the trees, the pipe led into the heart of the explosion. The blast was a dome of fire, bright and yellow and huge. It had swelled out to consume the first trees at the edge of what was the compound, and was now rising, shrinking back, like a flaming jellyfish rising ten, twenty, thirty stories into the night sky as black pustules of smoke burst out over its body. She stared, eyes wide at the beautiful violence of it and felt this night sun sear her face.

As it cleared into the sky, the fireball left desolation. The trees were burning just a few metres up the path from Celeste. Their lush, wet rainforest leaves combusted instantly from the heat into smoking, steaming flame. Beyond them, the tower swung for a moment, one of its legs blown outwards in a twisted stump, then twisted and pitched towards her, crashing down across the courtyard, folding the scattered iron boxes of the buildings like paper.

Another explosion from the centre of the drill, and a fountain of fire sprayed out from under the tower like a flamethrower aimed straight up into the sky. Around it, the torn out, eviscerated remains of the drill, the generator, the solid cast metal engineering of the camp and its machinery were lying smoking across the compound.

And she'd thought hacking the school had been bad. She'd really done it this time.

She could see no bodies, but there must be bodies. She just hoped Peter and the others had made it out, and that Zoila and Drier hadn't. That one moment of eye contact as she'd run past Drier in the compound had told her everything she'd needed to know about him. He was too clever - too focused to be caught up in the explosion. Besides, she couldn't be that lucky.

Celeste became aware that she was staring, hypnotised by the slow rising of her darkening fireball. A second later, the trance was broken by the shock of a bath-sized chunk of metal thudding out of the sky, embedding itself half a metre deep into the mulch just two steps away from her.

Celeste shook herself, scrambled to her feet and grabbed the laptop. She had to get to the boat. If any of them had made it out. If Josh had decided not to abandon them at the first hint of trouble, there might be a way out of the jungle.

She blanked out the pain from her shoulder and her chest, dismissed the trickle of dirty blood from the red raw scratches on her hands, the scorching sting on her cheeks and forehead. She staggered down along the pipe's channel towards the river.

After the fire's bright flare, her eyes were a swirl of orange after-image. She was stumbling into pitch darkness. Her ears were still ringing from the sound. Deaf, blind she forced herself on. Going by the softening of the ground and its downhill slope and the smell of oil and water, she knew the river must be close. Her dulled senses were hopelessly inadequate in this hostile environment.

She wiped a hand across her eyes, not daring to stop. The boat was her only chance, and she had to get to it. The last the others had seen, she had been running into the centre of the compound. A couple of minutes later, the whole place was burning. If they got to the boat first, they would make the logical call. They would assume she was dead.

Her ears were starting to clear now, the ringing now replaced by the singing cicadas, the beating blood by another, deeper sound she couldn't quite place. Was it water? Was it growling? Her eyes were beginning to clear too. Tiny pinpricks of light danced between the trees up ahead.

Something clicked in her mind and she started to run. The lights were phone torches. The sound, an outboard. She pushed into the undergrowth, leaves a soft tangling maze she had to scoop and scramble her way through, gasping for breath. She tried to shout, but the sound that came out was a rasping smoke-strangled whisper. As though in a dream, she floundered forwards, downwards. Finally, the leaves gave way and she pitched out, her foot sinking into ankle-deep mud on the overhung shore of the river.

Out in the water, she could see it. The dinghy. Four figures inside, moulded and huddled together in the darkness under hoodies. She could see one was Robert, and Rain's figure was unmistakable. A third figure could have been Peter, or Seb. She couldn't be sure. Either way, one of the two was missing.

Celeste shouted her hoarse, struggling yell. Waved her hands desperately. The last figure seemed to look up. Gaze out in her direction, his hand on the tiller. It was Josh. She could have sworn he saw her. Maybe not.

He looked away. Back to the water ahead. He opened the throttle and the boat sped away.

Celeste's legs folded under her. Her ankles still trapped deep in the mud, until she hit the ground with a soft, wet slap. She lay there, exhausted, feeling the mud seep through her clothes as the too-long ignored pain seeped outwards from her aching bones to her stinging skin.

Her limited googling of the rainforest told her there were anaconda here. There were pumas. There were black caiman - six metre crocodilians capable of dragging prey far larger than her into the water. All good reasons not to be alone in the jungle in the dark, but no clues about what to do if you were. She tensed her stomach, fighting her exhaustion. She had to get up. To move. But why? There was nowhere to go. No way out. She was done.

She heard voices just upstream and turned her head to look, resting it in the petroleum-poisoned silt under the waste pipe's outlet, but that motion was all she could manage. She could see the source of the voices. Another betrayal was taking place a few metres further up, lit by the headlights of a jeep parked up on the makeshift jetty. She watched it through the intermittent dribble of black ooze still draining from the pipe.

Drier had made it up the pier to the bunkering boat. Its engine was chugging. He was pushing another figure in front of him. Behind him, Celeste could see Zoila leap out of the jeep, and run towards the boat. Drier spun around, pulled a gun. Zoila stopped abruptly, shock on her face. Drier gestured, shouted. She stepped back onto the bank, protesting. He laughed a dry laugh, gestured again, back up the road towards the flaming remnants of the compound hidden behind the trees. Celeste couldn't hear the words, but the meaning was clear enough: her mess, her problem. Drier would deny he was ever there, and the fewer people left alive to disagree, the better.

He jumped on board with his captive, leaving Zoila alone in the jungle. Lying in the mud, Celeste watched her begging, pleading as Drier took the bunkering boat gently away from the jetty and down the river. It chugged past where Celeste lay, and she watched it go, heavy in the water, weighed down by full barrels of oil loaded in preparation for Drier's triumphant declaration of his newly opened well - at least she'd taken the tarnish off that for him. That was something.

As the boat passed, the captive figure on board turned to look up, and the moonlight caught his eyes. Peter!

Celeste let her head fall back into the soft mud. It felt like a pillow. She felt her eyes closing. The jungle sounds drifting away. She let the feeling take her, and consciousness slowly slip away.

45.

Celeste woke with a jolt. It was deep night and the smell of smoke and oil was still on her. The wet mud had soaked through her clothes, pressing them slick against her skin, but she was alive. That was something. That pain in her chest was still there. A hard pressure as though a tight bandage were wrapped around her. Maybe she broke a rib when the blast threw her through the trees. Maybe worse.

She had the sense that she had been out for just minutes, though there was nothing to tell her so in the darkness. She lifted her head painfully, the mud peeling away from her face, the hair matted against her head. There were eyes staring at her from the jungle. Two sets of bright shining reflections of the moon bouncing off the water. Both round and deep. She froze, staring, breath held, and waited for the grey shapes to clarify the shape of whatever predators were stalking her.

She recognised the monkey first. Something in the way its eyes bobbed, tilted, curious and jittery. The boy's stillness made him harder to see, but slowly his outline emerged, until she felt she could see his face. He looked down at her. Expression unchanged. Impossible to read.

Did he understand what she had done? Did he even understand the concept of revenge? Perhaps all he saw was another outsider bringing death and fire to his world. Perhaps that was all she was in the end.

The boy stepped forward. He gripped his spear in both hands, turned it sharply, bringing its point up level with her face, centimetres away. He held it there, motionless.

"If you're going to kill me, get on with it," she whispered, hoarsely. "I'm going to die soon anyway."

The boy just held his spear level. Celeste focussed on its point. It was a rough weapon, little more than a sharpened stick, but it would do the job quickly enough. She looked up at him, and waited, but he still didn't move. He seemed to be waiting for something. He looked at the spear, then back at Celeste. Slowly, it dawned on her. He wasn't threatening her, he was offering his help.

She reached out, grabbed the end of the spear, and pulled herself up onto her feet. He leaned back, allowing her to haul first one foot, and then the other, out of the gripping mud until she stood in front of him on the firm ground of the bank. How must she look to him? A half-dead creature of mud and blood and smoke.

"Thank you," she said. The boy didn't acknowledge what must, to him, have been a meaningless noise. Instead, he turned and took two steps back into the jungle. She hesitated. He turned back, waited for her to follow, then moved on.

She struggled after him through the jungle. Him in front, limping, heavily, leaning against his spear. Her behind, wheezing. Clutching her chest. The monkey running back and forth, scampering and swinging amongst the trees.

The ground was rising. He was leading her uphill, away from the river, and it was hard. She was on her hands and knees in places, hauling herself up one step at a time by grasping at the tangle of roots and hanging vines. Her fingers felt raw and tired, fighting to hold her grip. They seemed to be climbing forever, higher and higher up the side of the river valley. The boy ignored Celeste's protests and kept on climbing up and up.

The forest was thick, dark and huge. Without the boy, she would already be hopelessly lost. She thought of the guards and the workers fleeing the compound, blind panic on

247

their faces. In her mind she tried to count them - maybe there were thirty or forty. Seb, Rain and the others knew what was coming - that was how they had survived. Drier and Zoila's cunning had got them out. The rest - she thought of the dumb, slope-shouldered thug, the laughing, smoking guards blundering over Rain's toppled barrels when she rigged the forklift. If there was a gene for survival, they didn't have it. Those who weren't caught in the explosion would be lying, stunned and wounded and lost in the jungle by now. A stub of sympathy and guilt rose in the pit of her stomach, but then the image of the bodies in the boy's village flowed in around it, and it sank beneath them. The workers knew what they were doing here. They deserved everything they got.

Finally, the ground levelled off. The trees thinned out and they broke through the ground cover onto a sharp ridge of rock at the top of the valley. At last, Celeste could stand upright, and they both paused for a moment. From claustrophobic green darkness, they had emerged suddenly into a night of silver-blue clarity and a view over a pitching, rolling sea of dark trees beneath a sky peppered with more stars than she had ever seen.

She stood battling something like vertigo as the infinity of the sky and the forest flooded into her. The boy was still too, the stars and the moon in his eyes. He looked back down the way they had come and she turned to follow his gaze. Behind them, the burnt orange fire of the wrecked oil drill was still rolling thick, black smoke into the pure sky. Beyond it, the river was a thick silver snake winding through the valley.

If this were your world, she thought, how strange to have it suddenly ripped apart by invaders with their strange technology. She looked down at the laptop. Somehow she had hung onto it, though she wasn't sure why anymore. It was no use here. No WiFi.

"What are we doing here?" she said. The boy said nothing, but he raised his spear, levelling it towards the horizon in the direction of the river. A tiny white light bobbed in the centre of the river at the far end of the valley: Drier's boat, weighed down by a full load of oil barrels, was trying to navigate the river at night, single handed. He was making slow progress. And somewhere on that boat was Peter. She felt her heart leap against her broken ribcage. She hoped he was causing Drier trouble. Maybe it wasn't too late.

She looked back to the boy. "What can I do?" she said. "I can't get to him."

The boy raised his spear and turned, pointing with it down the other side of the valley. Celeste squinted into the dark, trying to work out what he was showing her. It just looked like an ocean of trees. She shaded her eyes from the brightness of the moon, and slowly the darkness resolved itself.

Amongst the trees beyond the ridge below them was a geometry that did not belong. A straight line. A flat, even, black line sliced through the trees running off into the distance. Tarmac. A road! The drillers had been building a road to take their oil back to civilisation, and they had almost made it. It must lead straight back to the coast, back to the river mouth. The road ended in a mess of construction just a couple of hundred metres downhill from where they were standing. She could just make out the shapes of abandoned earthmovers. If they could make it there, then maybe...

46.

It took just a few minutes to reach the road. Celeste plunged downhill through the jungle, the boy trailing behind, and burst out into the playground of hulking yellow machinery. There were forklifts, diggers. A crane. All too slow. Too hard to drive. She needed something that would get her the tens of kilometres back to the town before Drier got there and his hostage became a liability. She needed a truck maybe, if she could figure out how to drive it - or a car - or... and then she saw it.

Leaning on its stand at the side of the road. Maybe it was there to courier packages back and forth to the town. More likely one of the workers just enjoyed burning up and down the virgin tarmac of the empty jungle road. Either way, the keys were in the ignition, and nobody was coming back for it now.

Celeste ran her hand over the sleek leather seat. The futuristic angles of the gleaming black bodywork hunkered down over two silver-rimmed wheels like a strange insect - a mosquito perhaps, or a black wasp. This would do. This would do very well.

She pushed the laptop up under the front of her hoodie, and put her hands on the motorbike's handlebars, swinging her leg across the seat. It felt comfortable, moulded to her. She flicked the key and the headlight carved a tunnel down the smooth, black road between the trees.

She turned and looked back at the boy leaning heavily on his spear, in the shadow of the mess of earthmovers. It was clear he was in a lot of pain. His tribe were all dead, and that leg would not get better on its own. She nodded towards the back of the bike.

"Come with me," she said. The boy looked at her, then at the leather seat. He hesitated for a second. "Come on! Get on the bike!" Celeste yelled at him. "We have to get out of here." The boy stared back. They locked eyes. A realisation spread over Celeste. He wasn't coming.

If he stayed in the jungle, he would be dead inside a month. People were already dead because of her. Who knew how many. She had lost her friends. She had abandoned her parents. She had left the rainforest burning - done more damage to the jungle in a moment than Drier and Zoila had managed in six months. From the whole mess, this boy was at least something she could save. Something to make it worthwhile. He had to come.

"Don't be stupid!" she almost screamed, feeling tears pricking suddenly from nowhere at her eyes. The boy just stood and stared back. "Get on the damn bike!" He didn't move. Didn't blink. She saw it. Knew it. This was his home. He would rather die here than leave. A flash of Milton Highbury lit up in her brain. Did anybody feel that way about that place?

She wiped her eyes with her sleeve, swung her head back to face the road. If she left with nothing, so be it. She still had the laptop. She could still bring Drier down.

"I take that!" The voice was in English, thickly accented. It came from the jungle. Celeste swung the handlebars so that the headlamp scanned the trees like a searchlight. The figure it found was Zoila's. She stood, her smart 'best' business suit now filthy with dirt and smoke, and oil, her eyes manic. She held a small handgun out in front of her, trained on Celeste. "I take the bike!"

Celeste hesitated, her fingertips touched the ignition key. She could fire it up, open the throttle, try to make it away before the woman fired. Was it worth a shot?

No. There was an element of desperation in Zoila's eyes. In the headlight, Celeste could see the sinews in her gun-hand twitching. She was shaking, unsteady, but from this range she could not miss. Celeste would be dead before the engine caught.

"No tricks! We understand each other, no?" She waved the gun, gesturing for Celeste to move away from the bike.

Celeste swung her leg back over the saddle, and released the handlebars, slowly raising her hands, her eyes still locked on Zoila's. The woman stepped forward into the road. She smiled slightly, relaxed, just a little, and then levelled the gun, taking aim at Celeste's chest. Celeste clenched her fists. Waited.

It was a small gun, and Zoila didn't know she had the laptop under her clothes. Maybe it would stop the bullet. Maybe. If it did, she'd have a couple of seconds before Zoila understood what had happened. Dive, roll, grab it the gun. It wasn't much of a plan, but it was all there was. She tensed.

The impact came in a sudden thud, but it was not the impact she was expecting. Zoila's hand jolted suddenly to the side as the boy's spear hit. The spear smashed into the gun, sending it spinning out of her hand and rattling across the tarmac. Before Zoila even knew what had hit her, Celeste dived at the ground, snatched the gun into her fist, rolled, and was back on her feet, the gun trained on Zoila. If the boy's throw was intentional, it was a skilled shot. If he had been aiming to kill her, it was a poor one. Zoila was left gripping her grazed hand, but was otherwise unharmed. Celeste edged sideways to where the spear lay at the side of the road, and threw it back, shaft first towards the boy. He caught it neatly, and swung it to level at her again.

Zoila straightened, turning defiantly towards Celeste. "We want the same thing," she said. "Drier. Take me with you. We find him!" She stepped forward. Celeste shook her head. "He will kill your friend," said Zoila. "Feed him to the camen. You need me."

"No," said Celeste, "I don't."

Zoila turned back towards the boy. She looked him up and down, her eyes fixing on the black wound in his shin. "Your friend's leg. It needs attention. I know. I was once a nurse."

Celeste almost laughed. "You should have stayed as one," she said.

"It is infected. He will die slowly," she said. "I could help him." Another tactic, thought Celeste. This one never gave up. It was almost admirable.

"It's not me you need to convince," said Celeste. Zoila looked at the boy again. He didn't move, didn't blink. He was like a tree.

"We are the same, you and I," said Zoila quietly. She was looking at the boy, but speaking to Celeste.

Celeste shook her head. "We are not the same. You killed all those people."

"Not my decision," said Zoila. "Drier."

She probably really believed that made it ok, thought Celeste. She felt her hand tighten on the gun, her finger curling on the trigger. It would be so easy.

"You going to kill me now too?" said Zoila.

Celeste caught herself. Took a breath. Put the gun into her pocket. She mounted the bike.

"If you leave me here, you might as well," said Zoila. "It is the same."

Celeste clicked the ignition. The bike rumbled under her. Zolia's body language changed in a second. She drooped. Hung her head, her shoulders sagging as though Celeste starting the engine had drained the energy from her. "It's over," said Celeste.

"You can't leave me. I'll die here." Zoila's voice was breaking now. Desperate. Pleading. She let out a sob.

Celeste let her face harden. Allowed her lip to pull into the hint of a sneer. "Not my decision," she spat.

She kicked the bike's stand away, turned the throttle, and felt it pull forward, the sound of the engine drew itself around her like a bubble, blotting out the jungle.

Just before the blood red rear light dimmed on Zoila and the boy, she glimpsed them one last time in her wing mirror. Zoila was stepping forward, bending towards the boy's injured leg, palm out in a gesture that looked like an offer of help. The boy was staring back at her. Spear still levelled, wavering slightly.

Maybe there was a chance there for both of them. Probably not.

Celeste opened the throttle, and the motorbike tore away down the pristine asphalt, trees blurring on either side in the harsh headlight.

47.

It was like riding through a tunnel. On two sides and above, the trees arced around her in a flickering play of shadows. Below, the flat black of the tarmac rushed up.

She felt the hot, damp air in her face like a hairdryer, and every other second, the stinging impact against her face of bugs attracted by the light, hitting her face and making her screw her eyes up. Some tiny, exploding like wet tears on her face. Some huge, bouncing and making her wobble.

She rode as fast as she dared into the storm of insects. Every second, Drier was getting closer to the mouth of the river. To his ship and to escape. In a week he'd be able to cover his tracks, and by the time the world discovered the dead natives and the poisoned forest and river, he'd be able to claim he knew nothing about it. Zoila would be dead, and she could carry the can. Celeste herself had played her part, torching most of the evidence. She didn't doubt that even the laptop would be discredited once he'd had a chance to prepare his excuses. Worse than that, the moment he was safely out into open sea, Peter would become more inconvenient than useful.

She gripped the throttle and opened it a little further, trusting her tired reactions to cope with the twisting of the road as it wound, rose and fell through the jungle. In the darkness, walls of trees suddenly loomed as the tarmac swerved, and Celeste leaned in, fighting to stay on the road, passing within centimetres of the jungle thicket on one side and then the other.

Slowly, as she rode, she felt the ground begin to rise again. As the road opened out onto a high mountainside, the canopy dropped away to her left and she saw the first rays of the morning sun break suddenly across the forest, illuminating the silver hairlines of the river, shimmering in to join into one

255

great snake ahead before widening out into the delta, and eventually the ocean beyond.

At the point where the river met the sea, Celeste could just glimpse the squared off-yellow lights of the town, and in the centre of the river, the multi-coloured glow that just had to be the Green Crusader. The concert was still going on. That meant the hippies didn't yet know what their children had been up to - that Josh and the others hadn't made it back to the ship yet.

The road dived back down into the thickness of the jungle, and she lost sight of the town again, winding left and right, down and down towards the river.

She swerved back and forth, almost feeling the road as it passed, reading its turns almost before they came. Then in an instant she was at the bottom of the mountain, and the road straightened out. Through the trees, in the growing dawn, she glimpsed the river running parallel to the road just a few metres away.

She glanced sideways at the river and there it was - just for a second, just a flash, but she recognised it: the boat. Moving faster now, in the open river, its black shape low in the water. She felt a swooping in her stomach that could not be explained by the motion of the bike underneath her. If she were lucky, Peter was still on that boat. If she were very lucky, he was still alive.

Celeste judged they were maybe four or five kilometres outside town. She might just make it to the river opening before them. What she'd do when she got there, she had no clue, but she could see ahead now too, and the road was dead straight. She tore the throttle open fully. The speedometer dial climbed. A hundred and fifty kilometres per hour. A hundred and seventy. Two hundred. The trees rushed by.

The road veered away from the river and, in a flash, the jungle fell away behind her. A couple of seconds of rough-cut stumps where the clearing of the rainforest for farmland had begun but been left unfinished, and then wide, dizzying open space under a huge pale blue-grey dawning sky. Fanned-out feathered leaves stretching away in neat lines to the distance. Palm plantations. The human need for another kind of oil, slowly biting into the forest from the outside, while the search for crude oil poisoned it from within.

Celeste powered ahead until the road curved, joined another and the brand new asphalt gave sudden way to pitted brown mud. She lurched, breaking hard, skidding, wobbling, and just recovering. The potholes came fast and deep, each bump jolting her chest and hips, reminding her of those bruises.

There were buildings on both sides now. Low tin sheds at first, then brick. Half-built structures were everywhere, scaffolding the main architecture. The town was rebuilding itself on the promise of oil money. A promise she had left in churning ashes and twisted molten metal. More collateral damage, she told herself.

She pressed on. The streets were a mess, but they were at least straight, and above the engine, the sound of hard rock guided her down towards the water. At the end of the street, the road opened out abruptly into a mud beach on which a scattering of fishing boats were moored to a wooden jetty.

Before she even hit the end of the road, she spotted the familiar shape of the orange dinghy. Standing beside it were Robert, Josh, Seb and Rain. They had made it out. She skidded to a stop, and dumped the bike.

The four were huddled, so deep in conversation they didn't notice Celeste marching up the jetty towards them.

Out beyond the pier, in the middle of the estuary, the shape of the Green Crusader hovered in a pool of flashing green and red lights. Music pumped and pulsed from her. To Celeste's left just up the beach, the quayside rose in pitted concrete and beyond that the wall of blue steel that was the hull of Drier's tanker waited.

On the concrete in its shadow, a crowd had gathered to drink, dance, or just watch the protest in bemused wonder, and, ranged along the quayside, the spidery legs of a dozen camera tripods were lined up, dark bored figures guarding them - the press waiting for the one image that would tell their story. Right now they must be wondering whether it was going to be an image of the Pale Riders, reformed after thirty years to protest against the destruction of the rainforests, or a photo of Drier, triumphantly straddling his oil barrels and declaring the Amazon open for business.

Either story would play well. Unless Celeste could give them something better.

In front of her, Rain suddenly looked up. "Thank God you're alive!" she said, flinging her arms wide.

"No thanks to you!" said Celeste. "I saw you leave. I was waving, shouting. Why didn't you see me?" she demanded. Rain, Seb and Robert shook their heads.

"I did," said Josh from behind the other three. "I did see you."

The others spun around and stared at him.

"What?" said Rain, horrified. "Why didn't you tell us?"

"Because you would have wanted to go back!" said Josh. "You'd have got us all killed!"

"So you left me to die."

Josh shrugged. "You'd have done the same."

"No, I wouldn't!" said Celeste. She shoved him hard with both hands. Josh staggered back, but then recovered. The others stared at each other.

"You know you would," he said.

"It was not your decision to make." said Seb.

"You three were half-dead. I had to get you out."

"Had to get yourself out more like!" said Celeste.

"I save who I can is all," said Josh. Celeste glared at him. He looked away. "But - I'm glad you're alive," he said. "Peter?"

She shook her head. "Drier has him." Rain looked horrified.

"Where?" she said.

Celeste pointed. Out in the distance behind them, where the estuary narrowed, and the brown river rolled away into the jungle, the bunkering boat was just swinging into view. It was some way off yet, but they had to act fast.

"If he makes it to his ship, Peter is dead," said Celeste.

"We can't stop him with this," said Seb, gesturing at the inflatable.

He was right. She looked at the Green Crusader. On board a huge screen showed a closeup of the lead singer. The old rock god was in his element. The world could be ending. He wouldn't have known. On the quayside, the row of cameras had their long zooms trained on the ship.

"No," said Celeste. "But there may be a way. I have something he wants." she pulled out the laptop from under her hoodie. If it was still working, there was a chance.

"What do you need?" said Josh.

"I need the Green Crusader," said Celeste. "And I need everyone off it right now."

Josh jumped into the inflatable. "Let's go," he said.

Celeste hesitated.

Josh fired up the engine. "You trust me, or no? You choose now," he said.

48

"I don't know what to make of you," said Celeste as she and Josh bombed across the water towards the thumping sound of the Green Crusader. "I don't know whose side you're on."

Josh adjusted the engine. "I'm on my side," he said. "We all are."

"Are you going to tell me how you're going to clear the ship?" said Celeste, She looked back to where Seb and Rain watched them from the jetty. No point risking everyone. Somebody had to upload the pictures if everything went wrong. Someone would have to explain it to the parents.

Josh nodded. "Fire alarm," he said.

"The fire alarm's bust," she said. "It goes off all the time. They'll just ignore it."

Josh smiled. "Not if there's a fire," he said. "You just get to the bridge."

He pulled the little boat up alongside the hull of the Green Crusader where the steel rope ladder hung down into the water. Josh started climbing immediately. Celeste followed just behind. She was glad he couldn't see her wincing with pain with every step. Each time she reached for a rung, the stretching sent knives of pain through her chest. Each time she gripped the ladder, she had to force her tired fingers to close, and lock in place. Her head was starting to spin with the tiredness. When she last slept they were only just clearing the Panama Canal. It seemed so long ago.

She missed a rung with her foot, and her body slammed against the side of the ship. She had to focus. Push back the black clouds of unconsciousness creeping in at the corners of her eyes. Below her the little boat was drifting away. It was too far to fall.

Above, Josh hopped over the side and vanished. Celeste forced herself to take another step and another, her legs as leaden as her brain.

Eventually she reached the top, flopped over onto the deck beside the crane and scrambled to her feet. From where she stood, she could peer through the railings to the stage. The Pale Riders were just coming to the end of a song. They looked tired. The crew had been expecting the oil boat to chug out of the jungle hours ago - and they knew their protest would be for nothing if they stopped before it made its appearance. Not that playing all night seemed to be bothering them. This was their first gig together for three decades. It would take a fire to get these old pros off the stage now.

Around the stage, the skeleton crew of the Green Crusader milled. She scanned their faces. Happy, self-satisfied. On the other side of the deck, Dad was fiddling with the sound desk, balancing the bass for his favourite band. Closer, Mum and Rose were dancing a couple of metres from the stage. If her parents and their hippy friends had planned their lives out at the age of seventeen, this moment, right here, right now was what they would have hoped for.

For a second, Celeste felt something in her gut. She wanted to run to Mum - to throw her arms around her. She choked the feeling back. Not the time for sentiment. The crew had no clue their children were even missing, and it was best kept that way. She had a job to do.

She turned away, and crept along the gangway. At the other end, the metal steps rose to the door of the cockpit.

Celeste took them as quickly as she could. It would not be good to be discovered before she got control of the ship.

She grabbed the door and yanked it open. Inside was something she did not expect.

"What you want?" The captain, Peter's father, was half-sitting, half-lying slumped in the chair. Beside him, Tequila. Two bottles. A dribble of liquid was left in the bottom of one. The other was empty. It had been a long night. The captain's eyes focussed and then gradually widened in dawning shock. Celeste knew what she must look like. Filthy, smoke-blackened, mud-covered and speckled by the remains of squashed bugs, she realised that even to this drunk, it must be obvious she hadn't spent the night in her cabin.

"What..." he started again, his voice slurring. Celeste's mind raced. If she told him what had happened to his son, she might get him to understand. She might even get him to help if he was capable. But it would be a long story, and she didn't have time to tell it. She put her hand in her pocket. It touched something hard and angular. Right now, it was her only option.

She pulled out the handgun and leveled it at the captain.

"Out!" she said. "Get off the ship now, and say nothing." The captain blinked at her in surprise. His mouth fell open.

At that second, there was a bright, blue flash from outside the window. The crack and spark of electrical overload, and the deep boom of the bass speakers maxing out and then dying. The sound of the band cut out, and the captain staggered to his feet. A second later, the fire alarm sounded harsh and piercing. Josh was right on time.

"Out, NOW!" said Celeste, gesturing at the door with her gun. The captain swayed, and staggered out, and down the steps towards the life-boats. Celeste looked after him.

Towards the stern of the boat, electric sparks were thrashing and erupting like fireworks. She could see the reflections of yellow flames in the new paintwork the crew had spent the last month applying. The crew themselves were pouring out from behind the stage and leaping into the lifeboats.

Josh's face appeared at the bottom of the stairs.

"What now?" he shouted over the alarm.

"Get to the engine room!" Celeste shouted back. "We need to cut Drier off."

Josh looked back. The last of the crew, the captain and the band had made it into the lifeboats, and the automatic crane arms had started to swing them out. By now, the blue sparks from the stage fire had ceased, but black smoke was pouring up, and the fire was licking its way out around the bulkheads. "Not much time left."

Celeste nodded. "We'd better be quick then."

Josh turned and fled down the stairs towards the engine room.

49.

Celeste stood at the ship's wheel, watching through the window as the captain, the crew and her parents powered away in the lifeboats leaving her and Josh alone. She could smell the growing fire as it crept slowly towards her. She thought of the first time she had been in that room, Peter's hands guiding hers on the wheel. The feeling of control. She was captain now, and that feeling was long gone.

She reached down and flicked a control on the console to raise the anchor. Out in the estuary, she could see the low shape of Drier's boat now. It was powering across the water towards the tanker at the quayside. She grabbed the intercom.

"Josh! What's taking you so long?" she said. "We have to move, now."

Josh's voice crackled from the speaker. "Is a mess down here," he said. "Some idiot rigged the generator's power to the stage lights instead of the engines." Celeste rolled her eyes. That would be one of Dad's bright ideas.

"How long?" she said.

"Got it!" said Josh. At that instant, Celeste felt the engines turn over. The familiar vibration under her feet.

"OK, get up here now!" she said.

She dropped the intercom mic and jammed the engines up to full power. The juddering throb from below rose and she felt the ship pull forward, picking up speed. She yanked the wheel to starboard and the room tipped as the ship hauled itself around in the water to face in towards the quay.

Up ahead, and to the right, Drier's boat too was turning in towards the tanker on the dock. She could see Drier standing up on the open deck. One hand was on the wheel. The other, pointing what must be a gun at a figure slumped beside him. Peter.

Right now, the lenses of the photographers on the dockside would be training on them, Drier would be able to get on board his tanker without facing the press, but he'd have to get rid of Peter before he got in range of the cameras.

If she could pull across to block them, there was just a chance. It was a straight race.

The Green Crusader should have been much faster than the heavily-laden bunkering boat. But her engines were straining, they were closing the gap painfully slowly. Whatever Dad had done to the generators, it was going to take more than Josh could do to get the ship back up to full power. Meanwhile, every second, Drier got closer to the tanker.

Josh appeared in the doorway. "I've done all I can," he said.

"Take the controls," said Celeste. "He's heading for the tanker. Try to cut him off." She pulled the laptop out from under her hoodie. It looked battered. Soaked with her sweat. She slammed it down on the ship's console and flipped it open.

"What are we doing? We ram them?" said Josh, grabbing the wheel.

She shook her head. "That boat is full of oil. If we hit it we'll kill Peter and ourselves too."

"Good to know you're trying to avoid that. You're learning." He looked back, suddenly serious. "Whatever you're going to do, you better make it good."

"Well let's find out." She hit the power button, and after a heart stopping second of blue flickering, it powered up. So far so good. "We need something to bargain with. Something that ties him to the massacre."

She scanned the drive. There had to be something. The screen filled with files. Emails, back and forth between

Drier and Zoila. All bland corporate operational stuff. Celeste flicked through them.

"What have you got?" said Josh, correcting the ship's course. They were closing now, but Drier was getting closer to the tanker every second. Up ahead, the big ship was lowering a ladder on the side facing away from the quay. If Drier made it there, he'd be able to remain blocked from the view of the cameras, and nobody but Celeste and Josh would be able to see what he did with Peter.

"Nothing!" said Celeste. "He's too clever to discuss anything that puts him in the frame over email."

"He must have given the orders somehow." said Josh. "Keep looking."

Celeste stared at the screen. What was installed on the machine maybe that would give a clue. She listed the apps. Email, office stuff. Video conferencing. That was it! If he'd given his orders over video, there'd be no paper trail, but Zoila was smart she'd have her own insurance...

Celeste, opened the file browser and in a couple of seconds she had it. Dated videos. Zoila had recorded every conference call. She opened the most recent, and Drier's face popped up onto the screen. She scrubbed into the middle of the conversation.

"Kill them!" he was saying. "Kill them all." Celeste grinned.

"Got it!" she said. Outside the window, the two boats were converging. The Green Crusader pushed on, flames and smoke pouring from its stern, forcing Drier's boat to run closer to the shore and the press cameras.

"Whatever you're going to do, do it now!" said Josh, bringing the boat around to get the last few metres of advantage on its rival. Out of the window, Celeste could see

Drier now, almost alongside them, using the Green Crusader as cover from the camera as he desperately tried to guide his laden boat through to the tanker.

Celeste swiped her phone and put in a call to Rain on the jetty. "I need you to dump the last 10 photos on your phone into this email address right now." She read off the laptop's email address, while at the same time, logging the device into the Green Crusader's Wifi.

"Ok" said Rain, "but I don't understand -"

Josh wrenched the ship's wheel round and the Green Crusader tipped and swerved again, veering in front of Drier's boat, forcing him to cut its engines to avoid a collision.

Celeste rang off, grabbed the laptop and ran out of the cockpit and down the steps to stare over the side of the ship. The two boats hung in the water, a few metres apart. Drier's, heavy in the water, laden down with its cargo of crude oil. The battered old protest vessel, ruined, burning, blocking its way. From the deck of the oil boat, Drier stared up at Celeste. Beside him, Peter was slumped on the floor.

"You?" Drier shouted.

"Yeah, me!" Celeste shouted back.

Drier hauled Peter to his feet, and trained a gun directly at his head. "Let me though or I'll kill him!" he shouted across the water.

Celeste held up the laptop. "Let him go or everything on this goes public!" she yelled back.

Drier laughed. "You're bluffing, little girl. You've got nothing." he said. "Now get out of my way!"

"What now?" shouted Josh from the doorway of the cockpit. Celeste looked from the laptop to Drier. He was quite capable of shooting Peter where he stood.

"Move the ship," said Celeste. "Let him through."

"What?" shouted Josh. "He kill the moment he's safe."

"I said let him through," said Celeste. She lowered her voice. "Only, do it slowly. Give me two minutes - and turn the stage to face the cameras."

"What you gonna do?" said Josh. Celeste looked back at the stern of the ship where the fire was starting to consume the stage area.

"I'm going to put on a show," she mouthed towards him.

A sneer grew across Drier's face. "I knew you were bluffing!" he shouted.

Celeste gripped the laptop, and ran, keeping low, down the gangway and towards the fire. She stepped out onto the cargo deck. Above and around her, the flames had taken full hold. The whole middle of the ship was burning, the communications mast engulfed in tendrils of flame. The smell of burning electrics was sharp and acrid in her nostrils. The fire had snaked its way up the lighting gantries to form an arch above, electrical insulation cable was dripping down in a molten fiery rain around her, and the heat was intense. She could feel her face burning, her clothes stinging against her skin.

She looked around, squinting into the smoke, and there it was. The sound desk, tucked away at the back corner of the deck. If the fire hadn't reached it, and if it still worked, there was a chance.

She made her run, dodging left and right between pools of fire, ignited from the droplets of burning electrical cable rubber, fed by the oil and paint and detritus of the deck. Mid-way, her path was blocked by a wall of black smoking flame where cabling had been taped across the floor. She leapt through it, landing hard, staggering, putting a hand out, and feeling it sear as it touched the scalding deck.

Somehow she made it to the sound desk, and slapped the laptop down on it, firing it up. Eyes stinging, she dived into the mess of cables behind the desk to find the one she was looking for - a single, black wire, wound diagonally with gold stripes. And there it was, feeding from the sound desk, and out across the deck towards the stage. The stage itself was burning. The cabling leading to and from it had taken a lot of damage. Out along the lighting gantry, wires were hanging down. Others stripped of their insulation were glowing red hot. If this worked, it would be a miracle.

She yanked the wire out of the desk, and shoved it into the back of the laptop, clicking and dragging frantically, drawing in the photos from Rain's email with a couple of other files from the hard drive into the fastest slideshow mashup she'd ever made. She hit play.

50.

The computer stuttered, its screen flickering as it struggled to recognise the device being plugged into it. Celeste stared at it. Come on!

Suddenly, from above, the sound of groaning metal tore through the fire alarm's shriek. She looked up just in time to see the scaffolding of the lighting gallery, twisting out of shape. One of the struts holding up had given way, and was bending forward, causing the whole structure to buckle, pitching towards the deck.

Celeste dived away from the sound desk and across the cargo deck under the falling scaffold. She could feel it toppling above her as she stumbled, half-blind in the smoke back towards the side of the ship. As she ran, she could feel it above her, the downdraft of superheated air, rushing under the falling metal. She could hear it, creaking metal, roaring flame hurtling down towards her. Then the crash, shaking the deck as the metal structure slammed into the ground so close behind her running heels that the sparks sprung forward to sting the backs of her legs.

In front of her, the buckled strut, pulled down now by the structure it was built to support, twisted down in front of her, and caught, diagonally, blocking her way at chest height to form a flaming metal cage, but she was running too fast to stop. She ducked, slid and rolled under its falling weight, clothes smoking instantly from the heat of the deck, hair melting as it touched the hot metal.

The momentum of her dive carried her forward under the steel framework as it fell, and she scrambled to the edge of the deck, throwing herself down onto the gantry where she was shielded from the worst of the heat.

She got to her feet just in time to hear the sound system boom behind her, and she span around to look back.

It was working.

The huge screen, held above the burning remains of the stage, flickered into life. Drier's face from Zoila's secretly recorded video-call, as high and as wide as a house, filled it. Every pixel. Every nose-hair. His voice beamed out with the power of a stadium speaker system.

"Kill them! Kill them all!" it said. The screen flicked to a montage of photos from Rain's phone. The boy's village. The bodies lying in the jungle. The children. The gunshot wounds.

Celeste spun back to look out over the edge of the ship and down at the bunkering boat. Drier was staring wide-eyed at the screen, a terrible realisation spreading over his face. His mouth hung open. The montage cycled back to the video call "Kill them! Kill them all!" He staggered backwards as though the force of the bass speaker blasting out his confession was a physical impact, and stared at the screen.

The realisation turned to panic in a flash, and he hauled his gun around so that it was pointing up at the Green Crusader's deck. He fired, once, twice, three times. Celeste flinched, thinking, for a second that he had shot her, but no. She turned to look back at the screen. Three crazed bullet holes had appeared in the glass. Three dark blotches in the centre of Drier's forehead. He had shot his own image, but the video still played. The sound still blared out.

"If you don't have the stomach for this work, I've got people who have," it was saying.

Celeste turned back to the real Drier. He was raging now, firing off bullets one after another into the screen. Unaware that while he had been watching, the boats had turned, drifted so that he and the screen were now in full view of the press cameras only a few tens of metres away on the quayside.

Beside Drier, Peter took his chance. Without turning, he threw himself sideways over the side of the boat and into the river. Drier spun around, fired twice into the water, missing Peter by centimetres. On the third shot, the gun clicked but did not fire. He was out of bullets. Drier threw the gun aside, and for a second stared manically back and forth between Peter, now swimming frantically away from the boat, and his own bullet-marked face booming from the flaming deck of the Green Crusader. He was caught in panicked indecision. Camera flashguns exploded like lightning on the water.

Gripping the wheel of his boat, Drier jammed his hand down on the controls. Instantly, the boat, just a few metres from where Celeste was standing, jerked and started powering forward towards her. Celeste's heart lurched. The madman was going to ram them!

She ran for the prow of the ship yelling up at Josh in the cabin to get out. The door opened, Josh emerged, and thundered down the steps. She grabbed his arm and dragged him, stumbling, towards the front of the vessel. That rusted safety rail Peter had been threatening to fix since the day they'd first met - she prayed he hadn't got around to it.

As she pushed him forwards, Josh started to struggle, panic spreading across his face.

"No! No!" he was shouting, fighting against her in blind fear. "Not in the water!"

Looking back, she caught a glimpse of Drier, hand still on his boat's wheel, face twisted in panicked fury, lit by the billowing flames from above. She hurled Josh forwards. He hit the railing and it gave way instantly in a shower of rust. Josh vanished over the side, and Celeste propelled herself after him, running at the edge of the ship. There was a jolt as Drier's boat embedded itself in the side of the Green Crusader, and Celeste leaped out as far from its hull as she could.

The explosion changed from a grinding crash to a chain of fireballs as the bunkering boat's cargo of barrels detonated one after another, tearing the hull apart, peeling great ripped sheets of metal around her as she plummeted forward through the orange billowing flame and hit the ocean. Instantly, she found herself sealed in cold, silent water.

She was sinking. She shook herself, swimming forward, staying as deep underwater as she could. Around her, knives and bullets of shrapnel from the ship's hull tore through the water, but she swam hard and fast until her lungs burned and her stomach clenched. Above her, she could see the blurred yellow of oil fire. She forced herself onward. Maybe she was swimming away from the vessel, maybe she was swimming underneath its collapsing hull. There was no way to know in her streaming world of water and fire and mud.

She felt herself slowing. The pain in her chest, and the constriction of her clothes limiting her movement. Exhaustion flooding in around her, covering her like a heavy blanket. The weight of her hoodie, and her combats and her boots were dragging her down. Could she even make it to the surface now? Starting to panic, she fought her way upwards, reached forward, pulling the water back and down around her as she struggled towards the air.

Above her, she could see the surface, but however hard she fought it seemed only to inch closer. She kicked, and floundered, the absurd urge to open her mouth and breathe in the water blotting out everything else in her brain. She gave one last kick, reaching upwards, scooping at the water above her with both hands, and burst out of the water, gasping at the air.

It was a mistake. All around her the water was layered with patches of burning oil. Thick black poisonous smoke filled the air but she could do nothing to stop herself gulping it down. She choked and coughed, arms waving frantically in the black film, coughing, retching, her desperate lungs filling, searching for molecules of oxygen in the suffocating clouds of filthy petroleum smoke. Her head swam, spun. She could see smoke, flame, water. Over in the distance, the shape of the Green Crusader lolled on its side, pitching towards her as it started its final fiery descent to the seabed. There were voices too, shouting, distant as though in another world. She felt them falling further and further away, as the fire and the water and the blue morning sky darkened, and dimmed to cold, empty blackness.

51.

Consciousness returned slowly like a settling dust. That moment of panicked memory of the hideous choking, burning, drowning fell away as she was rocked awake by the familiar motion of the inflatable. Before she was consciously aware of it, she felt the firm solidity of its floorboards against her back and the blue brightness of the sky through her closed eyelids above her and she knew that she was safe.

There was another feeling too. Air being pushed into her lungs. Life being breathed into her. The pressure of lips on her lips. Confusing at first, but slowly resolving. She opened her eyes, eyelids prickly, hot. Blinked against the blue sky. Focused on the face above her, a smile spreading across it.

"You gave us a scare there." It was Peter. Hair and clothes soaked. Curls plastered to his head.

Celeste coughed. Tried to speak. A hoarse meaningless whisper was all that emerged. The smell of smoke filled her nostrils.

"You owe me a ship," said Peter. He grinned down at her. She opened and closed her mouth, trying to speak again, then gave up, lifted a hand, put it behind his neck, and pulled his head down until their lips met again in a kiss that lasted until she passed out again.

EPILOGUE
THREE WEEKS LATER

Celeste threw off the bedclothes and pulled on her combats and a top. The fan in the grimy hotel room that had been home to her since the Green Crusader went down was turning laboriously above her making a grating rattle she had learned to ignore. She dropped her laptop, phone and charger into her rucksack. On a whim, she stuffed a change of clothes in there too. You never knew. She hefted the bag onto her shoulder.

As she headed for the door, she glanced into the other room where Mum and Dad were sleeping. How they had managed to convince themselves that she, and the rest of the group had never even left the ship that night, she'd never know. The press had got plenty of shots of the video Celeste had played on the flaming deck, but they hadn't got a clear shot of her, and the others had managed to take her away in the lifeboat before the press had worked out what was going on. They'd been hiding out ever since.

As far as the rest of the crew were concerned, the kids had got bored of the concert preparations and retired to their rooms to play videogames, or whatever it was teenagers did these days. When the fire had broken out, everyone had put it down to an electrical overload on the Green Crusader's already decaying systems.

Zoila's incriminating laptop had gone down with the Green Crusader, but with both Drier and Zoila herself missing, the story of the massacre and the illegal dumping soon started to unravel. When the Sharkgirl photos - Seb's beautiful, haunting evidence of the poison in the jungle, and the shots he'd snatched of the explosion at the rig had started to appear strategically online (courtesy of the mysterious Logician), the

276

world had been shocked and captivated.   Rain and Peter's phone shots of the massacre at the village had followed - all strategically edited by Celeste to turn herself and her group into dark, mysterious outlines - and the full horror began to unfold across the world's media.

The company's stock began to plummet in value, and news of environmental abuses in oil wells all around the world started to surface as journalists became suddenly interested in the industry's failings.

If her parents and the rest of the stranded crew had checked the online news a little more closely, they might have recognised the six shadowy vigilantes who brought down the multi-billion dollar oil giant. However, with Celeste herself the digital expert of the crew, she had managed to act as their online content filter, so far keeping her and her group's part in the adventure away from their parents. It wasn't even that hard to steer them towards stories that focussed on the Pale Riders, so that the adults owned a part in the story. After all, the success of their concert was what they really wanted to hear about - and local anger gave them a good reason to keep a low profile while they tried to arrange passage out of Colombia.

But this new message was unexpected.

Celeste slipped out of the hotel room and closed the door quietly behind her.   The Logician's email had been characteristically cryptic.

I have set up a #SHARKGIRL crowdfunder, it read. **Anonymous donations to your cause have exceeded expectations.**

What cause? Celeste had asked.

That would be your decision. The answer had come back. **Unable to send cash without alerting authorities. Have therefore arranged a gift.**

What are you talking about? Celeste had typed.

Come to the quay.

Celeste ran down the narrow street towards the river, through the white blocky concrete of the permanent town, and the gaudily-painted tin-roofed shacks of the fishermen's quarter. It was early, and the market was just setting up as she dodged through the stalls. What did he mean, a gift?

When she got to the quayside, the others were already there. Rain and Seb holding hands, grinning. Robert smiling, looking around. Josh nodded at her as she arrived, panting. Peter serious, thoughtful.

"Well," she said. "Where's this gift, then?" She scanned the concrete quay. Apart from the six of them, it was empty.

Robert blinked at her. "Can't you see it?" he said. "It's right there!" He pointed behind him. Celeste gasped. She stepped back.

"You cannot be serious!" she said.

The ship was shining black and trimmed with silver chrome. It's hull sleek and streamlined as an arrow. Smaller than the Green Crusader, but with a cargo deck big enough to hold two solid inflatables, three brand new black jetskis, and even a two-person sub. A set of silver steps lead down onto the quayside. The name on the side read "Silvertip".

"She's all yours," said Peter.

Celeste didn't know much about ships, but one look around the cockpit of the Silvertip and she knew this was no ordinary boat.

"This must have cost millions!" said Josh, behind her. The others filed into the pristine control room. The gleaming white console was layered with buttons and displays. The ship's wheel was a stylish frame set into a chrome console, and behind it, a wall-sized video screen glowed into life.

"What's this all for?" said Celeste. "What are we supposed to do?"

On the screen behind her, a message began to type itself.

From: @thelogician

This ship is yours. Paid for by tens of thousands of anonymous donations. People all over the world have been inspired by your work. There is enough fuel, and enough food on board to take you anywhere in the world. You must do as you please.

However, you may wish to consider information I have received that the North Korean government is planning to test a nuclear bomb on an island in the Pacific. This illegal test will destroy all animal life on the island, and contaminate the sea for miles around. If you wish to travel there, you would need to leave within the hour.

They all stared at the screen.

"Mum and Dad would be better off without me," said Celeste, eventually. "As long as I'm with them they can't go home."

"I'm in," said Josh. "I'm not staying in this town. Is a dump."

"Me too," said Robert.

Rain and Seb looked at each other. Both slowly nodded. Celeste felt a smile growing. Her heart swelled. The start of something. She turned to Peter, but his face was dark and serious. He shook his head.

"Dad took losing the ship badly. He's drinking more than ever. He knows he'll never captain a boat again," he said. "I can't leave him. He needs me."

Celeste felt a warm dull pain spread out across her chest, as though her heart had been punctured and was pumping its blood out into the cavity of her ribs.

"I understand," she said without looking at him.

"I'm sorry," said Peter.

"We go and do the pre-checks," said Josh. "Come on, leave them." He led the others out, and down towards the engine room, leaving Peter and Celeste alone.

"You'd better go too," said Celeste. "We have to leave quickly. Tell my parents, will you?" she said. "Try to make them get it."

He nodded. She smiled. They'd never got anything else she did -why should they get this?

The two of them walked out and down to the top of the steps leading off the ship.

"Well, goodbye," he said. He reached out. She put her arms around him, but avoided the kiss. She didn't think she could take it. When the embrace ended, there were tears in both their eyes. Peter spoke first.

"You don't need me," he said.

"I know," said Celeste.

"You're Sharkgirl."

She laughed. "You know, back in the Atlantic, when I was caught in that sharknet, with the great white hanging there next to me, there was this moment..."

"I get it," he said, "a connection."

"Yes," said Celeste. "It was like I suddenly realised the shark wasn't the real predator."

Peter nodded. "Humans are the predators all right," he said.

She watched him walk down the steps, and step off onto the quayside. The steps folded themselves neatly away into the side of the boat and there was water between them. Only a few centimetres, but it might as well have been the whole ocean. She turned and walked away up to the cockpit, and took her place at the ship's wheel.

She hadn't told Peter but he had got it wrong. She hadn't hung there, eye to eye with the shark, and realised that humans were the predators all along. Her revelation had been nothing so predictable - nothing so sentimental. What she had realised was that she was the predator.

Celeste herself was the most dangerous thing in the ocean. Whenever there was blood in the water, she had no choice but to follow it to its source. The sooner she came to terms with that, the better.

She pulled out the communications mic and spoke into it.

"Let's see what she can do," she said.

Under her feet the engines started, and she pushed the throttle forwards. In the morning light, Sharkgirl and the Silvertip slid out of dock and out towards the open ocean.

I really hope you enjoyed this book.

If you did, please take a moment to put a review on **Amazon**, mention it on **social media**, or just **tell a friend**.

It really helps to spread the word.

Thanks so much,

Christian Darkin
Author.

You can also email me directly at
christian@anachronistic.co.uk
Or tweet **@animateddad**
I'd love to hear from you.

Printed in Great Britain
by Amazon

82612009R00160